Also by Iain Lawrence

THE WRECKERS

THE SMUGGLERS

Ghost Boy

Iain Lawrence

DELACORTE PRESS

Published by
Delacorte Press
an imprint of
Random House Children's Books
a division of Random House, Inc.
1540 Broadway
New York, New York 10036

Visit us on the Web! www.randomhouse.com/teens
Educators and librarians, for a variety of teaching tools, visit us at
www.randomhouse.com/teachers

Library of Congress Cataloging-in-Publication Data
Lawrence, Iain.
   Ghost boy / by Iain Lawrence.
      p.   cm.
   Summary: Unhappy in a home seemingly devoid of love, a fourteen-year-old
albino boy who thinks of himself as Harold the Ghost runs away to join the
circus, where he works with the elephants and searches for a sense of who he is.
   ISBN 0-385-32739-0
   [1. Albinos and albinism—Fiction. 2. Circus—Fiction. 3. Runaways—
Fiction. 4. Elephants—Fiction. 5. Self-acceptance—Fiction.] I. Title.
   PZ7.L43545 Gh 2000
   [Fic]—dc21   00-025590

The text of this book is set in 12-point Adobe Garamond.
Book design by Julie Schroeder

Manufactured in the United States of America
October 2000
10 9 8 7 6 5 4 3 2 1
BVG

For my mother

Chapter

1

It was the hottest day of the year. Only the Ghost was out in the sun, only the Ghost and his dog. They shuffled down Liberty's main street with puffs of dust swirling at their feet, as though the earth was so hot that it smoldered.

It wasn't yet noon, and already a hundred degrees. But the Ghost wore his helmet of leather and fur, a pilot's helmet from a war that was two years over. It touched his eyebrows and covered his ears; the straps dangled and swayed at his neck.

He was a thin boy, white as chalk, a plaster boy dressed in baggy clothes. He wore little round spectacles with black lenses that looked like painted coins on his eyes. And he stared through them at a world that was always blurred, that sometimes jittered across the darkened glass. From the soles of his feet to the top of his head, his skin was like rich white chocolate, without a freckle anywhere. Even his eyes were such a pale blue that they were almost clear, like raindrops or quivering dew.

He glanced up for only a moment. Already there was a scrawl of smoke to the west, creeping across the prairie. But the Ghost didn't hurry; he never did. He hadn't missed a single train in more than a hundred Saturdays.

He turned the corner at the drugstore, his honey-colored dog behind him. They went down to the railway tracks and the little station that once had been a sparkling red but now was measled by the sun. At three minutes to noon he sat on the bench on the empty platform, and the dog crawled into the shadows below it.

The Ghost put down his stick and his jar, then dabbed at the sweat that trickled from the rim of his helmet. The top of it was black with sweat, in a circle like a skullcap.

The scrawl of smoke came closer. It turned to creamy puffs. The train whistled at Batsford's field, where it started around the long bend toward Liberty and on to the Rattlesnake. The Ghost lifted his head, and his thin pale lips were set in a line that was neither a frown nor a smile.

"It's going to stop," he told his dog. "You bet it will."

Huge and black, pistons hissing steam, the engine came leaning into the curve. It pulled a mail car and a single coach in a breathy thunder, a shriek of wheels. It rattled the windows in the clapboard station, shedding dust from the planks. The bench jiggled on metal legs.

"I know it's going to stop," said the Ghost.

But it didn't. The train roared past him in a blast of steam, in a hot whirl of wind that lashed the helmet straps against his cheeks. And on this Saturday in July, as he had every other Saturday that he could possibly remember, Harold the Ghost blinked down the track and sighed the saddest little breath that anyone might ever hear. Then he picked up his stick and his jar and struck off for the Rattlesnake River.

The stick was his fishing pole, and he carried it over

his shoulder. A string looped down behind him, with a wooden bobber swinging at his knees. The old dog came out from the shade and followed him so closely that the bobber whacked her head with a hollow little thunk. But the dog didn't seem to mind; she would put up with anything to be near her master.

They climbed back to Main Street and trudged to the east, past false-fronted buildings coated with dust. The windows were blackboards for children's graffiti, covered with Kilroy faces and crooked hearts scribbled with names: Bobby Loves Betty; Betty Loves George; No One Loves Harold. And across the wide front window of May's Cafe was a poem in slanting lines:

> *He's ugly and stupid*
> *He's dumb as a post*
> *He's a freak and a geek*
> *He's Harold the Ghost.*

In the shade below the window sat a woman on a chair with spindly legs, beside a half-blind old man with spindly legs sitting in a rocker. Harold glanced at them and heard the woman's voice from clear across the street. "There he goes," she said. "I never seen a sadder sight."

He couldn't hear the old man's question, only the woman's answer. "Why, that poor albino boy."

The man mumbled; she clucked like a goose. "Land's sakes! He's going to the river, of course. Down where the Baptists go. Where they dunk themselves in the swimming hole."

His head down, his boots scuffing, Harold passed from the town to the prairie. The buildings shrank

3

behind him until they were just a brown-and-silver heap. And in the huge flatness of the land he was a speck of a boy with a speck of a dog behind him. He walked so slowly that a tumbleweed overtook him, though the day was nearly calm. In an hour he'd reached the Rattlesnake.

In truth it was no more of a river than Liberty was a city. The Rattlesnake didn't flow across the prairie; it *crawled*. It went like an ancient dog on a winding path, keeping to the shade when it could. But it was the only river that Harold Kline had ever seen, and he thought it rather grand. He splashed his way along the stream, a quarter mile down the river, until he reached his favorite spot, where the banks were smooth and grassy. Then he sat, and the dog lay beside him. He put a worm on his hook and cast out the bobber. It plunged in, popped out, tilted and straightened, like a little diver who'd found the river too cold. A pair of water striders dashed over to have a look at it, and dashed away again.

The dog was asleep in an instant. She hadn't run more than a yard in more than a year, but she dreamed about running now, her legs twitching.

"Where are you off to?" asked Harold the Ghost. His voice was soft as smoke. "You're off to Oregon, I bet. You're running through the forests, aren't you? You're running where it's cool and shady, you poor old thing." He looked up at the sun, a hot white smudge in his glasses.

The dog went everywhere Harold did. It seemed only natural to him that she would dream of the places he dreamed about.

4

"We'll get there," he said, leaning back. The grass and the water and the blue of the sky made a pleasant blur of colors around him. "David will be on the next train, maybe. Or for sure the one after that. And he'll take us away. You bet he will."

The sun seemed to float on the pool of the Rattlesnake, a little white ball shattered by the branches and leaves. Harold squinted at it, watching the bobber as it suddenly dipped in the river. He tugged on the string, but nothing tugged back, and when he gathered it in he found that the worm was gone.

He picked through his jar and took another one out, hating to see the way it slithered and thrashed at the touch of the hook. His brother had told him worms couldn't feel pain. "Don't worry, Harold," he'd said. "They don't have brains or hearts or anything."

But still the Ghost winced at the sound of the hook squishing in. "I'm sorry," he told the worm. And he let it catch its breath before he lowered it into the water.

He stared down, and for a moment it seemed there were two suns floating on the pool, before he realized it was his own face he was seeing, broken into bars of white by the ripples of the hook.

He was shocked to see himself; he never looked in mirrors. He never looked at window glass or shiny pots, at anything that would show how white he was.

"Oh, gosh," he said, and jerked his head away. The reflection zoomed across the pond. Then he dropped the bobber and plunged his hands into the river; he shoved them down below the surface.

The water, brown from prairie dirt, gave his skin a golden tan. He looked at his fingers, swollen by refraction but the most beautiful color he had ever seen, and he wished he really looked like that. He thrust his arms deeper, and deeper again, until his sleeves floated up in bunches almost to his shoulders. Then he took handfuls of the brown water and flung them over himself; he poured it across his legs and head, until it sopped through the helmet and dripped down his face and there were rainbows in his glasses.

He didn't hear the horseman come. Hooves trampled on the grass so quietly that even the dog didn't wake. They stepped in the water, and the horse lowered its head to drink from the Rattlesnake.

"It won't wash off," the horseman said.

Harold stood up, the river dripping from him. The horse was chestnut colored, with white socks up to its knees, and high on its back the rider rippled with black and red. Harold turned his head away to see more clearly; nothing looked right if he stared straight at it.

"You're the way you are," the horseman said. "Some things can't be changed."

He was an Indian, old and wrinkled. His face was cracked by sun. He wore a feathered headdress with a tail that curled across the horse's back and fell again along its flank. He sat on a blanket but not a saddle, and his legs were cased in buckskin, his feet in beaded moccasins. He held a lance eight feet long bundled at the top by clumps of jet-black hair and eagle feathers tipped with white, all tied with crimson wool. He might have ridden out of the painting of Custer's last stand that hung above the bar in the Liberty Hotel. He might have ridden out of time, somehow.

"Who are you?" asked Harold. His dog was still asleep.

"I was named Thunder Wakes Him," said the old Indian. He smiled. "Some people call me Bob."

"Where have you come from?"

"Where does anyone come from?" he asked.

"Then where are you going?"

"I follow the circus."

Harold frowned. He couldn't remember a circus ever stopping in Liberty. "What circus?" he asked.

"Hunter and Green's," said the old Indian. "Hunter and Green's Traveling Circus."

"But it hasn't gone by."

"Sometimes I follow ahead of it," said the old Indian. He leaned forward, his elbow on a bundle that he carried between his thighs. "You've got a fish there, son."

The bobber was half underwater. Only the tip of it showed, running at a slant across the pond. Harold groped for the string and found it with his hands. He pulled it in, one fist over the other, squinting against the sun that glared back from the water. A big sucker fish clung to the hook, its odd mouth agape, and Harold hauled it onto the grass. The dog finally woke and sniffed at it. Then Harold looked up, and the old Indian was gone.

He climbed up the bank and stared east across the prairie, then west, down the faint ruts of an ancient wagon road. And down the faded trail went the old Indian, a tattered shape with his feathers and scalps. The chestnut horse high-stepped through the grass, its white stockings flashing.

The ruts were a hundred years old. Harold could follow them, he knew, all the way to Oregon, through fields and cities, from hills to mountains, up through forests of pine. And he gazed at the old Indian with a feeling of sadness and longing.

Chapter
2

In late afternoon a song came to Harold. It drifted across the prairie and into the gully of the Rattlesnake, and he climbed up the bank to listen.

It was calliope music, a faint little song that came in whistles and wheezes, a cheery song that sang of circuses. And it called to him like a piper, just as it called to every child throughout the whole, flat county.

Harold collected his fish and his stick, his jar of worms, and the dog stood up behind him. And together they went down the old ruts of the Oregon Trail, into a breeze that carried the song in waves across the grass.

From a long way off he saw the circus tents in Batsford's field. They made castle shapes with colorful spires, with banners of crimson and gold. To Harold it seemed that a new town had sprung from the stubbled grass, a town so bright and cheerful that it made Liberty look dreadful beside it.

He plodded along, into the smells of cotton candy and toffeed apples, of sawdust and horses, and corn on the cob. They washed over him on the breeze, along with sounds he'd never heard: the flutter of celluloid birds, the thrumming of canvas, the high and heart-tingling trumpet of an elephant. And above it all, the calliope played, tootling out a circus march with its steamy sighs.

His lips cracked into a smile. His watery eyes gleamed behind their round lenses. He walked down a line of enormous old army trucks, some still in khaki and white stars, others gaudily painted, all smeared with the dust of the road. There were Fords and GMCs and a monster-sized Diamond T, then a silvery Airstream trailer and—last—a bright yellow jeep. Harold passed them all, then wandered on toward the tents. And in the open there, the children found him. They circled him like wolves around a deer.

"It's Whitey!" said one. "Hey, Maggot!" cried another. And three at once shouted out, "I guess he's going to the freak show!"

Harold said nothing. It had been a mistake, he knew, to start across the field so boldly. He put his head down and stared at his boots; he stumbled along, and the children swarmed him. They taunted him with ghostly cries, looming up toward his face, swirling all around him in blurs of brown and gray. "It's the Ghost," they cried. "It's Harold the Ghost." One leapt in and snatched away his helmet; another took his little jar of worms. They shrieked and laughed and pushed him from behind, jostling him along to the row of sideshow tents. The dog stayed with him, her clouded eyes wide with fright, her tail between her legs. Harold felt his stick being pulled from his hands. Someone plucked the fish from his shoulder. And when he turned, wheeling back at the tug on the string, feet entangled in his and sent him sprawling in the dust as the children laughed and shouted.

10

All the time he never said a word, and his expression never changed. *I'm the Ghost,* he told himself. *I'm Harold the Ghost.* And he tried to make himself small and invisible, to vanish into the crowd. He repeated the little chant he'd invented, his eyes closed tight behind his glasses.

No one can see me, no one can hurt me. The words that they say cannot harm me.

Then, like the sudden passing of an August storm, the children were gone again. Harold lay by himself in the grass and the dirt, in the bright shadows of a sideshow tent. It rose above him, the roof hauled up like skirts around the frame of poles, a canvas wall that the sun shone through. The dog nuzzled against him, and he let her take hot, slobbery licks at his nose as he picked up his helmet and his little round glasses and put them on again. He didn't know why he'd been left alone until, looking up, he saw the shadow on the canvas.

Whatever cast it was huge and shaggy, more a beast than a man. Hair-covered arms spread across the canvas, and the cloth puckered in sharp little points, as though the thing had claws for fingers. The sun twinkled through pinholes in the old, faded cloth, and the shadow moved sideways, flickering across the tent like a cartoon phantom on a movie screen.

The head was huge and wild with hair. It pressed against the canvas, blotting out a pinhole.

The dog barked. Harold took hold of her collar. "Come on," he whispered. "We'd better go, you bet."

He set off down the tent, and the shadow went with him, pace for pace. Harold hurried; the shadow hurried. Then it bounded before him and vanished in the doubled thickness of a tent flap. The canvas bulged, an arm reached through the gap. The creature really *was* matted with hair. Its fingers really *were* claws, and they clutched on to Harold's shoulder and pulled him into the tent.

Chapter 3

Harold blinked through the glasses at a swirl of shadows and shapes. At his back, the creature held him by the elbows. His dog howled like a lunatic beyond the canvas wall.

"Say, you're scaring the boy," said a lady from the corner. "Let him go, you big lug."

The claws came away from his arms.

"And bring that dog in, for heaven's sakes. It's barking its head off out there."

The creature stepped around from behind him, and Harold saw shoulders as wide as a doorway, hands and feet so thick with black hair that they might have been covered in fur. The thing swept open the tent flap, and Honey came slinking inside.

"Say," said the lady, "that's a pretty swell dog. Hey, puppy, come here."

"She won't," said Harold. "She won't go to anyone else but me."

The dog came slinking past the creature, then bounded toward Harold, and he held his hands to catch her. She was running, he saw, really running for the first time in years. And she ran right past him, to the lady in the corner.

"Yeah, he's swell all right," the lady said. "Oh,

you're such a pretty dog. You're just the cat's pajamas."

Harold took off his glasses and folded them into his hands. Nearly half the tent was a cage. But the door was open, as though the beast had just wandered out. Beyond it, in a corner where the shadows were darkest, stood a platform draped in velvet. At its center was a little chair, and in it sat a tiny lady no bigger than a doll. She was leaning forward, her head at the same height as the dog's, her little fists buried in its hair.

Harold rubbed his eyes. He couldn't believe he was seeing right, a woman as small as that. Her face was the size of a child's but as old as an adult's. It was hard to look at her, but impossible not to.

"What do you call him?" she asked.

"She's a girl, not a him," said Harold. "Her name's Honey."

The lady laughed. "And look," she said. "She's sort of honey colored." She grinned at Harold. "You're so clever. I would have called her Muffy."

Harold shrugged. It bothered him that the dog had gone to her and not to him. "Honey," he said, reaching out. "Come here. Come on, girl." But the dog didn't move.

"I like dogs," said the lady. "Not like Samuel there." She was quite fat for her size, her black dress swelling down from her shoulders like a small, dark balloon. Then she raised her voice. "Say, Samuel, where are your manners? You're standing around like a lamppost, you big nut. Why don't you get the boy a Coke?"

The big, shaggy figure went shambling to the end of the tent. He rummaged through boxes, his back toward Harold. There was a clinking of bottles; then he straightened. And turned.

Harold gasped. The man was hardly human at all. He had great, thick brows and the flattened nose of an ape, his ghastly face covered all over with hair as coarse as string. He put the bottle in his mouth, between teeth that were crooked and sharp. There was a little snapping sound as he tore off the cap, and the Coke fizzed from his mouth in a froth, tumbling in brown foam down his cheeks and his beard. He thrust the bottle at Harold.

Harold would have run from the tent in a moment if the thing hadn't been blocking his way. The bottle hovered between them.

"Take it," said the woman. "You'll hurt his feelings if you don't."

Harold took it; snatched it, really. It disgusted him to feel his hand scrape against the hair on Samuel's fingers, as stiff and bristly as a scrubbing brush. He didn't want the Coke; he felt he couldn't swallow a drop of it after seeing that bottle—a third of its length—inside the creature's mouth.

Samuel stared down at him through small black eyes. And then, for the first time, he spoke. He said, "It's not very cold, I'm afraid. It's the heat here, you see; you can't keep anything cold in this heat."

It was a sad little voice, even more shocking for Harold than the sight of the creature, half man and half ape, that towered above him. He stared up at the gruesome face, trying to make sense of it. But Samuel turned away and threw himself down on a little round pillow.

"Have you taught your dog any tricks?" asked the woman.

"Some." The Coke still fizzed from the mouth of the bottle. It was warm and sticky on his fingers.

"Come and show me."

He sat at the edge of the platform and made the dog shake hands. She shook hands with the little woman. "Sing," he said, but Honey only looked at him.

"Sing," said the little woman, and Honey put back her head and wailed.

The little woman laughed. "That's something else," she said. "Say, Samuel, wouldn't you like a dog like this?"

Samuel grunted. "No," he said.

"Oh, posh. So, what else can your dog do, kid?"

"Lots," said Harold. But he didn't feel like showing her. He was frightened that the dog would do tricks only for the woman. "Can I go now?" he asked.

The woman smiled at him. "You can go whenever you want."

"Come on, Honey." He snapped his fingers. The dog looked at him but pressed closer to the lady, whose chubby little hands tweaked at Honey's ears.

"Say," said the small woman. "That shouting we heard. Was that about you?"

Harold nodded.

"I thought so," she said. "It's tough, isn't it? We know what it's like to be different."

He wasn't *that* different, he thought. At least he wasn't three feet tall; at least he wasn't half an ape.

"Maybe you should come with us," she said. "You and your dog."

The beast grunted. "Don't tell him that," he said.

"He's got a home, a mom and dad. Don't fill his head with notions."

"Don't listen to *him*," she said to Harold. "He's just a big stick-in-the-mud. We're going west if you want to come."

"To Oregon?" Harold asked.

"Why, sure. We go there every year."

"Have you seen the forests?"

"Gosh, yes! There's forests that go on forever."

"And mountains?"

"This big!" She stretched up her tiny arms. "They're covered in snow right through the summer. And the ocean! Oh, don't get me started."

"Too late," said the beast.

"I'm going to go there," said Harold. "To Oregon."

The lady smiled. "You are?"

"You bet," he said. "When my brother comes home he's going to buy us some horses, and we're going to get on them and ride right to Oregon. We're going to live like mountain men, fishing for trout and hunting for deer." Forgetting himself, he took a drink from the bottle. "He's in the army now, and some people say he's not coming home, but he is."

"Sure he is, kid."

She didn't believe him; he could see that in her eyes. She looked away from him, over at the beast. "Couldn't we take him, Samuel? I could square it with Mr. Hunter."

For a moment Harold was happy. He saw the convoy of trucks heading west, the big silvery trailers. He saw himself at a window as the prairies went by and turned into forests and then into mountains. He saw himself rattling through the great cities, thousands of children standing to watch, waving at him—at Harold the Ghost, the whitewashed boy. And the picture melted away. He looked at the tiny little woman perched like a bird on the platform. He turned his head and saw Samuel there on his pillow, watching him with those animal eyes.

"No," he said. "No way. I'm not going off with a freak show."

"Gee, kid, that's not what I meant."

He put the bottle on the floor. "If I leave now," he said, and nodded toward Samuel, "will *he* try to stop me?"

"Of course not," she said.

He got to his feet. "Honey, come on," he said. But the dog didn't move. "Honey, please."

The small woman took her hands from the dog, but still Honey wouldn't move; she only stared at him with her head tipped sideways. Harold felt tears come to his eyes. Then he turned and ran for the tent flap.

Chapter

4

His big boots carried him over the field, over the gravel and up to the dust of Main Street. The wind was furnace hot, and dust devils swirled before him, blotting out the writing on the windows. The tilted sign of Kline and Sons banged against the wall, and Harold the Ghost went into the doorway below it.

In the days before the war, his father had kept the building painted and clean. Its big yellow front had sparkled in the sun, so that Kline and Sons, the dry-goods store, had stood out among all the other buildings. But now it was the dustiest building on Main Street, as hollow as an old pumpkin. And Harold reached through the hole where a window had been, and turned the brass knob to let himself inside.

The store was warm but not hot, the dry air thick with a smell of old paper and wood. Spiders had spun skeins of thread from every wall and every corner and shelf. Mice had built enormous nests of ledger pages, heaps of paper in little bits of yellow, white and blue. All around the room great chunks of gypsum had been knocked from the walls so the laths showed through like the bones of the building.

There were times when Harold thought his father still kept the store, tending to a ghostly business in the quiet and the shadows. He had seen his shape standing at the counter, had heard his footsteps and the cheerful little songs he whistled, again and again.

Now it was just a sad place to come to when he was sad, a place to wrap himself in sadness. He sat on the floor, facing the street. He sat for a long, long time. Then a smear of sun appeared across the dusty window, and another below it, a square of sun with a man in the middle, rubbing at the glass. It was Hopalong John, lame in one leg, holding a bundle in his left hand, a cloth in his right. He peered through the window, then came to the doorway. He spoke through the missing pane.

"I didn't know you was in there," he said. "If I'd knowed, I'd have asked."

"Asked what?" said Harold. He went to the door.

"Posters," said Hopalong, lifting his bundle. He carried rolls of paper bound by string, and he stepped clumsily back as Harold opened the door. "I'm putting up posters on windas."

Harold came out beside him.

"Where's your dog?" Hopalong John stared past him into the building. "Don't think I've ever seen you without that dog nearby. It's like the sun come out and you ain't got no shadow."

"She's at the circus," said Harold.

"Guess everyone is." Hopalong scratched his head. "They're giving out jobs like the Fuller Brush man gives away brushes. They've got me putting up posters, you see?" He pulled out a poster and let it unwind, and the breeze stretched it flat on the air.

Hunter and Green's Traveling Circus, it said across the top. There was a picture of an elephant carrying a dozen children on its back. A man standing beside it barely reached the knees.

"That's one big critter there," said Hopalong John. Harold squinted at it.

"I knew your daddy wouldn't mind if I put this on the winda."

Harold shrugged. "Go ahead."

Hopalong put up his poster, and they both stood back to look at it, Harold with his head at a slant. He could see a circus tent and rows and rows of wagons behind the elephant. In the distance were the mountains, just barely there, a bit of jagged blue.

"I guess if I was younger, I'd go traveling with the circus," said Hopalong. "If I didn't have a bum leg, I'd be up there on the tightrope, see." He pointed at the poster. Under the elephant's trunk, so small that Harold couldn't really see it at all, was a figure in a leotard balanced on a line as thin as a thread.

"Damn the war," said Hopalong. "Damn it all to hell."

"You weren't in the war," said Harold.

Hopalong squinted. "I was thinking of you. Look what it did to you. Took your daddy and killed him. Took your brother, David, and never gave him back."

"He's coming home," said Harold.

"Don't I know it?" Hopalong gathered up his bundle, his cloth, the little bucket of paste he'd set below the window. "Why, he's probably sitting in Tokyo now, figuring out how to get back." He jabbed a paste-speckled finger at the poster. "But don't you think that looks like him? That little guy there in the tights?"

Harold stood so close to the picture that his nose almost touched it. The tightrope walker, he saw, did

21

look like David, tall and slim and bulging with muscles. He gazed at the figure, remembering things he was afraid he'd forget: splashing through the Rattlesnake with David, swinging from the fence rails, just walking down the street and feeling big as Gary Cooper. No one dared to tease him then, with David right beside him.

"What else have you got there?" he asked.

"Well, I'll show you." They started back along the main street, and on every window was a poster. The pictures hung askew on doorways and wrapped around telephone poles. There were clowns. There were people on trapezes, a juggler and a bareback rider.

"And look at this," said Hopalong, coming to the credit union.

It was an enormous poster, and across its top it said Freaks of Nature. And there was the tiny lady and the ugly giant of a man that she'd called Samuel. Princess Minikin, the poster said; She Lived Among the Crowned Heads of Europe. And beside that: The Fossil Man! Is He an Ape or a Man? He's the Missing Link, a Living Fossil Direct from Darkest Africa!

"I met them," said Harold.

"Did you, by gosh? You met a living fossil?"

"I guess I did," said Harold.

"And did you meet the Cannibal King?"

"Who?"

"The King! The Cannibal King!" He hopped up on his one good leg. "Well, come and look, Harold."

Even limping, Hopalong John went faster than Harold. He scuttled ahead, waited, then scuttled along again, to the corner of the drugstore. "Well, here's your dog," he called. "Here she comes after you, sure as pigs follow the slop bucket."

She came around the corner, but Harold didn't stop. He would ignore her, he thought; he didn't care if she followed or not. And then he looked back, to show that he didn't care, and Honey was lying flat on her stomach with her paws on her nose.

"Oh, come on, then," he said, and she trotted up by his side. He bent down and ruffled the fur between her ears. He cuffed her ribs the way she liked.

"What's that she's got in her collar?" asked Hopalong. "See there? She's got something stuffed in her collar."

It was a piece of white paper folded in three, with a ticket inside for the circus. Harold held the ticket in one hand, the paper in the other, and read the writing that went in a crazy scrawl.

> *To the boy from Libberty*
> *Deer boy,*
>   *Jist to show theres no hard fealings heres a tikket to the circus. We are jist going to bee hear for only one nite so you better come to nite. Drop by and see us if you like to. We hope you will.*
>   *Your freinds,*
>   *Samuel and Tina*

"Geez, it's your lucky day," said Hopalong. "Now you can meet him."

"Who?" said Harold.

"The Cannibal King! Come on and look."

23

They went halfway down the building before Hopalong stopped. The poster was close to the ground, and he beamed at it so proudly that he might have painted the picture instead of only pasting it up on the wall.

"You see?" said Hopalong. "There he is. The Cannibal King."

The man on the poster was wearing a leopard skin and a necklace of bones, a round white shell for an earring. His hand was held high, and dangling from it by its hair was a shrunken head. He stared ferociously out of the picture.

"You see?" said Hopalong John.

Harold nodded.

"He's just like you."

"Yes," said Harold.

The Cannibal King was an albino.

His skin was white, his hair a woolly shock, like a feathery cloud on a summer day. But what a cloud! It rose like thunderheads, billowing out in wild array, a huge white mass of hair. His eyebrows were the same, and his hands were like blocks of ivory.

"You see what it says?" said Hopalong. He pointed at the poster, reading out the words. "He's the strange king of a strange tribe—the Stone People, from the jungles of a Pacific island. They hunt for human food! They boil their hapless victims and shrink their heads for trophies! And now he's here on his first world tour, the Cannibal King of Oola Boola Mambo!"

Hopalong took down his finger. "Lordy!" he said. "I didn't know there was *anyone* looked like you. Not anyone."

"No," said Harold. All his life he'd felt alone.

24

"You've got to meet that fella, Harold. You've just got to."

"Where do you think Oola Boola Mambo is?"

"Oh, miles away," said Hopalong. "Maybe he'll take you there." Then he frowned. "Do you think he's really a cannibal?"

"If it says it's true, it must be true," said Harold. "You can't say it's true if it's not."

"I guess so," said Hopalong.

"But maybe he's not *always* a cannibal." Harold looked sideways at the bones and the shrunken head. He wasn't sure if he wanted to go to Oola Boola Mambo. But he was certain of this: He had to meet the Cannibal King.

Chapter 5

Mrs. Beesley, Harold's mother, was as big and as shiny as a 4-H pig. She sat in the middle of the front steps, fanning herself with *The Liberty News*.

"Where have *you* been?" she asked as Harold came up the path.

"Fishing," he said. "I got a sucker, Ma."

"I'll sucker you," she said, and stopped fanning. "What have I *told* you about going off without telling us? Huh? Your father had to go looking for you."

Harold stopped at the foot of the steps. "He isn't my father," he said.

"Well, he's *trying* to be," said Mrs. Beesley. "And if you gave him so much as *half* of a chance, you'd find out he's a very nice man."

There was nothing nice about Walter Beesley as far as Harold was concerned. He sat in the chair that belonged to Harold's father, slept in his bed, ate with his knife and fork. A tall, weedy man, Walter was a banker in the daytime, at night a collector of stamps. He spent hours at that, bending over a scatter of stamps that looked all alike to Harold, demanding silence as he fumbled with the tiny hinges and fixed the stamps in place.

"He's got a heart of *gold*," said Mrs. Beesley.

26

Harold looked at the ground. Quietly he asked, "Then why did Daddy never like him?"

"Oh!" she said. "Oh! You've got a *real* smart mouth on *you* today." She fanned herself quickly. "Then tell me, *Mr. Smartmouth,* if you went fishing, where's your pole? Huh? If you *really* went fishing, where's this *world-famous* sucker of yours?"

"I lost them," said Harold. He scrunched up his eyes to keep from crying. He hated coming home.

"You can't go out without losing *something.*" She shook her head, her mouth in a frown. "You'd think money grew on *trees,* the way you treat the things we buy you."

"It was just a crummy old stick," he said.

"And why is *that*? Huh?" Mrs. Beesley tugged at her dress; it was stuck to the steps with sweat. "Because you *lost* your good one. You lost your *reel* and your *knife* and your *net*." She counted the things off on her fingers, whapping her hand with the paper. "Two pairs of *shoes* and *eight* pairs of mittens over the winter. Where have they gone? Huh? Where have they *gone*?"

Harold shrugged. "I don't know," he said. It wasn't a lie. Everything she'd named had been snatched away; he didn't know where they were.

"You don't know *nothing,*" she said. "I should send you out like Farmer Hull's old *beat-up* Dodge, all tied together with bits of string and wire."

He couldn't help it then. He started to cry, and the tears rolled out from under his little dark glasses. He missed his father terribly, his father and his brother. They had never shouted at him, and in those days neither had his mother. Hopalong John was right; the war had ruined everything, and the war had made her crazy.

"And what's *that* in your hand?" she asked.

Harold looked at the paper as though he had never seen it before. "A ticket," he said. "To the circus."

"Huh!" she cried. "And I suppose you caught *that* while you were fishing."

"I was given it," he said.

"Well, if you think you're going off to the circus, you've another think coming," said Mrs. Beesley. "Your father's not going to stand for your going to the circus."

Harold said stubbornly, "He isn't my father." Then he climbed up the steps and went right past his mother, into the house and through to the kitchen. Honey went behind him.

Strips of brown tape hung from the ceiling, matted with the bodies of flies. They spun slowly in the drafts of warm air that came through the window screens. Harold filled Honey's water dish and watched for a while as she drank. Then he opened the white slab door of the refrigerator and found a jug of iced tea inside, with wedges of lemon and lime bobbing on the surface.

"I wondered how long it would take you to sniff that out," said Mrs. Beesley, suddenly filling the doorway. "Now you just keep out of that icebox, you hear."

"It's a refrigerator, Ma."

"Oh!" she said. "Well, you just keep *out* of it, because that iced tea's for your *father*, you hear? He's going to be hot, and he's going to be tired, because he's out there in this *devil's heat* searching all of God's acres for you."

28

Harold didn't answer. He closed the door with his hip.

"And here he is now," she said, hearing his step on the porch. She fussed at her dress, at her tangles of hair. Suddenly she was smiling. "Oh, all right," she said. "You can have one glass. A *little* one, mind. And bring a large one for your father."

Walter Beesley had blisters on his feet and a mass of burrs clinging to his pants. "I walked right to the Rattlesnake," he said. "Clear to the Rattlesnake."

"You poor thing," said Mrs. Beesley. She sat him down in the big armchair, beside the card table covered with his albums and stamps. She knelt on the floor and untied the laces of his banker's shoes.

He leaned back, exhausted. He could barely lift an arm to take the glass from Harold. "Well, at least the boy's here," he said. "Doesn't seem any worse for wear."

"He *claims* he was fishing," said Mrs. Beesley. She pulled off the shoes and arranged them beside the chair. "He *claims* he was down at the Rattlesnake."

"In this heat? And the sun like a blowtorch?"

Mrs. Beesley nodded. "He claims he was *fishing*," she said again. "But he came home with a ticket to the circus. He came home not half an hour ago, all *het up* about going to the circus."

Harold stood and watched as they talked about him, the boy who wasn't there.

"I know a thing or two about circuses," said Walter Beesley. "And they're dens of evil, that's what they are." Walter held the glass of iced tea against his forehead. "They're the haunts of Gypsies."

"You tell him," said Mrs. Beesley.

Walter rolled the glass back and forth across his brow. "I know a thing or two about Gypsies. And there's nothing good to be said in that department." He flexed his toes in his thin black socks. "No, I think the circus is not a fit place for a boy like you. A gullible boy."

Harold felt very small. He felt too small to answer.

Mrs. Beesley glared at him. Her fat white fingers kneaded at Walter's feet. "You hear that?" she said. "Your father's made a decision."

"And stay out of the sun," said Walter. He shook a thin finger at Harold. "A boy like you, you're different from the others. The sun will kill you, don't you know that? It'll burn you like old, dry grass. It'll make a blind man of you before you're twenty-one."

Mrs. Beesley smiled. "You see?" she crowed. "There'll be no more fishing. No more *gallivanting* across the countryside."

Harold felt smaller and smaller and smaller.

"I've tried," said Walter Beesley. "Lord knows how much I've tried." He turned his eyes to the ceiling. "I'd hoped to interest you in philately, in books and accounting, in pursuits more apt for a boy like you. I know a thing or two about albinos, and I'll tell you this: They spend their lives inside. They don't go traipsing around the country."

Harold thought of the Cannibal King. *On his first world tour.*

"You're not a normal boy," said Walter Beesley. "You're not like the others, who can go off playing for hour after hour. You're—" He raised his voice. "Look at me when I'm talking to you."

Harold turned his head away, looking sideways at his stepfather to keep his vision focused.

"Look at me!" shouted Walter.

"I can't," Harold cried, and fled to his room.

From the window there he watched the sun go down. He saw the smears of color changing and looked forward to the darkness. He liked the shadows more than light, the coolness more than heat. What Walter had told him was true; the sun did terrible things to his skin and made his eyes burn with unbearable pain.

The shadows thickened and filled around him. The huge, flat horizon of the prairies turned to purple and then to black. And Harold sat in a silence so oppressive that he heard the ticking of the clock in the room below his own and the squeaking of the hinges in Walter Beesley's rickety folding table.

He stared through the window, over the roof of the station, and saw the circus big top glowing with light. Then, so very faint that they were hardly there, came the first wheezy notes of the calliope. It was a cheerful song, whistled the way his father would have whistled it among the shelves of Kline and Sons. The music swelled and filled the air, and a swarm of fireflies rose from the garden, twinkling in the hoot and shriek of the song. And then the people started passing, streaming down to Batsford's field, and he watched them from above, the little children holding hands with parents as the calliope played them to the circus.

Chapter
6

Harold lay on the bed on his back, gazing up at a jagged, toothy line of baseball pennants. Beside him was a gun rack holding Louisville Sluggers instead of rifles. And beside that was a shelf eight feet long crowded with trophies, with a catcher's mitt stuffed inside a mask, a fielder's glove bound by string around an oversized softball that was painted red and yellow.

They were David's; everything was David's. "Don't cry because I'm going," he'd told Harold the morning he left for the war. "Ghosts never cry," he'd said, and punched Harold's arm lightly.

"I'm frightened," Harold had said. "I'm scared you won't come back."

David had laughed. "Of course I will. And we'll get a couple of horses and follow the Oregon Trail like Dad always talked about doing. We'll see the ocean."

"And the mountains?"

"And the forests," David had said.

"And we'll live like mountain men?"

"Sure." David had laughed once more. "On the weekends we'll ride down to the ocean."

Then David had put on his soldier's cap and picked up his duffel bag. "Look after Ma," he'd said. "And don't go touching my junk." And Harold never had.

Every week he dusted, whisking at the pennants and the trophies with a big feather duster, taking great care that nothing was moved.

Only one thing was gone: the top bunk of the pair. His mother had taken it away more than a year ago, but still it was strange for Harold to look up from the bed and see the ceiling high above him instead of the boards of his brother's bed.

"He's gone," his mother had said. She was just starting to change then, getting fat, going crazy.

"He's not," he'd said. "He's missing, that's all. Just missing in action."

"But he's not coming back," she'd told him. "And it's high time you faced up to that." Then she'd taken the bed in pieces because Harold wouldn't help—the headboard and footboard, and then the big hollow base that boomed on the stairs as she dragged it down by herself.

Harold gazed at the pennants. He watched them flutter in his poor, weak eyes. And he waited, and the calliope played.

At ten o'clock there were heavy thumps in the hall as his mother went off to her bed. At eleven Walter went too.

Harold got up. He pulled his pillow out of its slip and stuffed the bag full of clothes. He worked as quietly as he could, glancing at Honey to see that she didn't come awake. He stepped around her, back and forth, sorting out socks without holes, the best of his shirts, the cleanest of his underwear. From the shelf he took the fielder's glove, knowing that David wouldn't mind; Harold had worn the glove as often as his brother. "I'll never make the majors,"

David had said. "But *you* might, Harold. You're a natural."

A natural. Even then, Harold had known he wasn't that. David had got the biggest ball he could find—a softball, the sissy's ball—and painted it as yellow as sunflowers. Then on top of the yellow he'd painted red stripes, so that even Harold could see it. And then he'd spent hours pitching the ball as slowly as anyone could—never laughing, never getting angry—until Harold learned to catch it and hit it as well as anyone else.

Now the paint was cracked, the white of the softball showing through the yellow. It nestled in the glove like a colorful egg about to open. *Take it,* David's voice said. *It's yours. Just take it.*

Harold shoved the ball and the glove into the pillowcase. He squashed it down and tied a knot with the corners, and it weighed half a ton with all the things he'd packed. So he stepped across Honey one more time and took a bat from the wall to slip through his knot for a handle. Then he stood at the door, staring back at his dog.

She slept in a ball, her head on her paws. One hind leg was crooked out behind her like a frog's, but she had slept that way ever since Harold could remember. He watched her breathing, her eyelids just barely fluttering. And he smiled at her, aching to touch her again. "So long, old girl," he said. "You be a good dog, you hear?" Then he turned the knob as slowly as possible, listening through it for sounds from his mother's room. With a tiny click the latch sprang open.

And Honey came awake.

Her feet tangled in the blanket and scratched

34

against the floor. Maybe the sight of the baseball bat made her young again; maybe it was just the open door and the sense of excitement that came through it with a faraway drumroll—faint as crickets—beating from the circus. But she bounded across the floor like a puppy and banged against Harold. And in her eagerness she barked.

Across the hall, bedsprings squeaked.

"Hush!" said Harold. He blocked the door with his leg, and again she barked. "Oh, Honey," he whispered. "You have to be quiet."

"What's going on out there?" asked Walter Beesley from the bedroom.

"Nothing," said Harold. He stood half in the doorway and half in his room, the pillowcase at his feet with the bat resting across it. Honey sniffed and whined, then raised her head.

"Don't bark," whispered Harold.

Her chin quivered. And he hit her.

It was the first time he had ever hit her, and he heard her teeth knock together as his fingers slapped her nose. She reeled away as though he'd done it with a sledgehammer, slamming her head against the door. It rattled on its hinges, and she barked again, and yelped. And Mrs. Beesley, half asleep, said: "Get that fleabag back in bed!"

Honey cowered on the floor, and Harold threw himself down beside her. "I'm sorry," he said. "Oh, I'm sorry." He put his hand out to stroke her, but she cringed away, her eyes flickering shut, fearful he would hit her again.

"Oh, gosh," he said. "Gosh, I was frightened, that's all." He stretched out on the floor, the same height as

Honey. He threw an arm across her back; he pressed his cheek against her nose. "I've got to go," he said in a whisper. "I've just *got* to go, and I can't take you with me. I wish I could, you bet I do, but I can't, you poor old thing."

Honey shuddered under his arm. She whimpered, almost like a baby.

"Oh, don't cry," he said. "Don't cry because I'm going."

He stroked her in all the places she liked to be stroked. He told her he'd be back, that David would come and they'd *all* go out to Oregon. But he couldn't help thinking he was seeing her for the last time.

There was white and gray in her muzzle. Her eyes were clouded, crusty in the corners. There were pink warts on her paws that were spreading, month by month, across her back and shoulders. She lifted her head and gazed at him. And he blinked his eyes; he fussed with her blanket, pressing it around her, making a pillow of folds for her chin.

"I love you, Honey," he whispered. And once more he patted her. "You be a good dog, you hear?"

Then he sniffed; he wiped his nose on his sleeve. "And don't go touching my junk."

He didn't look back. He went to the door and pushed the pillowcase out with his foot. He listened for a while to the sound of his mother breathing—almost snoring—in her bed. And he wished not that he could go and say goodbye but that he *wanted* to say goodbye.

He closed his bedroom door. He padded down the stairs, through the living room, out to the porch and the summer night.

White and helmeted, Harold the Ghost stole through the darkness. He hurried from house to house, from walls to fences to hedges. The bat on his shoulder, the bag against his back, he made his way to Main Street and the row of buildings there.

He stopped and listened. But there was no calliope music, no murmur of a crowd.

From the prairie to the west came a single spot of light growing larger on the road, then the rattle and bang of an old truck. Harold waited at the side of May's Cafe as it came steadily toward him, not slowing for the town. Bits of stone and gravel shotgunned off the sides; dust rose up behind the light. And Farmer Hull went hammering past in his truck with one headlight and no fenders, intent on his driving, hunched over the wheel. Then Harold the Ghost crossed the road, passed the station and made his way to Batsford's field.

He found it empty; the circus was gone.

There were long, greasy ruts in the grass, like the faint tracings of the Oregon Trail. Everywhere lay ticket stubs and candy wrappers. Crows pecked at chewed-away corncobs and hamburger wrappers, and Harold the Ghost put down his bundle. He sat on the grass in a thin circle of sawdust where the big top had been.

The moonlight shone down on him, a little white dot in the vast, empty field.

Across it came the horseman, the old Indian, his feathers fluttering and the fringes of his buckskin tapping on the horse's hide. He came up beside Harold.

"What was it?" he asked. "What sort of fish did you catch?"

Harold looked up. "A sucker," he said.

The old Indian nodded. He looked to the west. "Do you want to ride with me?" he asked.

Harold passed up his bundle, and the old Indian balanced it on top of his own, on the cream-colored mane of the horse. He held a big red hand toward Harold, and the boy climbed up behind him. Then the horse started forward, across the field and onto the prairie, down the grown-over path of the Oregon Trail.

They didn't talk. Harold slumped down until his head was on the old Indian's shoulder, his hands resting lightly on buckskin-clad hips. The crickets chirped and the horse swayed along. The grass whispered past, and soon Harold was sleeping.

When he woke again, he was twenty miles from Liberty.

Chapter
7

The old Indian built a fire by a little stream. He made it out of sticks and grass, and the smoke went up in a spiral. From his bundle he got a pot that he filled with water and set by the fire to boil.

He had taken off his headdress and left it lying across the horse. His hair was gray and very long, tied in double braids. He crouched by the fire and the smoke wrapped around him, thick as woolen blankets. It covered him completely, then drifted on and up.

"How old are you?" asked Harold.

"Very old." He looked all around, across the stream and across the prairie. "There's nothing you can see that was here when I was born."

"The grass?" asked Harold.

"It burns and grows again."

"The river, then," said Harold.

"It rises from a pond that was dug by cattle herders. Fifty years ago it wasn't here."

"The Oregon Trail," said Harold. "The ruts the wagons made."

"I remember when they passed." The old Indian smiled. He threw a bunch of yellow grass onto the fire, and the smoke came up through the stems. "I saw them from a distance. I thought they were clouds floating on the ground."

Harold squinted at him through his round glasses. "That was more than a hundred years ago."

"It seems like yesterday," said the old Indian.

Harold stood up to see farther. Bands of grass, one after another, rolled for miles around him. There were clouds far to the west, low in the sky, like enormous sheep grazing beyond the horizon. And the faint lines of the Oregon Trail led toward them like a mystical road.

"My grandmother wasn't born then," said Harold. "*Her* mother rode in the wagons, and she was only thirteen."

The old Indian grunted. "Maybe I met her," he said.

It seemed impossible to Harold. His great-grandmother had kept a diary of the trip. He had peered at her penciled writing until his eyes ached, puzzling out stories of broken-down wagons and river crossings and buffalo by the million.

"I remember when the ground was covered with buffaloes," said the old Indian, as though reading his mind. "I remember thinking they would last forever."

"I wish I lived back then," said Harold.

"It was the best time to be alive, I think."

Harold sat beside him, close to the fire, smelling the grass that was burning. "Did you meet Jesse James?" he asked.

"Only once. Didn't care for him much."

"And Custer?"

The old Indian stretched out his leg. He pulled the fringes aside and pointed to a button that kept the

40

leggings fastened. "That was Custer's," he said. He rubbed the button with a gnarled old finger, and the tarnish came away, showing silver swords. "I wove a string from his yellow hair, but it turned to brown and then to black, and I threw it away. People laughed; they said it was my own hair, not the Son of the Morning Star's."

"Did you know Crazy Horse?"

"Like a brother," said the old Indian. "He used to sit me on his knee and tell me legends."

"What sort of legends?"

"I don't want to talk about it," said the old Indian. "We've talked enough."

"Just tell me one," said Harold. "Tell me why they named you Thunder Wakes Him."

The old Indian placed his grass on the fire, and the smoke became so thick that Harold couldn't breathe. He staggered from it, blinded and choking, but the old Indian stayed where he was. The smoke wrapped him up and made a ghost of him as he poked at his pot of water.

They ate their breakfast, slept and carried on.

All that day they rode to the west. As the sun rose higher their shadows shortened ahead, as though they somehow overran them and, at noon, trampled them under the hooves of the big chestnut horse.

And then the old Indian spoke, the first time since that morning.

"All right," he said. "I'll tell you one." And he began the legend of Buffalo Woman.

Harold wriggled forward. He pressed himself against the old Indian and *felt* the words that rumbled from his chest.

41

"She appeared before my people on a summer's day," he said. "She came walking from the clouds, dressed in white skins. A warrior saw her and thought she was so beautiful that he would carry her off and take her for his wife. But a cloud descended on him, a swirling cloud that caught him up and turned him into dust and bones. Then Buffalo Woman came to the village, and she showed my people how to live in peace, all together, all the people and all the animals and all the world we shared. And then she left again, and she rolled once across the ground and became a black buffalo. She rolled a second time and became a brown buffalo. And the third time that Buffalo Woman rolled across the ground she rose again as white as snow."

The old Indian raised his arm. "She went across the prairie at a walk and then a run. She left the ground and galloped through the sky." His hand rose higher. "She ran up and up. A white buffalo calf running through the clouds. She vanished in the clouds."

The old Indian's fingers closed in a fist, as though he clutched at the sky. Then he lowered his hand and took up the reins. "The legend is that one day she'll return. And the buffalo will roam again, the fences will be gone. It will be as it used to be in the days I can't remember."

"Will she come back as a buffalo?" asked Harold.

"I believe so. But who can say?" The old Indian shifted on the horse. The lance, in his left hand, tilted toward the west.

They came to a fence of barbed wire stretching as far as they could see to either side. The posts seemed to shrink away, as though the fence was only inches high everywhere but right before them. A tumbleweed was jammed below the lowest wire, and a clump of fur clung to the one above it. The old Indian got down from the horse. He closed his big fists around the upper wire and popped the staples loose. He held the wire down and whistled to the horse, which stepped across beside him. And on they rode toward the west.

"Where's the circus now?" asked Harold.

The old Indian pointed over the horse's ear, a little to his right.

"When do we get there?"

"Not tonight. Tomorrow, maybe."

The grazing clouds were coming closer. The wind that drove them bent the grass and lifted the feathers on the old Indian's lance.

Harold smelled smoke on his buckskins. "Why do you follow it?" he asked.

"I'm in it," said the old Indian. He sounded a bit offended.

He was small and withered. Harold couldn't imagine him performing in a circus.

"I do some fancy riding," said the old Indian. "I whoop and holler and dash around the ring a bit. It's just a show; it's what the people want."

Harold smiled. "How long have you done that?"

"I started with Buffalo Bill. In that Wild West show he had."

Harold straightened; his head came up from the old Indian's back. "You knew Buffalo Bill?"

"No one knew Bill," said the old Indian. "He was a different person for everyone he met. He was full of himself. Read too many of those books."

"What books?" asked Harold.

"The ones about himself." The old Indian bent his shoulders back and straightened them again. "He was always reading them. Sometimes he'd laugh and sometimes he'd say, 'Yeah, I remember that.' Didn't matter if it never happened. He lost himself inside himself. Not like the Cannibal King."

"What do you mean?" asked Harold.

"You will understand when we find him."

It was all the old Indian would say. They rode along, and the tumbleweeds went sailing by on the waves of grass. The buildings of a town rose up far to the north and vanished again behind them. They spent the night on the open prairie and heard the coyotes calling.

Chapter

8

The morning clouds were thick toward the west. Blue and black, smeared with yellow, they made the sky look bruised and battered. The feathers of the old Indian's headdress flapped like wings, and Harold was forever fending them off.

"He's a good man," said the old Indian suddenly.

"Who?" asked Harold.

"The Cannibal King."

The old Indian glanced back. He saw the feathers fluttering and took off his headdress. He added it to the bundles, folding it carefully as the reins hung slack across the horse's neck and the animal plodded along.

They crossed another fence, and a third, a dirt road running north to south between them. Again they ran their shadows down and trampled them at noon. And then the sun went on ahead, and the clouds came up to meet it.

Darker than before, the clouds oozed across the prairie, pressing on the grass. Lightning flickered through them, faint in the distance. And they drove before them a herd of tumbleweeds that bounded in fright. They drove black streaks of crickets, songbirds by the hundreds and a flock of whirring crows.

Harold sat closer to the old Indian, until they

shared his tattered saddle blanket. He heard the wind passing through the feathers on the lance. His helmet straps slapped his neck, and he heard the snorting of the horse's breath.

"We'll have to stop," said the old Indian. "We'll have to find a shelter."

They rode west toward the lightning and the hollow sound of thunder, toward a belt of purple clouds. The old Indian turned the horse, and the wind blew sideways at them. The rain started, warm and heavy, and soon was thicker than the Rattlesnake. The old Indian hauled his deerskins around his shoulders; he made a hood that covered his head. Then the horse stepped down into a shallow bowl of grass and dirt where a buffalo skull—half buried—lay staring at the sky.

It was there that Harold the Ghost and Thunder Wakes Him took shelter from the storm. Side by side they lay, one as bright as whitewash, the other dark as terra-cotta. In an ancient buffalo wallow, worn into the prairie by the trampling and scraping of a million shaggy hooves, they lay with a blanket around them as the wind tore at the mane of the chestnut horse.

The rain slashed across the hollow, driven by the wind. For Harold, it was like looking at a river flowing past above him. Waves of rain went by.

The wind howled from the west, and suddenly from the south. It came with such a strength that the horse tilted up on two white-socked feet, with a roaring and a scream that made Harold press his helmet against his ears. He felt himself grow lighter, lifting from the ground. But the old Indian stretched out an arm and held him down, his other fist clamped into the empty eyes of the buffalo skull.

A pillar of clouds passed beyond the rim of the hollow, a dark and swirling pillar that writhed along its length like a shaken bit of rope. It swayed and straightened and traveled on, brown with dirt, green from the grass of the prairie.

And the rain fell harder and flooded the ground. In rivulets and trickles, and then in little streams, it drained across the prairie and into the shallow bowl. It carried a dead cricket and a leaf ridden by a ladybug, spilling them down beside the buffalo skull. A yellow feather, thumbnail-sized, sledded past the old Indian, then a beetle on its back, and then a snakeskin—old and brittle—that tumbled down in coils.

The old Indian plucked it from the ground. He got up and crouched on his ankles, and Harold crouched beside him. He smoothed the snakeskin along his leggings, flattening the curls. "This is powerful," he said, shouting from the hood that his deerskins made. "It is a good sign." Then he passed the skin to Harold.

It crinkled in his fingers. Harold too stretched it out, seeing a faint shimmer in its wonderful pattern of diamonds. He wondered why the snake would shake off a skin as beautiful as that. But he envied it because it could. He wished he could do that too.

His eyes closed, he pictured himself squirming on the ground, writhing like Houdini coming out of his straitjacket. He saw his skin peeling loose from his fingers and toes, from his arms and his legs. It would fall away from him, his snow-white skin, his tuft of hair as bright as sunlight still attached at the top. It would lie in a heap and he would step from it all tanned and dark like the old Indian, or as freckled as Dusty Kearns, the rancher's kid from the north of Liberty

47

with a face like a piebald horse. He would love to look like that. No one teased Dusty Kearns; no one laughed just to see him.

"It's powerful," shouted the old Indian again. "The snake that had that skin, I think that maybe he was white."

The water streamed down every side of the hollow. It rose above the horse's hooves and up its four white socks. It lapped at the boots of Harold the Ghost, at the beaded moccasins of the old Indian. Swiftly, steadily, it filled the ancient buffalo wallow and drove away the boy and the man and the horse.

They traveled on toward the west as thunder rolled around them and lightning came in hot white flashes. The old Indian wrapped his deerskins tightly, so that every inch of him was covered. He looked like a wind-blown tent pitched atop the horse, and Harold huddled behind him.

The horse found its own way, tramping over the prairie, splashing down the ruts of the Oregon Trail. It carried its riders into the swirl of cloud, into the storm and the darkness of night.

For hours at a time Harold could only dimly see the old Indian right before him, and the horse's head not at all. Then the rain stopped, and the old Indian threw off his deerskins. He took the reins again and turned the horse to the north. And in a moment a light appeared, a tiny spark at first.

"We've found him," said the old Indian.

"The Cannibal King?" asked Harold.

"I think so, yes."

The light grew brighter and larger. It broke into two and then into three, into square little windows that seemed to float in the darkness like the cabin of an airliner.

Harold thought of the man in there, a savage who had grown in his mind to a giant, with bulging arms and a chest like a barrel. He would look at Harold and greet him like a son. "Come with me," he would offer. "Come home to Oola Boola Mambo. You belong with the Stone People."

The light from the windows spilled on the ground. But the night was so dark that Harold was nearly beside them before he saw the rounded bulk of an Airstream trailer and the shadowy shape of the truck that pulled it.

"I was wrong." The old Indian stopped the horse. "It's not the Cannibal King."

"Who is it?" asked Harold.

"Princess Minikin. It is good the storm guided us here. You will travel faster with her."

Harold slid down to wet, spongy grass. He held his hands out to take his bundle.

"I liked riding with you." The old Indian's fingers circled the bat. "We will meet again, my friend."

"You're not stopping?" asked Harold.

"Not here," said Thunder Wakes Him. "I am too wet to sit and visit." He passed Harold's pillowcase down.

Their hands nearly touched on the baseball bat. Harold squinted at them, trying to make sense of what he saw. His eyes, always twitching, blurred the color of his own hand with the redness of the larger one. For a moment it seemed that his was darker now, compared to the old Indian's, or not so shockingly different. But the light was faint and yellow, and it was hard for him to see at all. Even the old Indian's face, high above him, seemed blotched with paler patches.

Thunder Wakes Him put his headdress on. The wind made the feathers flutter. He tossed up his lance and caught it near the base. Then he touched his moccasin heels to the horse's ribs and vanished into darkness.

Chapter 9

The trailer was rounded at the ends and domed at the roof, all smooth and shiny, like an enormous toaster set on wheels. It sounded hollow and tinny when Harold tapped on its side.

"Say, there's someone there." Tina's squeaky voice came faintly through the walls.

The trailer rocked on creaking springs. The door flew open and Samuel burst out, squeezing sideways—bent double—through its oval shape. "It's the boy," he said. "That boy from Liberty."

"Gosh!" said Tina. She came to the doorway, her little arms stretched to touch its sides. "It's a happy day!" she cried. "Oh, it's such a happy day. Give him a hug, Samuel. Give him a great big hug for me."

Harold cringed as the arms encircled him, the big hairy arms that nearly squeezed his breath away. But they felt so safe—so tender—that he closed his eyes and let himself be hugged. Not for years had he been greeted so warmly.

"Now bring him in," said Tina. "You big dope. You knucklehead. Say, he must be starved to death."

They gave him the only chair in a tiny living room that had only that and a sofa. He sank between its overstuffed sides, into cushions as soft as clouds.

Samuel towered over him, his head cocked sideways under the ceiling. Tina brought him sandwiches of thick white bread filled with chicken breast, then perched beside him on the arm of the chair.

"How did you find us?" she asked. "Who brought you here?"

"Thunder Wakes Him," said Harold.

Tina laughed. "Oh, isn't he the sweetest guy? Say, where is he, anyway?"

"He didn't want to stop," said Harold.

Samuel grunted. "He likes to be alone. It's funny he would take you."

"And you came through that great big storm?" asked Tina. "Just you and Bob and a horse? Say, don't you know the rivers are flooding? Don't you know the circus is scattered all across the land?"

Harold shook his head.

"It's a mess, all right," said Samuel. He folded himself onto the sofa, his enormous, ugly head tilted back. He put his clawed fingers over his eyes. "A bridge washed out; a road was closed. The big top's in one place and the Cannibal King's in another. And Lord knows where the Gypsy Magda is."

"Oh, she'll be all right," said Tina soothingly. The trailer rocked in a gust of wind. Rain pattered briefly on its top, and Tina looked up at the sound. "Don't you worry, Samuel. She'll be fine out there."

The trailer was cozy and warm. Harold nodded off, then jerked awake; finally he slept.

He dreamed the old dream, the one that came to him more than any other. He was standing in the doorway of a crowded room, full of people from wall to wall. He saw them very clearly—men in farmer's

52

clothes and business suits, ladies in fine, flowing dresses. They were gathered in bunches—some standing, some sitting—and the room shook with the sound of their talk. Then he stepped inside, and the faces turned toward him. The businessmen touched their spectacles; the farmers chewed tobacco and peered at him with weathered eyes; the ladies held their fingers at their throats. There was one more peal of laughter, and then the room was silent.

Harold, in the dream, saw his hands, and they were tanned by sun. Then he wasn't in himself but was looking down *at* himself. His face was almost golden, his hair as dark as iron. And he realized that he wasn't really white at all, that he never *had* been white. Someone shouted, "Don't be shy!" And all the men and all the ladies waved him in; they beckoned for him to join them.

He woke from the dream, as he always did, with a feeling of tremendous joy to know he wasn't such a freakish white. But a moment later it turned to sadness when he remembered that he was.

The big, comfortable chair hugged him with its softness. Blankets had been tucked around him, tight as a cocoon at his feet. The trailer walls rose in a curve to the shiny dome of the ceiling. And there he saw himself, as he had in his dream, but small and white and lonely.

"He's awake now," shouted Tina. He hadn't seen her on the sofa, as tiny as she was, camouflaged against its beige ulphostery in a shabby housecoat. "Say, we thought you'd sleep the day away."

"I'm sorry," said Harold.

"I don't know why you should be. You have to sleep,

you know." She laughed. "It's not like we're going anywhere."

"Why not?" asked Harold.

"Well, take a look outside." She gestured with her little hand vaguely toward the window. "It'll clear your head. Go on and take a look."

He folded his blankets and left them on the chair. Then he pulled on his helmet and stumbled out through the door, down a step to sodden grass.

The storm had passed, and the sky was full of ragged clouds. The truck and trailer were pulled off beside a dirt road—now only mud—that ended just yards away, at the edge of a swollen river. Water swept around the stumps of a washed-out bridge and covered the road from shoulder to shoulder. Samuel stood there, but to Harold he looked like only a stump, until he turned and came across the grass.

"Almost drove right off the road," he said. "The rain the way it was, mud all over the headlights, I couldn't see a thing. Not a thing." He was rubbing his hairy fists together. "I just hope old Bob saw it. What if he rode himself straight into the river?"

"The horse wouldn't let him," said Harold.

"Maybe not. Maybe not." Samuel's claws clicked as he wrung his hands. "No, I suppose you're right. Of course that's true."

The river went by in a dark, silent rush. Harold watched it oozing through the grass, and he thought what a sad, tiny thing the Rattlesnake was. And suddenly he felt very far from home, and remembered his dog and his mother.

Samuel was watching him, staring down from his great height. "What's wrong with your eyes?" he asked.

54

"Nothing," said Harold.

"They're kind of moving. They're jumping like Mexican beans."

Harold blushed. He felt in his pockets for his glasses.

"Do things look wobbly?" asked Samuel, bending closer. "Is everything you see sort of moving?"

"No," said Harold.

Samuel straightened. "Can you see what I look like?"

He was the ugliest thing that Harold had ever seen. Below the big, thick brows his face was squashed and flat. The hair that grew from it hung in tufts, thickened by dirt and rain.

"Can you?" asked Samuel again.

"Not really," lied Harold.

"You're lucky." The little eyes seemed sad. "You wouldn't believe how lucky you are."

THE CLOUDS BROKE UP and the sun came out, but the river didn't fall; it rose higher. Samuel drove a stick into the ground at its edge, and they sat on a bit of canvas—the midget, the monster and Harold the Ghost—watching the water creep up the stick. It spread through the grass toward them.

A milking stool went past, and then a chicken coop turning circles, with a rooster crowing at its top.

"If a rocking chair goes by," said Samuel, "I'm going to fetch it. I always wanted a rocking chair."

"And a chest of drawers," said Princess Minikin. "With a big old mirror that tilts and turns. That's what I'd like." Then she looked at Harold. "What about you?"

Harold leaned back on his arms. He thought of all the things he wanted, and imagined it would take a raft to hold them all. He tried to picture it coming slowly down the river, stacked with fishing poles and Daisy rifles, towing kites with long tails of red ribbons. He saw a television set and an army of toy soldiers. He saw a huge heap of boxes. And then, balanced on top of it all, his brother, David, was sitting in his uniform, waving as he came, and there at the front was Honey. He even heard her bark.

Suddenly he was crying. He wasn't making a sound, but tears were trickling out from his glasses. The raft disappeared and he saw Honey instead, lying on the floor where he'd left her.

"Say, I'm sorry," said Tina. "Gosh, I didn't want to make you feel bad."

"I guess he misses his home," said Samuel.

"Of course he does, you lug."

Samuel shifted to his knees. "Jolly jam!" he said. "Let's give him a jolly jam."

They closed around him, Tina standing up to throw her arms around his neck, Samuel folding down to take him in those enormous, hairy fists. They crushed him from either side; they rocked him back and forth.

They squeezed the sadness from the Ghost. They squeezed it up so it filled him at first—more than it ever had—then poured from him like the sour juice of a lemon. In its place came a glow of warmth and peace, and Harold smiled and hugged them back.

"You see?" said Samuel. "That's what he needed. A good old geezer-squeezer." He smiled, his teeth so sharp and crooked, his eyes bright as little stars. Harold stared back at them, and for the first time saw something other than ugliness. He saw—or thought he did—a normal person inside those eyes, a different person trapped in all that hair and sagging flesh. It was a funny little man in there, one he would love in a moment if he looked the way he should.

Tina's hands clung to Harold's wrists. "Don't you worry," she said. "Everything goes for the best. The Gypsy Magda said it would. Tell him, Samuel. Didn't she say that anyway?"

Samuel nodded. "Yes, she did."

"She said a boy would come. He would be on a journey, she said. He would start in the dead of night, and at the end he would find contentment."

"I've never met her," said Harold.

"Say, you think that matters? The Gypsy Magda sees visions. She can look at your hand and tell you everything that's happened and everything that will."

"She's never wrong," said Samuel.

They sat in a row, facing the river. It crawled through the grass and rippled past Samuel's stick, hardly an inch from its top.

"Where's the Gypsy Magda now?" asked Harold.

Samuel grunted. "I guess she's lost. She's always getting lost somewhere."

Chapter 10

The river crept higher, and then no farther. It flowed past like a great moving lake, carrying whole trees from a distant forest, carrying a horse trough and a bucket and an old wagon with its wheels poking up in the air.

Then the sun went down, and a silver curve of moon drifted up behind it. Far away the coyotes called.

"Listen," said Samuel suddenly.

The prairie seemed to hum with the noise of the night. The crickets, the frogs, the river in the grass; a rush of tiny noises churned in Harold's ears.

Samuel stood up. "The Gypsy Magda's coming."

Harold felt a tingle through his back and down his arms. Walter Beesley had made him scared of Gypsies; he saw them as thieves that came crawling in packs.

Above the prairie noises he heard the growl of the engine and looked up, to the east. A prick of light floated there, between the land and sky. It split in two, a pair of yellow eyes. They glared down the road and shone in leaping flashes on the trailer. And Samuel ran to meet them. He sprinted through the grass, hunched and gangly, like something prehistoric. The eyes caught him and pinned him on the road, and his shadow stretched for a quarter mile, rippled on the river.

The truck slowed, grinding through its gears. It shimmied sideways, straightened again, then stopped beside the other one. It was shorter and fatter than the Ford that Samuel drove, clotted with mud around its fenders. The lights went out and the engine stopped. A door creaked open.

"That boy, is he here?" said the Gypsy Magda. "That boy on his journey, that traveling boy. Is he here?"

"Yes," said Samuel. He stood below the door, reaching up into a void of shadows. "We were worried about you," he said.

"Has he seen the Cannibal King?"

"No."

"Much I have to tell him."

Samuel stretched his arms toward the cab. A hand floated out of the darkness, a face above it, but nothing to join them. The hand fluttered down like a moth and lighted on Samuel's shoulder. He took the woman in his arms and set her down on the grass.

She came into the light from the trailer windows, a woman dressed all in black, in layers of scarves that flowed around her. She was thin and shriveled and gray; her arms were nothing but bones. But on her wrists and her ankles she wore silver bracelets, and bells below the scarves, and she walked with a jingling and a tingling of metal. Tina ran to greet her, and the Gypsy Magda dropped to her knees to hug the little princess.

"Where have you been?" asked Tina.

"She's so big, this land of America," said the Gypsy

Magda. "I drive and drive across her steppes. The same fence post, thirteen times he passes me." Her face turned, gaunt and yellow in the light. She found Harold in the darkness, and her eyes seemed to burn. "Why does he stand in shadows?"

"He's kind of shy," said Tina.

With a shimmering of bells the Gypsy Magda stood. She beckoned to Harold, and he went to her, his arms in a cross on his chest, his feet scuffing, as though she *dragged* him to her.

"Yes, you're the one," she said, and smiled a toothless grin. "Let me see your hands."

She didn't wait; she snatched them. She took them and turned them sharply over, and her thumbs—with thick, yellow nails—scraped across his palms. Then she shook, and her bracelets rang. Her voice went high and keening, and it shivered through his skin. "Beware the ones with unnatural charm. And the beast that feeds with its tail."

Gooseflesh rose on Harold's skin. He saw his snow-white hands, her dark thumbs laid across them. He saw her head roll back. And again her voice scraped at his spine like a fiddler's bow.

"A wild man's meek and a dark one's pale. And there comes a monstrous harm."

Her voice faded off. Then a coyote called, and then another, in the same shrill and eerie tones as the Gypsy Magda. A third answered them, and a fourth in the distance, as though they sang her warning across the prairie, from den to lonely den.

"Gosh!" said Tina. "Jeepers, that was good." Her little face was smiling, her adult's face like a child's again, gazing up at Harold. "Say, didn't I tell you she was something else?"

Harold couldn't answer. He felt a heat from the old Gypsy's thumbs, but it was the look in her eyes that startled him. The Gypsy, he thought, was frightened.

Chapter
11

They sat at the trailer's small table, in rickety chairs that squeaked and chattered on the floor, a tall one for Tina, a low little stool for Samuel. They drank the Gypsy Magda's tea, a wicked brew as dark as the night, from china cups with painted roses on the side. She had cast a handful of leaves in the pot, and they swirled on the surface of each white cup.

Samuel was happy, even jolly. He towered above the Gypsy, his china cup like a thimble in his hand. "We might as well make the best of it," he said. "We could be here for days."

"Why?" asked the Gypsy Magda.

"The river. It hasn't even crested yet." He drank his tea in slurps, spilling it down his beard. "It'll take three days at least to fall. There's not a chance we'll cross before that. Not a hope in the world."

"Ach," said the Gypsy Magda. "She's nothing, that river. Just a trickle, just a nothing."

Samuel laughed. "Then it's a whole lot of nothing," he said, and finished his tea. He put the cup on the table and poked it, with a claw, toward the Gypsy Magda.

"Not now," she said.

"But you always read my leaves." He sounded disappointed, so pathetically so that the Gypsy Magda in all her scarves took his cup and set it upside down.

She turned it slowly; four times she turned it, so the handle faced north and then west, south and then east. Her lips shrunken in around her toothless mouth, she chanted as she turned. "Withershins we go. Back to where we start. Withershins we turn. To see inside the heart."

Samuel leaned forward as she picked up the cup. "What does it say?" he asked.

"I see a storm. Much rain, much thunder. I see trouble, a person in trouble."

"Me?" asked Samuel.

"Someone else. He comes to you with trouble."

"When?"

"Soon," she said, and put down the cup. "That is all."

"It wasn't very much," he said, pouting.

She shrugged. "You spill too many leaves."

"Now me," said Tina. "You did Samuel, you've got to do me." Her cup seemed too big, her fingers loose inside the tiny handle. She put it down and slid it over the table.

Bracelets jangled. The Gypsy Magda turned the cup onto its brim. There was a stain of tea on the table. Again she turned it, and again she chanted.

Tina grinned at Harold. Little fists clunked together, knuckles to knuckles. The Gypsy Magda took the cup in her hands.

"What do you see?" asked Tina. "What do you see?"

"Happiness. Great happiness." The Gypsy Magda leaned forward, peering at the cup.

"What else do you see?"

63

"Kindness. Love. It is dripping from you, this kindness."

"Money? Do you see money?"

"No."

"Nuts!" said Tina. "What else?"

"A game. A great game and much laughing."

"What kind of a game?"

"It is hard to see." The Gypsy Magda tipped the cup. "You are running. Shouting." Suddenly her head shot back. She looked sharply at Harold. "That is all."

"What do you mean, that's all?" asked Tina. "Say, what's in there anyway?"

The Gypsy Magda shook the cup, hard. Leaves sprayed across the floor in a smear of black and tea. She tugged at her scarves, at her bracelets. "It's not enough, this happiness? You will be more happy than you ever dreamed. But it's not enough?"

"Sure," said Tina. She sat back, not as happy as Harold might have thought.

He held his cup close to his chest, tightly in his hands. He wasn't sure if he wanted to know what was in there.

"I'm tired," said the Gypsy Magda. "I must sleep." She pushed back her chair and stood wobbling by the table. "The boy, he will walk with me."

They went out into the darkness and the soft chirruping of crickets. The Gypsy Magda slipped her arm through Harold's, and they walked across the grass.

"Are you frightened of me?" she asked.

"No," said Harold.

"Of the future, then?"

He nodded. She leaned against him, her weight not half of his.

Her bracelets and her bells made a music in the night. "It is good you ask no questions. You are brave to go in darkness without the lamp to show your way."

Harold shivered. He wasn't brave. He was scared to know his future.

He helped the Gypsy Magda into the high, covered back of her truck. There was a little door that she crawled through, into a cave that smelled of spices and candles. She looked down at him from above.

"Hurry back," she said. "Your friends, they have something for you."

He walked through the darkness, into the trailer, and saw that his friends had gone to bed. Down the narrow corridor, underneath the cabin doors, slits of light sprayed across the floor. But in the little living room a blanket was hung from the ceiling, suspended in front of the sofa. Pinned to it was a piece of paper, and on it was written Harrolds Rume.

The cabin doors banged open. Samuel came through one, the princess through the other. "Surprise!" she shouted, her hands in the air. "Do you like it?"

Harold squinted at the bit of the paper and the curtain. "What is it?" he asked.

Tina frowned. "Why, it's your room," she said. "What do you think?"

He was touched by the gesture. The Airstream trailer was small and cramped, but this little bit of it was his. He thought of the tiny woman and the monstrous man, and how they must have planned it out, then waited for a chance to give him this small surprise.

He pulled the blanket aside and sat on the sofa; there wasn't room to stand. His bundle of clothes had been opened, everything unpacked and set neatly on little shelves. The baseball bat, the glove and the painted ball, everything was there. A coverlet and pillow were laid out for him.

Harold the Ghost stretched out on the sofa, in the first room that had ever been his own.

"You like it?" asked Tina.

"Very much," he said. "Thank you, Samuel. Thank you, Princess Minikin."

Tina laughed. "You don't have to call me that," she said. "Just call me Tina, okay?"

Chapter

12

The Gypsy Magda was right. In the morning the river was gone. Just a thin, dark line of water flowed through its wide channel, the banks and the prairie on either side blackened with mud and debris.

The trucks started in coughs of smoke, with rattles of fenders and cowlings. They lurched across the river, spewing mud from whirling wheels, and staggered up the other side. They gained the road and headed west, with the morning sun behind them.

"I love traveling days," said Tina, wedged between Samuel and Harold. She sat on an apple box, her fat little legs braced across it. "Sometimes I wish we could travel forever."

The day was hot and bright, the roads covered again in dust. It rose from the wheels in feathers at first, and then in a cloud that thickened behind them, bubbling over the trailer.

All that day and all the next they drove toward the west. They sang "Roll Out the Barrel" as the telephone poles went whooshing past and the wind came hot through the windows. They sang "When Johnny Comes Marching Home," and Samuel made the sound of a drum with his fist on the wheel, and Tina had tears in her eyes.

Then Harold saw the mountains. He pushed back his helmet and gazed at them rising from the prairie far ahead, a blur in his poor, bad eyes. "The mountains!" he cried, and pointed. "That must be Oregon, I bet."

Tina laughed, and so did Samuel. He laughed so hard he started coughing, and the big truck wandered toward the ditch before he brought it straight again.

"Those aren't mountains," Tina said. "They're only hills."

"Only hills?" asked Harold. They seemed enormous.

"When you see the mountains you'll know it," she said. "And, say, you know what we'll do? We'll stop and have a party. Won't we, Samuel? We'll stop in the middle of the road if we have to, and—jeepers, creepers!—we'll have ourselves a party." She squirmed atop her apple box. "There's nothing better than seeing the mountains when all you've seen is prairie."

They came to a farmhouse that afternoon, and a big barn with gaps along its walls. In a moment they were past it, and the fence posts went by in a ragged, crooked line.

Then Samuel pointed suddenly and cried out, "There! Look there!"

A piece of paper was stapled to a post. Tattered by the wind and rain, it curled across itself, a square of red and an arrow in the middle.

Samuel touched the brakes, and the truck skittered, pushed by the trailer behind it. "Which way is it pointing?" he shouted.

Harold put his head from the window. His helmet

straps lashing at his cheeks, his white face looking back, he shot along across the prairie.

"Up!" said Tina. "Oh, it's a happy day."

When Harold pulled his head inside, his glasses were grimy with dust. He took them off and cleaned them on his sleeve. "What was it?" he asked.

"A sign," said Samuel. "The Cannibal King goes ahead and puts them up to mark the way."

Harold smiled. He faced ahead again, pleased to think he was going where the Cannibal King had gone, down the very same road, just days behind him.

Chapter
13

The truck labored up the hills, its motor overheating, steam wafting from the hood. Then it crossed the top and started down toward the valley, toward a little city that seemed tremendously big to Harold.

"We'll stop and get supper," Samuel said. "We'll have a bite to eat."

Harold turned toward the window. "I've got no money," he said.

Tina laughed. "Don't worry about that. We've got lots," she said. "Don't we, Samuel?"

"A bit," he said.

"You big lug, we've got lots." She slid from her seat and opened the glove box. She pulled out a thin wad of paper. "We sell these," she said. "After the show we sell postcards."

Harold squinted at them, inches from his eyes. There were pictures of Tina in a tiny tiara, signed in spidery writing, "Princess Minikin." There were pictures of Samuel in nothing but a pair of shorts, his chest and his stomach all covered with hair.

"We get to keep nearly half of what we make," said Tina. "Mr. Hunter's a swell guy."

There was a picture of the two together, Tina in

Samuel's arms. Another showed her on a pony. In every one Tina was smiling; in every one Samuel scowled.

The truck jolted down the hill. Samuel worked the gearshift, and the engine growled and backfired.

The last postcard was of the Cannibal King. It showed him sitting on a huge throne, surrounded by coconut palms. Harold frowned at it, bending forward, his nose nearly on the picture. The coconut palms seemed to shake as his eyes jiggled back and forth.

"Is this Oola Boola Mambo?" he asked. "All these trees?"

Tina laughed. "You crazy nut! Sure, that's Oola Boola Mambo, isn't it, Samuel?"

Samuel wiped his mouth, flattening a grin. "That's what it is, all right."

Harold stared at the picture. "What's so funny?" he asked, and they laughed all the harder. "I don't get it," he said.

"They're just such funny trees," said Tina.

The postcards were packed away as the truck came down toward the city. Harold goggled from the windows. He'd never seen buildings six stories tall; he called them skyscrapers. He marveled at the traffic lights, at the flashing neon signs. He was astounded by the traffic; he could count thirty cars at once, and it seemed to him like chaos.

If there was ever a time when Harold wished his eyes were normal, that time was now. He squinted so hard that his eyes hurt. He pointed to the left, to the right. "Is that a television set?" he asked, and Tina laughed. "It's a newspaper box," she told him.

The truck stopped at a light. A knot of people streamed past on the crosswalk. He heard a child shout, "Look at that!" and turned to look himself.

"Oh, yuck!" said the child, right below him. "Why's he so white? And look at the guy that's driving!"

"Roll up the windows," said Samuel. Already his thick, hairy arm was cranking the handle, and the glass was rising, sealing them off. "Roll it up!" he snapped.

All around, the people stopped. "Freaks," said a man. "They're circus freaks." And a woman said, "Oh, the poor boy!"

Harold couldn't move. Tina reached across him and turned the handle, and the window shut with a squeak. The people swarmed around them.

They stared through the windshield, up past the mirrors. A pimply boy stood on the running board and leered at Harold through the window. His fingers were flattened pink blotches on the glass.

"Look ahead," said Samuel. "Just keep looking straight ahead." The light changed, and he rammed the truck into gear, scattering the people. But at the next corner different people gathered, and at the third it happened all over again.

Harold sat perfectly still; only his chin was quivering. He stared straight ahead, as Samuel had told him to do. He was the Ghost again, Harold the Ghost, small and invisible. He chanted to himself, under his breath, the words that he used for a charm, his little incantation:

"No one can see me, no one can hurt me. The words that they say cannot harm me."

They didn't stop at a restaurant. They passed

through the city and traveled on. Bugs came soaring up and splattered on the windshield, and the engine droned beneath the hood.

Harold fell asleep, his head against the window, and the trucks went roaring through the night, chasing cones of yellow down the road. Small and white, the Ghost went flying across the prairie, dreaming his old dream of being a dark-haired boy.

Chapter
14

Harold's head swayed sideways and banged against the window. He came awake to find the truck lurching off the road, to hear the sound of gravel popping underneath the wheels. He saw a building with red and yellow lights, a bank of gas pumps waiting there like a row of little fat men, each with one skinny arm and one hand in a pocket.

The motor was oddly quiet, the voices in the cab little more than whispers.

"It's not quite empty," said Samuel. "A couple of people inside."

"It'll do," said Tina. "We've got to stop somewhere."

Harold yawned and stretched. "Where are we?" he asked.

Tina patted his arm. "We're just getting some gas. Something to eat."

A sign blinked redly at him: Gas. Food. Worms. It sizzled in the summer night.

Samuel parked beside the pumps. The Gypsy Magda drew up beside them, and the light glared off her windows so that it seemed the cab was empty.

They climbed down, Harold and Tina from one side, Samuel from the other. The Gypsy Magda, with her shimmering of bracelets, came around her truck, and they stood together in a little group below the crackle of the lights.

A bell jangled as the door opened in the building. A man came out, dressed in blue, walking quickly in leather boots with the laces loose. His head down, he wiped at his hands with an oily rag. "What do you want?" he asked.

"Gas," said Samuel. "Please."

The man lifted his head. "Jesus!" he said. He looked at Harold, at the Gypsy Magda, down at Tina and up at Samuel. He took a step backward. "Oh, Jesus," he said again.

"Have you got a bathroom in there?" asked Tina.

His mouth was open, his eyes as round as Harold's glasses. "Huh?" he said. "You're going to go in?"

"We'd like something to eat," said Samuel. "If it isn't any trouble."

"No," said the man. "No problem." He dabbed at his face with the rag. "But my wife's in there. And she's . . ."

"What?" asked Samuel.

The man fumbled with the rag. "Sort of scared. You know?"

"Yes," said Samuel. "Can you fill up both the trucks?"

"Sure. No problem." The man's face shone with sweat. "You're, uh—you're going to pay for it, aren't you?" he asked.

Samuel smiled with his horrid teeth, his little eyes gleaming. "Sure. No problem."

The man's hands shook so badly that gasoline sprayed across his boots. Harold laughed, until Samuel's hand clamped with its claws on his shoulder.

"Don't stare," Samuel told him gently. "It's not polite to stare." He put his hand on Harold's back and turned him toward the building.

It looked warm and safe in there, all the colors bright as fire. Through the windows Harold saw a rosy shine of padded chairs, the red of Coke machines, a fountain fizzing Orange Crush.

There were three booths at the window, and behind them a counter where a young girl sat on a stool of chrome and orange. She was six, or maybe seven, and she twirled a finger through her hair as she worked with crayons at a coloring book.

When the bell rang over the door, she looked up. Her eyes, full of wonder, flickered over Harold and Tina and the Gypsy Magda to settle, finally, on Samuel. "You're very big," she said. "You're more hairy than my grampa, even."

Samuel covered his mouth with his hand. He was smiling behind it, Harold could see, and hiding his teeth from the girl.

"What's your name?" asked Tina. "You're a sweetheart, kid."

"Doris," she said.

"What a pretty name." Tina waddled toward her. "We're just traveling through and we wanted something to eat. Is that okay?"

Doris frowned. "Well, I'm kind of busy."

"We can see that," said Tina. "You've got your coloring there and all. Say, why don't we just sit at a booth, and you can tell your mama we're here?"

Doris nodded.

"That's swell," said Tina. "Say, where should we sit anyway?"

The little girl sighed and tilted her head. "It really doesn't matter," she said so seriously. "We're not very full right now."

She turned the stool to watch the four go by. It squealed and tilted, and she looked down at Tina. "You're mighty small," she said.

"Gee, thanks, kid," said Tina brightly.

"And you." She pointed at the Gypsy Magda. "You make music when you walk."

Harold blushed. He felt a hotness rushing through his chest. He dreaded what the girl would say to him. And he turned away when she pointed at him with a crayon.

"You're an albino." She said it slowly, making three words out of one. *An al-bye-no.*

Harold felt sick, as though she'd called him a gargoyle. He hurried past and slipped into the booth. He saw his fingers clasping the table like white sausages and shoved them underneath. The Gypsy Magda sat beside him, her old face lined with worries. Tina scooted up the other bench, and Samuel squeezed in by the aisle.

Doris climbed down from her stool, sliding on her stomach. Her little crimson skirt rode up around her legs. She stood at the side of the booth. "He's a nice albye-no," she said. "And that other one was a big fat liar."

"What other one?" asked Samuel.

"I dunno." She shrugged. "He came in a big old car. As big as a boat almost, pulling an island behind him. And he didn't even pay for his gas."

"He didn't?" asked Samuel.

"No!" She shook her head solemnly. "He got really mad. Really, really mad."

"He did?"

"Yes! He got mad like this." She put her legs wide apart, her arms straight out from her shoulders, bent down at the elbows. She stomped up and down the narrow floor. "I'm not taking this," she said, her voice mockingly deep but childish in its shrill. "I'm the Cannibal King! I'm the Cannibal King!"

Tina shrieked with laughter. "That's him," she said. "That's him all right."

Harold only gawked. He saw the child somehow magnified, eight feet tall, bellowing in an awful rage. She *became*, for a moment, the Cannibal King, with a necklace of bones and the fierceness of a savage.

The little girl stomped and swayed, and behind her came a woman. She flew around the end of the counter on clattering heels. "Doris!" she said. "You get away from there!"

"Say, it's all right," said Tina. "She's not bothering us. She's a swell little kid."

The woman grabbed the child. She pulled her backward across the floor and whirled her around, holding the little face against her dress. The child burst into tears, and her mother was red with rage. "You bunch of freaks. You goddamn monsters," she said. "You stay away from her. Don't you touch my child."

Samuel's hands clenched into fists; Tina looked utterly shocked. The Gypsy Magda trembled all over, and Harold the Ghost—who had never fought back in his life—said, "No one touched your child."

He surprised even himself. His fingers were shaking under the table, and his eyes jittered madly behind his glasses. When he was nervous or frightened he could hardly see, and now the room and the woman blurred around him.

"What's she going to make of you?" the woman demanded. "A midget and a monkey man. An old witch and a boy like a ghost. What's she going to make of you?"

"Friends?" said Harold.

Tina clapped her hands. "Yeah!" she said triumphantly. "We were making *friends*, that's all."

Samuel's fists opened and closed. The heels of his hands pushed at the table's edge. "I think we'd better go," he said.

The woman laughed. "You're goddamn right you better go." The child was crying hysterically, almost climbing up her mother's skirt. "Go on, then. Get out of here."

Harold started to rise. But Samuel leaned across the table and pressed him back. "I changed my mind. We'll stay," he said. "The boy has to eat."

The Gypsy Magda stiffened. "The old man is coming on."

A door latch clicked. Footsteps echoed in the building. They grew louder, a heavy step. Harold pulled his glasses off and pressed at his eyes. He wanted so badly to see.

There were batwing doors behind the counter, and they swung open as the cook came through. He wore a battered fedora that was cracked down the middle like an egg. "What's all the noise?" he said. "What in tarnation is going on out here?"

The woman was staring down at the Gypsy Magda. The child still cried against her, blubbering now, "We were talking. We were only talking, Mom."

The cook put his hands on his hips. "You go on to the back, Betty," he said, ushering her away. Then his hands went into his pockets. "You're all with the circus, are you?" he asked.

"Yes," said Samuel.

He shook his head. "Fifty years I been here and never saw a freak, and all of a sudden you're coming like flies to the butter."

"The storm split us up," said Samuel. "It washed out a couple of bridges."

"You ask me, freaks belong in a tent." The cook sucked air through his teeth. "If I looked like you, I wouldn't be showing myself to no one, but that's me and you're you. I guess you've gone and frightened the daylights out of that little girl. So, here's what I'll do, and it's just what I told that other al-bye-no."

He rubbed his cheek, then scratched at his head through the slit in his hat. "I'll give you sandwiches, coffee, whatever you want. But you can't eat 'em here. What if someone respectable comes in? What would happen then?"

He rocked forward, and he smiled. He actually smiled. "So you just tell me what you want and then clear on out of here. I'll bring it to your truck, but you'll pay for it now, see."

He hauled out a little pad from his back pocket, a stub of pencil that he licked with his tongue. "Now let's see your money." He shouted at Samuel. "Do you understand English? Huh? Do you have any dough?"

Samuel looked sadly at the table.

"Can't he talk?"

"Sure he can," said Tina.

"Then what does he want? Ask him what he wants." And he added with a sneer, "Little lady."

Tina touched Samuel's hand. There was an awful, beaten look about her, a look of sadness and despair. She said, "You order, Samuel. I don't care what I get." Samuel looked back at her, and his eyes were wet. The Gypsy Magda sat shrunken into her scarves, her face blank, her eyes empty, as though she wasn't there.

"I don't have all day," said the cook.

"Denvers," said Samuel, his eyes still on Tina. "We'll have denvers."

"And you?" asked the cook. "You. Whitey."

Harold winced. He saw then that no matter how far he went from Liberty, it would never be far enough.

"What do you want?"

Harold straightened his shoulders and looked directly at the man, though all he saw was a blur. He said, "I want to be bigger, sir. I want to be darker."

The cook snorted. "You're a wise guy, huh? Well, I guess you're a pretty hungry little wise guy. Now get out of here. All of you. And I'll bring you *three* sandwiches."

"Two," said the Gypsy Magda.

"Huh?"

"Just two." She stood up, stiff and proud. Although she was shorter than the man by a third of his height, she was full of a great dignity that made her seem larger. "I want nothing from you," she said, and went past him, down the worn tiles, in a beautiful tingling of bells. And then Samuel got up from his bench, and then Tina. They waited for Harold.

He wished he was stronger, as big as the Cannibal

King. He would bellow and stomp; he would flatten the cook who stood there, openmouthed, in his stained and dirty shirt. But he wasn't big, and he wasn't strong, and he went without a word. Samuel's hand settled on his shoulder, and they went together to the door.

"Good riddance!" the cook called after them. "Get out of here, Whitey. You spook. Yeah, all of you go, you bunch of freaks. Bunch of goddamn freaks."

The gas pump hummed and whirred, a little red-and-yellow ball spinning in the fuel line. The man tending to it was just as nervous as before. In his overalls and floppy boots, he leaned against the Gypsy Magda's truck, holding the nozzle in place.

Samuel stood beside him. "That's good," he said. "It's full enough."

The nozzle clattered as the man pulled it out. He watched warily under his cap as the Gypsy Magda and Harold and Tina crowded around him. "You're not eating?" he asked.

"No." Samuel took a roll of money from his pocket. It was thick, green, bound by an old rubber band. They were one-dollar bills, and he peeled off a few; he paid for the gas, and for the Cannibal King's as well.

When the man reached out for his money, the Gypsy Magda took his hand. "Your wife," she said. "She has rambling blood. Ask her this: Where does she go in her prettiest clothes?"

The man looked at her, then up at the windows where the cook stood. He shoved the money in his pocket and went off like a crab, scuttling sideways.

The Gypsy Magda smiled at Harold. "I'm proud of you," she said.

"Yeah," said Tina. "That was great, what you said in there. I thought he'd have a fit. 'I want to be bigger,' you told him. Say, wasn't that swell, Samuel?"

"It was." The little eyes shone in that monsterlike face. "You're one of us now. For good or bad, thick or thin. Forever and ever, you're one of us."

Harold glowed.

"Jolly jam!" said Samuel suddenly, and they crowded around him in a mass of claws and little hands and cold, metallic bracelets. They tilted and swayed.

"Where does she go?" asked Harold. "In her prettiest clothes, where does she go?"

The Gypsy Magda laughed. "I don't know," she said. "I just make the trouble, I think." Then she climbed up into her truck. "The boy will come with me."

Chapter

15

The headlights cast their yellow cones into an empty land beyond the limits of the filling station. Windshield wipers flailed and squeaked, sweeping dust and bugs away. Then Samuel, like a gruesome pilot, raised his thumb and started forward. The Gypsy Magda followed him, hurling herself at the gearshift, tromping on the pedals.

Her headlights glared from the back of the Airstream, and she let it pull ahead a hundred yards, then fell in line so perfectly that a cable might have joined them.

"I grew up like this," she said. "On the road I was born, in a caravan pulled by horses. On the road, I think, I'll die."

She never really sat. She leaned on the edge of her seat as she stood on the pedals, her bells and bracelets jangling as the truck went throbbing to the west. The black scarves were slipping slowly down her arms, and in the pale green light of the instrument lamps Harold saw that her wrists were as bony as a skeleton's.

"I had a little cradle that my father made me. When the wagon moved, it rocked. Wagon stops, I cry." She slid her hand to the top of the wheel and, flinging herself sideways, shifted gears on a slope. "I remember this, my little cradle. Hung all about with pretty things and shining stars of metal my father cut from tin. Ach, the noise! I think it drives my mother mad."

The headlights lit the Airstream trailer. It hovered in the windshield, growing slowly larger.

"We traveled through the mountains and traveled through the forests. Every night we build a fire with big and leaping flames. The Roma—the Gypsies, you call them—they like the dancing; they sing and dance and circle round the fire. My young eyes, they see the fire dancing too, the flames dancing with the Gypsies."

She swayed on the pedals. The trailer seemed to slide across the windshield and back again to the middle.

"I had seven brothers. They are big and handsome boys. From my mother they learn to laugh; from my father they learn to work. We go all across the land." She was silent then, her face like stone in the trailer's silver light. "Ach, it's long ago."

"Do you ever see them?" asked Harold.

"Sometimes, yes. In the mountains. When the wind is high and the rain, it is splooshing in the windows, I see them standing by the road. All battered; torn and battered. They look like buzzards."

Harold frowned.

"They're dead," said the Gypsy Magda. "My brothers, my parents. All that I knew."

The trailer suddenly filled the windshield. The Gypsy Magda tromped on the brake. A hand shot out to brace against the roof, and the scarves tumbled down to her shoulder. And in the silver glare of the Airstream, Harold saw numbers tattooed along her arm.

"The Nazis," said the Gypsy Magda. "You know them?"

"Yes." It was the Nazis his father had gone to fight in Europe. It was the Nazis who had killed him.

"They were so powerful, so many. But they were scared of Gypsies. We were dark and wild and free. They made it a crime to be a Gypsy, and they hounded us all across the country. We went west, the way all souls will go, toward the falling of the sun."

Harold sat sideways on the seat.

"We went to the mountains," said the Gypsy Magda. "We went high in the mountains where the lovely Danube rises. We made a camp, and the wolves were calling in the night."

She spoke slowly as the truck threaded through the darkened hills, close behind the Airstream trailer. The light glaring back made gruesome shadows on her face.

"My father, my poor old father, he said we were close to the passage to the underworld. He said the wolves were dogs, the nine white dogs that guard that path of souls."

She shifted gears; they turned a corner. The headlights flashed across the truck ahead, and Harold wished that he was in it.

"We were happy there," said the Gypsy Magda. "We dance and sing. We live the old ways and let this war go past."

The trailer slid far across the windshield.

"Then comes the night, the dreaded time. Nine soldiers come to our camp. They are big, blond soldiers, very white. Ach, so pale and white. My father, he says,

'The dogs have come!' My mother tells me to hide myself, to hide under the caravan, in the space where the water barrel goes."

Harold clung to his seat as the truck leaned around the corner, as the trailer crept back across the windshield. The numbers on the Gypsy Magda's arm were square and squat and ugly.

"The soldiers have black coats, big black boots. White hands and white faces, and all the rest is black. They take the men, the boys, and put them on this side, the women on the other. And then I hear a terrible sound: The guns are fed with bullets."

She took her arm down and shook the scarves across the numbers. "I see them shot," she said. "My father first, my brothers in a row. My mother—I still hear her screaming when they carry her off." The Gypsy sighed. A stone bounced with a clatter from the truck. "A soldier takes a stick from the fire; he comes down the wagons and sets them alight. They are canvas and wood, they burn very fast, orange and roaring. I fall from my place and my dress, she is burning. There are men crying, horses shrieking. But the Nazis, they laugh to see a Gypsy burn."

For a long time she was silent. "What happened then?" asked Harold.

"I don't remember after that. I'm put in a camp, the dreadful place. The smoke of burning bodies comes black from the furnace. I see graves where bodies swim in mud. I see dead people sitting, talking. I will never forget what I see."

Her bracelets rang as she covered her cheek with her hand.

"Killing is a game the Nazis play, but the Gypsies they keep alive. We dance for them; we play the tambourine. And somehow we are happy in the horror and the dying. We are Gypsies, after all." She touched her throat, the scarves around her neck. "But one morning the smoke is thick, the fires burning orange in the winter. The Roma, they are gone. And I am the last Gypsy; only I am left, I don't know why. They march us through the snow, through the winter, and the guns we hear behind us. In rags we march, dead we go. And at last I see the passage of the souls. It's small and dark, and I crawl inside and wait there for the ones who will come to take me on my way."

"And the soldiers found you?" Harold asked.

"You!" she shouted suddenly, glaring across the truck. "What happens to you is nothing. Nothing!"

Her anger was so sudden, so unexpected, that Harold cringed. He sank into the corner of the seat, looking up like a small, white animal.

"I would like so much to be you. Young, smart, free. You have everything, and still you don't know how lucky you are. You don't even imagine."

"You said you were proud of me."

"For speaking, yes. For waiting, no." She pulled viciously on the gearshift. The truck slowed, drawing back from the Airstream. "If you were there alone, without your friends, what would you have done?"

"I don't know," he said.

"Nothing. You would have sat and sniveled like the baby."

The light was growing fainter. The Gypsy Magda was shrinking in the darkness. "If you think that you are less than them, can you blame them for thinking they are better?"

Harold didn't answer. The Airstream was a dot in the windshield, and then it was gone. The blackness overwhelmed him, and the Gypsy disappeared.

"I smell death ahead," she told him.

J ust before dawn they stopped at a schoolyard overgrown by long grass. Swings with planks for seats
hung on tangled chains beside an old teeter-totter and
a little wooden roundabout. A flock of crows perched
on the moss-covered beam that held the swings.

The Gypsy Magda spread a blanket on the grass,
and she slept—they all did—until the wind woke
them at noon. It hushed through the grass and set the
swings creaking. The roundabout revolved slowly on
its hub, and the crows came down to ride it.

Harold, in a grassy nest, watched the clouds rolling
past the stalks above him. They were storm clouds,
which didn't surprise him; the Gypsy Magda had long
ago sensed the coming of a storm.

Of the death ahead, she had told him no more. He
had peppered her with questions: "*Who* is going to
die? *When* will it happen? *Where?* Can't you tell me
that?" And she'd answered mysteriously, "It is better
that you never think of it."

He lay on his back, his little round glasses reflecting
the sky, his helmet pulled close to his eyes. Hours he'd
spent like that, in the fields by the Liberty station,
David beside him and Honey between them, her
tongue hanging out from a run. He found it pleasant

to lie there now, and at the same time sad, his thoughts of home passing with the clouds. He saw in them the things he dreamed. A fat, rolling cloud was his mother pacing through the house. A thin one clocking along was Walter Beesley walking up the Rattlesnake, walking out to Bender's Corner, walking in his banker's shoes, searching in the bushes. And a fluffy one was Honey. He whistled to it, as he'd always called for Honey, and the fluffy head seemed to rise, as though the clouds had heard him. But then they turned and tumbled away, toward the east and Liberty. The legs snapped off, the tail broke loose, and the dog vanished into nothing.

Samuel sat up. His shaggy head was higher than the grass. "Listen," he said.

"What?" said Tina.

"Just listen."

But she was like a child. She stood, then shouted out to find the grass was taller than herself. And she leapt around the little wallow they'd made, springing up to see across the field, flinging out her arms to jump a little higher. The Gypsy Magda's bracelets jangled as she too stirred to hear the sounds. She stood, and the wind took her scarves, stretching them out.

"What is it?" asked Tina. "I can't see a thing. Say, what do you hear anyway?"

Samuel laughed. "Just listen," he said.

It was calliope music, so faint it was hardly there. It came through the grass like a whisper. And Harold imagined that he could smell the sawdust and the cotton candy, as though the notes were little balloons full of the sounds and smells of the circus.

"They must be close," he said.

Samuel shook his head. "Nothing travels like the music of a calliope." He called it a cally-ope. "You can hear a cally-ope for a hundred miles on a day like this, when the wind is right and the air is clear." He stood up. "But no, they're not so far away."

The music was chirpy and bright. "It's the breaking-down song," said Samuel. "They're on the move."

He trotted through the grass, his waist and legs below it, his arms swinging forward and back. He ran for the little roundabout and leapt up on its platform as the crows scattered in a black and cackling mass. And Tina ran behind him, down the trodden path he'd left, and she set the roundabout in motion as she leapt and staggered along its rim. Samuel, in the middle, turned round and round, his great arms up in the air. Then they were all at the roundabout, wheeling in circles, laughing to the ring of the Gypsy's bells.

Harold pushed, stumbling in his boots, his white arms stiff, a curl of white hair gleaming below his tattered helmet. The Gypsy Magda sat at the edge, trailing her scarves through the grass. Samuel hoisted Tina up to his shoulders, and she sat there, laughing, shouting, "Faster, Harold. Faster."

He turned it around and around, then flew off from the edge like a stone from a slingshot. He ran to the trailer and fetched his painted ball and bat. And they played Five Hundred in the long grass until the rain began to fall.

Then the trucks moved off along the road. Harold, in the big one again, with Samuel and Tina beside him, watched the wiper blades click from side to side. But the rain fell harder, and within an hour the wipers couldn't keep up. Samuel slowed the truck. The roads turned to mud.

At twenty miles an hour they crawled across a land of low and round-topped hills. The truck, the trailer, the Gypsy Magda, went weaving through the land.

Chapter
17

The rumble of the motor, the clacking of the wipers, put Harold half asleep. He was staring blankly from the window when Tina said suddenly, "My father owns a grocery store."

"He does?" asked Harold.

"No, you dope." She pushed him in the ribs. "It's a game. Just a game."

"Go on," said Samuel.

She sat bolt upright on her apple box, her legs poking stiff beyond it. "And in this store he has something that starts with the letter *A*."

"Artichokes!" shouted Samuel. And he laughed and picked it up. "My father owns a grocery store, and in this store is something that starts with the letter *B*."

"Bananas," said Tina, so quickly that Harold was sure they had played the game a thousand times, for mile after mile to while their journeys away. They went through the alphabet, to dates and elephants.

"*Elephants!*" said Harold, a moment after Samuel did. "He wouldn't sell elephants."

"He might," said Samuel defensively. He looked in the mirror for the Gypsy Magda's truck. "My father owns a grocery store, and in this store he has something that starts with the letter *F*."

"Figs," said Harold.

"Pharmaceutics!" shouted Tina, tossing up her arms.

Samuel bobbed his head. "*Pharmaceutics* wins. A bigger word is always better."

"But it doesn't start with *F*," said Harold.

Tina laughed. "Oh, you're just a sore loser," she said, reaching out to grab her toes. And the game went on, through oranges and pineapples.

"My father owns a grocery store," said Tina. "And in this store he has something that starts with the letter *Q*."

"Cucumbers!" yelled Samuel.

"No," said Harold. "That starts with *C*."

"Get away," said Samuel.

"It does. It really does," said Harold, so plaintively that it sent the others into gales of laughter, and Harold laughed himself. "It starts with *C*," he said.

"Gosh, he might be right," said Princess Minikin. "He's a real smart guy." Then she looked at Samuel. "She's going to like him, isn't she?"

"Oh, yes, she will," said Samuel.

"Who?" he asked.

"Flip," said Samuel.

"Who's Flip?"

Tina shook her hands. "Flip Pharaoh! You never heard of Flip Pharaoh?"

"No," said Harold.

"She's only the greatest bareback rider that ever was. She's cute as a bug too."

The game was forgotten. Tina opened the glove box and took out the postcards again. She shuffled through them, spilling them across the seat. Harold

95

saw the Cannibal King reaching through the bars of a cage, glowering down from a tremendous height. Then Tina put a card in his hand.

"That," she said, "is Flip."

He turned it in his hands; he held it close to the window.

The girl was blond and beautiful. In a shining skirt of spangles she stood astride a pair of horses that were absolutely white. She was smiling, bouncing up as the horses ran, the skirt lifting at the hem.

"Her name's not really Flip," said Tina. "It's—It's—Gosh, what is it anyway, Samuel?"

Samuel thought, and laughed. "I don't know," he said.

Harold stared at the picture as the truck slithered through the mud.

"She'll like you," said Tina. "She likes guys that are smart. Guys that are brave enough to go looking for something."

And guys that are white? he wondered. He shook his head. "No. I don't want to meet her."

"But you have to," said Tina. "If you want to travel with the circus, it's Flip you'll have to talk to."

"I thought Mr. Hunter ran the circus."

"He only owns it," she said.

"Then what about Mr. Green?"

Tina laughed. "Listen, Harold. If you want to join the circus, you'll have to talk to Flip." She stacked the postcards neatly and returned them to the glove box. "But don't worry. You'll do just fine."

In the last bit of daylight they drove past a church. It was small and white, with a bell tower topped by a lightning rod. Lined along the road beside it were buggies and buckboards, at each one a big farm horse standing patiently in the harness.

But through the clouds came a single ray of light, a golden beam that shone on the church and the buggies, on men in black and women in dresses that touched the ground.

It was like a painting, the little church with a graveyard of crosses, the grass cut short and green.

"I'd like to be married somewhere like that," said Tina, and Samuel smiled down toward her.

Already the church was behind them. Harold watched it slip away, the sunbeam vanishing like a spotlight shutting off. "Where are we?" he asked.

"Bible country," said Samuel. He twisted his fists on the steering wheel. "The people around here ride buggies and horses. They use machines only when they have to."

"Why?" asked Harold.

"Religion." Samuel shrugged. "They look like those old Bible people come to life."

He wriggled in the driver's seat. "But they don't believe in circuses."

Chapter
18

It was just as the Gypsy had said. With the night came a storm. The storm brought thunder and great sheets of white lightning, wind that buffeted the truck and screamed through the cracks of doors and windows. It brought the man in trouble.

But first the truck skidded off the road.

They were singing "Roll Out the Barrel" when Samuel suddenly wrenched on the wheel, spinning it in his enormous hands. The engine raced and the truck lurched sideways, toppling Tina from her apple box. Lightning flashed, and the crack of thunder came an instant later. The Airstream pushed against the truck and turned it faster. The truck wobbled, tilting up, and came to a stop at a terrible slant, with Harold jammed against the door.

Samuel clung to the wheel. He switched the engine off, but the windshield wipers clicked and clicked, and the headlights threw their cones up through the rain and the clouds.

"Is anyone hurt?" he asked. "Can you open your door?"

Harold pulled the handle. The door flew open, and he tumbled out with Tina behind him, down to the mud of the ditch.

The trailer pointed one way, the truck the other. It seemed impossibly stuck, a front wheel right off the ground, spinning slowly.

Samuel stood in the rain and the wind and banged his fists on his head. "I'm sorry," he said. "I don't know how I did it. Stupid! I'm just stupid."

"You're not stupid, you lug," said Tina. "No one can drive better than you."

The Gypsy Magda stopped behind the trailer, her headlights blinding on its silver. She climbed from the cab in her scarves and bracelets, with a blanket wrapped around her, flapping in the wind.

"The little truck will never pull us out," said Samuel. "We'll get them both stuck if we try." He kicked the trailer's wheel. "What do we do? What on earth do we do?"

"We wait," said the Gypsy Magda. Her hair streamed in tangles of gray. Her bracelets and bells tinkled in the wind. The lightning lit her like a skeleton in rags. "He is coming now, the man in trouble," she said. "He is on his way."

Chapter

19

The man in trouble came from the prairie, in a spot of light, as the Gypsy herself had come. He rode an ancient tractor that was huge and red, with metal wheels and a smokestack like a crooked finger, capped by a chattering lid. He sat high on a small metal seat, with a black Stetson on his head and glistening oilskins tumbling from his shoulders. On his lap he held a child, a girl, who lolled and tipped against him as though her bones had melted in the rain.

He drove down through the ditch and up to the road behind the Gypsy's truck, then turned to his right with mud spraying from the wheels.

It seemed he wouldn't stop. It seemed he would go right by on that enormous, bloodred tractor. But the Gypsy Magda spread her arms, and the wind thrashed at her scarves and blanket. Like a scarecrow, she stood in his way.

The farmer stopped. He shouted down, "You madwoman! You witch! Get thee behind me."

She stayed where she was. Then Samuel came forward into his headlights, with Tina behind him, and Harold the Ghost.

"Good God almighty," said the farmer. "Have you come to take her? Are you devils?"

"Gosh, no," said Tina.

"You are not of this world, whatever you are." He fumbled with the gearshift, jamming it forward and back. "Out of my way, I tell you!"

He stood on the tractor, black and gaunt against the clouds. The child's head rolled back as he raised an arm and shouted, "In the name of God I command you to go!"

Lightning seared across the sky. It made, for an instant, a world of white and black. The farmer in his oilskins, the Gypsy below him, seemed to smoke in that flash of hot light as the rain pelted off them in spray. Thunder boomed and echoed, and another flash of lightning cracked through the clouds. The light was blinding, the noise deafening. Harold could see or hear nothing for nearly a minute.

Then the farmer blinked down from his seat. "You are still here," he said.

Samuel stood against the small front wheels. As big as he was, he was dwarfed by the tractor. "We're circus people," he said. "That's all we are. We're stuck and we need some help."

"Circus people?" said the farmer. "Freaks, you mean? Is that all you are?"

"Yes. Yes, we're freaks," said Samuel, and Harold could see how hard it was for him to use that word. "We just need a push on the truck."

"I can't help you. I'm sorry, and God forgive me, but I can't stay to help you."

"The child!" said the Gypsy Magda. "You're frightened for the child."

101

The farmer lowered his head. Rain poured from the Stetson, down on his oilskins, on the face of the child, bare in the blankets.

"Give her to me." The Gypsy Magda reached up along the tractor's fender. Her bracelets scratched on the metal. "I can help her if you give her to me."

"My firstborn." He held the child closely, turning away as the Gypsy Magda groped across the fender. Her hand clutched at his boot, at the sodden cuffs of his pants.

Then her eyes closed. "She lies below a quilt you call the Drunkard's Path, under a picture her grandmother made. A cat, it sleeps by her feet. She dreams of giants and she cries out. The house, she says, it is spinning."

The farmer gawked at her. "How do you know this?"

"She knows everything," said Harold. He stepped up to the front of the tractor. "You have to trust her. You have to."

"You won't find your doctor," said the Gypsy Magda. "His gate is closed, his windows black. He rides across the prairie in a buggy, a bag at his side and hot bricks at his feet. A dog—a white dog—runs behind him." She reached farther up his leg, clawing at his oilskins. A flash of lightning showed her there, the fallen scarves around her shoulders, the numbers on her arm.

"The devil's mark," the farmer said. He shook her off and jammed the tractor into gear.

"It will be the death of her!" screamed the Gypsy Magda. "You will take her home, and the doctor—when he comes—will come too late."

The tractor leapt forward, and Samuel fell away on

the left side, the Gypsy Magda on the right. Only Harold stood in its path. The radiator grille, like rows of metal teeth, clanked toward him. "Stop!" he shouted, his hands held out. "You have to trust her."

The metal touched his hands. The tractor pushed him back, his boots skidding in the mud. The engine roared and clattered, and it seemed the teeth would swallow him whole. He fell to his knees, got up, fell again. And then the roaring stopped.

The farmer was crying. "She might be gone already. She hasn't moved or said a word." Rain hammered on his Stetson and his oilskins, and he hunched over his daughter, shoulders shaking with his sobs.

Samuel climbed up and took the girl. He didn't speak; he just lifted her from the farmer's lap and carried her through the mud and the rain to the Gypsy Magda's truck. And they all crowded inside it, the farmer in the doorway, as the Gypsy Magda lit her candles. "Open the blankets," she said.

Harold peeled them back. The girl was tiny, frail and very thin. Her eyes open, her lips apart, she seemed to be not quite alive and not quite dead, but somewhere in between, staring out from a lonely world.

"Oh, the poor thing," said Tina. "The poor little thing."

"No talking!" snapped the Gypsy Magda. "She must hear no words of pity."

The Gypsy Magda opened jars and stoneware pots. She ground powders in her palms, working in the candlelight with the din of rain against the roof. She muttered incantations as she stirred the powders into a paste, as she dabbed it lightly on the skin above the young girl's lips. It smelled strongly, and sweetly, of meadows and trees, of mushrooms and earth. She moved her hands along the small body.

"Breathe the world of the living," she said, and touched more of the paste to the child's lips. "Taste the earth, the plants." She pressed little balls into the girl's closed fists. "Feel the things you've left behind. Breathe and taste and feel. Breathe and taste and feel."

The Gypsy's chant, the rain on the roof, were the only sounds. Her hands were all that moved. Then the child's nostrils twitched, her eyelids fluttered, and the little fists closed tightly.

"Breathe and taste and feel," said the Gypsy Magda.

Thunder rolled, and a gust of wind shook the truck. Rain misted through the doorway, past the farmer's shoulders.

"Take her hand," the Gypsy Magda said to Harold. "Hold it tight and wish her better."

Harold did as he was told. The child's skin was cold and dry, the fist like a bundle of roots in his hand. But he held it and he wished. He imagined her playing in a schoolyard, laughing with her friends.

"And now we wait," said the Gypsy Magda.

Chapter
20

The child died, or so the Gypsy Magda said. She died and then returned from the land of the dead to the land of the living. The small eyes closed and opened, and a smile came to her lips. She looked at Harold and asked, "Are you an angel?"

"I believe he is," the Gypsy Magda said. "Yes, I believe that he is."

They settled the child into a nest of pillows, then traveled east, the way they had come, down a road that was thick with mud. The Gypsy Magda drove, with the farmer shouting directions, with Harold squeezed between them. From the back of the truck came laughter as Samuel and Tina and the child lolled on the Gypsy's cushions.

"Turn here," shouted the farmer.

The truck slowed and swung to the left, up a narrow lane toward a farmhouse in a field. Again the child laughed, and the farmer smiled. "She seems well," he said. "I cannot thank you enough."

"You must never talk of what was done," the Gypsy Magda said. "You must never ask her where she was or what she saw."

The farmer nodded. He fiddled with the Stetson that he held now in his lap, bending the brim into curves. "I am a patient man," he said. "A good man, I believe. But I would not have answered such rudeness as I showed you with the kindness that you gave."

"It was nothing," said the Gypsy Magda. "Nothing."

"It was the world to me."

"The child we helped, not you," said the Gypsy Magda. "We know what it is to suffer."

The farmer turned the hat upside down and balanced the crown on his knee. "And you," he said to Harold. "You put yourself right before the tractor. I could have squashed you; I nearly did. Yet there you stood, like Gabriel himself, all bright and shiny, white as goodness. Is it true? Are you not an angel?"

Harold shook his head. "No, sir."

"Then you are a saint. Or you ought to be." The farmer tipped the Stetson up against his chest. "You saved my daughter's life, and I'm forever in your debt. How can I repay you?"

Harold eyed the Stetson and wondered: Could he ask for that?

"Anything," the farmer said. "Only name it."

He almost did. It was on his lips to ask for that big, tall hat. But he saw the Gypsy Magda watching him as the lights of the farmhouse came swimming out of the rain. She had asked for nothing, and it was she who had really saved the child.

"Money?" asked the farmer. "I haven't much, but every penny that I own I'll gladly give to you."

"No," said Harold. He remembered the cook in his battered hat, the pride in the Gypsy's voice. And he said again, as grandly as he could, "I only wish I was a little bit darker."

The farmer laughed. "I sow the ground, but God grows the plants. I leave the miracles to Him."

THE HOUSE WAS SMALL and tidy, with scrolls of woodwork above the doors and windows. It looked like an overgrown birdhouse, a square little building with only one room. Water poured from the roof in a dreary black gurgling, into barrels that overflowed. But if a house could be cheerful, this one was. It seemed as safe and inviting as the Liberty church.

The Gypsy Magda parked the truck below it, beside a whitewashed shed where chickens squawked. A curtain cracked open in the farmhouse window, and a woman peered out, black against the light.

"Can you give me a moment," the farmer asked, "to tell the wife I have brought some . . . some company?" He fidgeted with his Stetson. His voice had a nervous crack. "She's not used to company. She—she might be alarmed. At company coming."

"We understand," said the Gypsy Magda.

He took his daughter and carried her up to the house. The door closed behind him, then opened soon after. And he waved, and they followed him in.

The farmer's wife was big and husky. Her face was brown and smoothly lumped, like a potato fresh from the ground. The farmer had prepared her well; she smiled at her visitors as though circus freaks called every day at her tumbledown home on the prairie.

"Sit," she said. "Please. I will bring you some food."

Harold saw that the floor had been quickly swept. A little pile of wood chips and bark and grass was pushed to the corner, behind a broom that stood on its tattered straws. Above it, on a loft that was reached by a ladder, two children stared down, as small as bats up there in the heat of the woodstove. A cloth had been thrown over the table, and an odd assortment of chairs placed around it—a rocker and a milking stool, a bench still wet from rain.

"Gee, this is swell," said Tina.

On their loft, the children giggled. The farmer's wife glared at them. "Those are the twins," she said. "They're supposed to be *sleeping*." Then she picked up the broom and bashed its handle at the side of the loft. "So, what do you think of this weather?" she asked, smiling, as she put the broom back in the corner.

They ate soup and chunks of fresh bread. The girl who had died sat beside Harold, squeezed with him into the rocker. When he leaned forward so did she, and they dipped their bread together into bowls of thick brown soup.

"Harold's an angel," she said.

"You bet he is," said Tina. "He's something else, that Harold."

He ate without talking. Then supper was over and the farmer's wife touched him on the shoulder. "Harold?" she asked. "Is that your name?"

"Yes, ma'am," said Harold.

"Would you help me out back for a moment? Will you be kind enough to carry the kettle?"

He stood up, and she gave him a cloth to wrap around his hand. It was a big, black kettle that steamed on the stove.

She took a lamp and led him through a low door to a shed behind the house. Along the wall was a wooden bench, a washboard propped on its side, and a washbasin under a red-handled pump. The farmer's black clothes stewed in a black broth in the basin.

"Sit," she said.

"Where?" asked Harold. There was nowhere to sit.

"Oh, mercy me," she said. "The stool's in the house, of course."

She pulled the clothes from their broth and hung them, dripping, on a little clothesline. Then she heaved the basin down to the floor and added water from the kettle. She opened a jar of foul-smelling liquid as black as molasses. And she dyed the white hair of Harold the Ghost.

He knelt on the floor and tipped like a bottle as her big strong hands kneaded and pushed at his head. He watched the water in the basin turn to black and froth. She spilled it out and filled it again, and rinsed him with a dipper. Then she grabbed his hair and lifted his head, and he could see that she was smiling.

"How do I look?" he asked.

"Like a count," she said. "Like an Eye-talian count." She gave him a towel and fetched a mirror, and took him close to the lamp.

He turned his head to look sideways, and she moved the mirror, and he turned his head again. They went around in a circle like a lord and a lady dancing. And then she laughed and gave him the mirror to hold for himself.

He saw a squinting, frightened, white-faced boy. Then he tipped the mirror and saw a black-haired boy, a suddenly grinning boy who didn't look like him at all. He touched his eyebrows and wished they were black instead of white, or not quite so ghastly white. He would have liked his skin to be a little darker, his eyes something more than clear. But for the first time in his life he liked the face he saw.

"Your own mother would hardly know you," said the farmer's wife. She put the lid on the jar and tipped out the basin. "You are a different person, sure enough. Now come, let's show your friends."

Harold stooped to go through the door, for it seemed that he was taller now, and broader. His boots didn't scuff or drag on the floor; they carried him across the kitchen in great, long strides. At the table faces turned toward him, and he tipped his head back a bit, so that the light might shine on his very black hair.

The farmer stroked his chin and nodded slowly. Samuel showed his crooked teeth. "Well, who is this?" he said. "Who's this handsome boy, and where has Harold gone?"

"Oh, you lug," said Tina. "You look terrific, Harold. You look just swell."

But the child, the farmer's daughter, wasn't pleased at all. "He looks like a goblin," she said. "I thought he was an angel."

"Hush!" the farmer said. "You will be off to your bed with talk like that."

Harold crumpled slightly. His hands, which had felt so strong, began to shake and sweat. But the Gypsy Magda rose from her place and came across to Harold. "She's only a child," she said. "She speaks without thinking. You look very handsome, very nice. But you have always looked handsome to me."

The Gypsy Magda came up on her toes and gave Harold a cold, dry kiss on the cheek. "You have got the one thing that you wished. You should smile; you should laugh. You were right to be happy."

The farmer's wife brought blankets and quilts, and the travelers bedded down on the floor. Harold listened to the rain pattering on the roof. He heard it stop at midnight, and was still awake when the farmer got up and roused them all. Dawn was hours away, but they dressed and drove back to the road, where the farmer hauled Samuel's truck from the ditch with his tractor. Then he stood in the glare of the tractor's headlights and solemnly shook hands with everyone. Last of all was Harold.

"You have a good lot of friends," he said. "You are blessed for that."

"Yes, sir," said Harold.

"Do you know what the Bible says about friends?"

"A lot, I bet," said Harold, groaning inside. The wind, at his back, blew strands of dark hair before his eyes. He felt new, different, at last like the snake he had envied for shedding its skin; he wanted to be off on the road, not listening to sermons.

"It tells you to be proud of them, and not to be ashamed of what they do."

Harold nodded. The farmer squeezed his hand with big, plow-strengthened fingers. The Gypsy, in her truck, was watching him.

"You are not listening; I can see that," said the farmer. "Go on, then, and be off with your friends."

He stood by the road, and he shouted after the trucks. "Good luck! Good luck to all of you!"

The truck left the farmer behind. It roared on to the west, into a world just starting to turn from black into gray. Harold rolled his window down. He took the old leather helmet that lay on the seat beside him, and flung it out across the prairie. It leapt and rolled like a little tumbleweed, falling back as the truck moved on.

Then Harold closed the window and leaned his dark head against the glass.

No one spoke a word.

Chapter

21

They drove west over flooded fields and swollen creeks. The sun rose behind them, and the sky turned the color of roses. And they came to a town that was still asleep.

There were only a dog and a milkman out on the main street, a wide avenue built for driving cattle. On either side, plastered to walls and windows, were posters for Hunter and Green's. But the paper had turned to mush in the rain, and the wonderful pictures of elephants and tightrope walkers hung in tattered strips.

"Where's the circus?" asked Tina.

"They've come and gone," said Samuel. "But they must have been here when we heard the calliope."

Already the town was behind them. Samuel shifted gears, bringing the truck back to its highway speed. Red arrows flitted past.

They followed the trail of the Cannibal King, across townships and counties, past fields of wheat that were battered down by rain and hail. They passed a field of Liberators, row after row after row of them, the silver bombers parked nose to tail, wing to wing, a crop of planes that seemed as useless as the broken wheat.

They drove to the north and back to the west,

through a bright shower of rain. Then they climbed a hill to its summit, and spread out below them, in a field at a bend in a river, was a gaudy cluster of circus tents.

At the center was the huge cook tent, its stack of rusted tin wafting curls of smoke. Spread in rings around it were the stable tents and the elephants' tent, the dressing tent and all the smaller tents the performers had pitched for themselves.

But the Cannibal King wasn't there. And neither was the big top.

"There's something wrong," said Samuel, slowing the truck.

"Maybe they're resting," said Tina.

Samuel shook his head. "They wouldn't be camped like this if there wasn't something wrong."

He steered onto the field, clinging to the wheel as the truck bounced across the grass. He parked it behind a line of others, and the Gypsy Magda parked beside him. Then they climbed down, the four travelers, and stood in a row, staring at the tents like explorers who'd stumbled on a strange little village.

"There's Mr. Hunter," said Samuel. He waved his arm and shouted, "Mr. Hunter!"

Harold squinted. He tipped his head sideways and gazed through his glasses. "Where?" he said.

"There."

All Harold could see was a pole, a stiff little pole with one arm flapping. Then it swayed and started toward him, and Harold blinked. The pole became a person, the thinnest one imaginable. Even taller than Samuel, Mr. Hunter was like a short man balanced on a pair of stilts; his legs seemed twice the length of all the rest of him.

"Mr. Hunter owns the circus, remember," said Samuel.

"You've arrived, I see," Mr. Hunter shouted across the field, down the row of trucks, in a voice so deep and loud that it could hardly have come from his thin little chest.

Tina smiled. "He *is* the circus, Harold."

He tilted over the rutted grass, just a strip of black to Harold, with a twinkle of gold where a watch fob swung against his waistcoat. "Greetings to you all," he shouted. "Grateful greetings, my peripatetic pair of prodigies."

"And he's the ringmaster too," said Tina.

Samuel put his hand on Harold's shoulder. "Stay here," he said, and shambled off, half in a run, with his wild hair flowing behind him. He took Mr. Hunter's elbow and turned him around, and their heads bent close as they talked. First one, then the other, looked over his shoulder. Samuel pointed at Harold.

"What's going on?" asked Harold.

"Don't you worry," said Tina. She reached up and squeezed Harold's hand. "Samuel's putting in a word for you, that's all. You've got it made, kiddo."

Harold was sweating. His hand shook in Tina's. "I'm the Ghost," he told himself softly. "No one can see me, no one can hurt me." Then he turned his head and saw himself in the shining side of the Airstream, his hair as black as the Gypsy's clothes, his glasses like black circles below it, on a face that was lost in the sun-lit metal. And he smiled to himself; he was different now, he thought. He had nothing to fear anymore.

Samuel and Mr. Hunter came together, side by side, stopping right in front of Harold. Mr. Hunter looked

115

down and the Ghost stared up, higher than he'd ever looked to see a person's face. It was gaunt and bright red from the sun, but it was a smiling, kindly face.

"Have you run away from home?" asked Mr. Hunter.

Harold frowned. He hadn't thought of it like that.

"You've come to join the circus, have you?" Long, thin hands rubbed together. "Well, you're living the dream of America, son. Footloose and free, following fortune where fortune is found."

"Yes, sir," said Harold. It seemed the proper thing to say.

Again Mr. Hunter stretched out his arms. "Welcome to my circus, son. Welcome to the great Hunter and Green's."

Tina clapped her hands. "He's got a job?"

"Oh, dear," said Mr. Hunter. "That's not up to me. That's out of my department."

"But if Flip says yes?"

"Well, certainly. If Flip says yes, it's fine with me."

Tina grinned up at Harold. "What did I tell you, kid? Come on, let's go."

She tugged on Harold's leg, but the Gypsy Magda stopped him with a glance. "Be careful," she said. "Remember what I told you."

Harold nodded; he would never forget. *Beware the ones of unnatural charm, and the beast that feeds with its tail.* But it seemed unimportant, even meaningless now. And he looked up at Mr. Hunter. "Thank you, sir."

Mr. Hunter smiled.

"Will there be a circus today?"

"Here?" said Mr. Hunter. "Who would come but the bees and the flies? No, son. Not today."

"What's wrong?" asked Samuel.

"Oh, it's been a lash-up. A proper snafu." Skinny fingers tangled in the watch chain. Mr. Hunter's head drooped to his chest. "We had a windstorm, Samuel. The blasting breaths of Boreas. They rent the big top right in two, and we're waiting here for the canvas boss. He's gone to fetch new panels—three new panels—the canvas boss and the rigger boy. And the Cannibal King has gone on ahead; I don't know where he is."

"Gee, I hope he's okay," said Tina. "I worry about him driving."

"He'd better be all right," said Mr. Hunter.

Samuel sighed. "What a tough season. The worst I remember."

"It could be the last." Mr. Hunter's voice turned sad and weary. "It could be the end for us all."

Harold felt sorry for him, the smiling face collapsing into wrinkles. But Tina pulled at his leg and led him away, slowly at first and then faster, until she trotted at his side.

They passed the trucks and crossed the field and hurried in among the tents. People sat on chairs of wood and canvas, looking up from books, from games of cards. Some didn't speak at all, and others called, "Well, there you are!" and "We thought you'd never find us." Tina laughed and waved her stubby arms, but Harold only stared ahead. He didn't like people watching him; he thought he'd never get used to that. To him, the faces that turned in his direction were like the coyotes he'd seen at the edge of winter fields, staring at cattle, waiting for a weak one to stray toward them.

He stumbled and caught himself. Then they walked behind the tents and into a different world.

Men in leotards bubbled up from a trampoline. A clown in baggy clothes, but with an ordinary face, juggled silver rings.

"Hey, Mr. Happy!" shouted Tina.

Harold stopped to watch as the clown spun his rings round and round, a wheel of rings ten feet tall. Then they stopped in midair, and the clown laughed at Harold's shock; the rings were welded in a circle.

"Come on," said Tina.

They passed a girl on a slack wire, a man doing handstands on a ladder. And at the end of the lot they found Flip Pharaoh.

She had her back toward them, poking with a rake at the wall of a red-and-white tent. She pushed at the canvas, then leapt away as rainwater spilled from the sagging roof. It splashed across the ground and across her clothes; she never leapt away quite far enough. And with each surge of water she gave a girlish squeal and a shiver as she stood on her toes. The tent ropes hummed like cello strings.

"Hi, Flip," said Tina.

Flip turned around, and Harold felt a lurch in his heart, a tremble that shook right through him. Blond and tanned, her cheeks puffed in a grin, Flip was more beautiful than the girl in the postcards, more beautiful than any girl he had ever seen. The water had soaked through her shirt, and it clung now to her shoulders and her chest in a skin of white and bright red frills.

Harold stared at her, his mouth hanging open, his

eyes jiggling madly. He felt light-headed, almost dizzy to see her. And she laughed. She plucked the shirt from her shoulders and laughed, but not with malice, not with the cruelty he'd heard so often in the laughter of the Liberty girls.

"I gotta get a longer rake," she said. "It's kinda cold, the rain."

Harold saw the sunlight fall across her, and wherever she was wet she seemed to shine and sparkle. He wished he had a jacket; he could give her his jacket and let her put it on.

"Who's this?" she asked.

"This is Harold," said Tina. "Mr. Hunter says he can have a job if you've got one."

"What kinda job?" asked Flip.

She was staring at him, studying him, her eyes flicking up his face and down. And for a moment he saw the look he'd seen so often, that awful wonder that came to everyone's face when they saw a boy as white as chalk. He was scared she would tell him to take off his glasses, terrified she would see his eyes—like drops of water— and that she would know his hair was only dyed.

But she smiled all the harder. She ran a hand under her yellow hair, lifting it up from her shoulders. "Gee," she said. "I don't know."

"Oh, please?" said Tina. "He's come all the way from Liberty. All this way, without a dime in his pocket."

"Why?" asked Flip.

"To see the King, of course," said Tina, her arms held high. "To see the Cannibal King!"

Harold groaned inside. His face, he knew, had blushed a brilliant red.

"Oh?" Flip let the rake rest on the ground. "And why does he want to do that?"

"Well, gosh," said Tina. "Because he's—" She stopped. Her mouth hung open, her eyebrows in a high, comical arch. She covered her lips with her fingers.

"Because he's an albino?" asked Flip, and Harold's heart sank. "Is that what you mean?"

Harold looked down at the ground, scuffing at it with the toe of his boot. His hair fell in shining black curls across his eyes, and he blushed even more to think how foolish he'd been to hope he could hide what he was.

"Because the Cannibal King's an albino? Sure, I can see that." She laughed gaily. "He wants to meet the King because he's never seen an albino before."

Harold turned his head to see sideways through his glasses. Flip stood on the rake, her cheek resting on the handle, and she smiled the most charming, the most beautiful smile. He raised his chin from his chest. He felt as though he had shrunk and grown again but was bigger now than when he'd started. It was true, he thought; he *was* different now. He was the dark-haired boy in his dream; he was an Eye-talian count, whatever that was.

She laughed again, and he smiled shyly back. She said, "I guess you don't see many albinos in Liberty."

"Not really," said Harold. He wished she would talk about something else.

"They've got white hair, if you can believe that." Flip leaned forward on the rake, her shirt sticking to her. "But I think he's real handsome, the Cannibal King. There's something—oh, *exciting* about albinos. They just give me the shivers."

120

Harold swallowed. He felt a shiver himself, as though it had leapt like a spark from her to him.

"You'll see what I mean," she said. "Just wait till you meet him."

Tina grinned. "You're going to give him a job?"

"Maybe," said Flip. "What can you do, Harold?"

He had to think. What *could* he do? "Well, I can't ride horses," he said. "I can't juggle, and I've never tried to walk on a tightrope." He shrugged. "I'm pretty good with animals. Maybe I could be a lion tamer."

She didn't move. She leaned on the rake handle and smiled at him. Then slowly she turned toward Tina, swiveling on the stick. "Is he kidding?" she asked.

"I don't think so," said Tina.

Flip swung back toward him. "Do you know how long I've been riding?"

Harold shook his head.

"Thirteen years, that's how long. I could ride before I could walk. I learned the language of horses before I learned English. I practiced eight hours a day, every day, for my whole life, and—man!—it bugs me when people say, 'Oh, I could do *that*.' Like it's so darned easy."

"That's not what I meant," said Harold, dismayed at her anger. He straightened his glasses, fiddling with the little round lenses. "I didn't mean I could *do* it; I meant I wanted to learn. Princess Minikin says you're the best in the whole world. She says you're famous, and maybe you'd teach me to ride."

"Yeah? Really?" Flip cocked back her head, her hair tumbling down from her shoulders. To Harold, she looked like a movie star posing for pictures. "Well, maybe I could. I don't know."

"Just give him a chance," said Tina. "That's all he needs, just a chance."

She glanced at Harold. "You're good with animals?"

"You bet he is!" shouted Tina. "He has a real swell dog that can do all sorts of tricks. He's just a sweetheart, just an angel."

"And what are *you*? His agent?" Flip pushed away from the rake. She propped it against the tent. "All right. I'll give him a chance. I'll see how he does with the animals."

Chapter 22

She showed him the horses first, six huge white horses that stood in stalls along a narrow tent, their heads thrust out to the aisle. They whinnied and snorted, reaching down with their noses for a pat or a hug from Flip. They looked all alike to Harold, big shadowy horses in the dimness of the tent. Of course he kept his glasses on.

Flip called them by the names of dead generals. "That's Sherman," she said. "And that's Jackson. This is Grant, and whatever you do don't go whistling Dixie around him."

Harold nodded gravely. "Oh, I won't," he said. "You bet I won't."

"It's just a joke," she said, and nudged him with her elbow. "You'll feed them oats and bring them water, and I'll show you how to comb them."

"I'd like to do that," Harold said. He loved the stable with its smell of warm hay, its amber light filtered through the canvas. He reached up to scratch the horses' noses, to pat their round and bulging cheeks. They rattled at the stable doors and shook their manes.

"It's true," said Flip. "They like you."

At the back of the stable was a burlap bag full of

peanuts. Flip filled a small bucket and carried it out into sunshine that was too bright for Harold. He squinted against it, stumbling behind her, past the cook tent and down another wall of canvas.

"Now let's see how you do with the roses," she said.

"What roses?" asked Harold.

Around the corner of the tent came a sound of rattling chains and then a low and ominous rumble. It was soft, then loud, broken by a high and eerie wail.

"*Those* roses," said Flip.

Harold stopped. The clouds closed in again and took the burning from his eyes, but Flip was just a shadow; he couldn't tell if she was smiling. "What sort of roses are they?" he asked.

"Just go and look," said Flip.

He poked his head around the corner. In a patch of open ground stood three enormous elephants. They grazed at the grass, pulling whole clumps of dirt and roots from the field. They swung them lazily over their heads and knocked them, in clouds of mud, against their shoulders. Each one had an iron collar fastened around a hind leg, a chain leading back to a stake in the ground. In a great circle around them the field was broken and torn, and the elephants pulled their chains taut to reach for the fresh, new grass at its edge.

"Those are *roses?*" asked Harold.

Flip giggled. "That's Canary Bird there. That's Max Graf beside him. And this big one here, this is Conrad Ferdinand Meyer, or Conrad for short. We name them after roses, see?"

"They're beautiful," said Harold. Their legs were thick as tree stumps, their skin a mass of wrinkles. But they had a majesty and a grandeur that came from more than just their size. They seemed exotic and ancient, half animal and half machine. They tore up the ground like bulldozers.

Conrad was the tallest by a yard. "He's a giant," Harold said.

"*She,*" said Flip. "Circuses only use females. But we talk about them like they were boys because they're so big and strong." She touched Harold's arm. "It's like they *should* be boys, you know?"

Harold looked down at her fingers curved across his sleeve. They made his whole body tingle.

"What do you think?" asked Flip.

He could hardly think at all. Then the fingers fell away and left little dents in his shirt, but the tingling stayed in his skin.

"I guess you've never seen elephants, either," she said.

"No," said Harold. They were so big, so different from anything else, that they made him feel small, and a little bit scared. They could pick him up in their trunks and knock him on their backs like clumps of grass if they wanted. Still, he wished he could see them better; he wished he could know what they felt like.

"Can I touch them?" he asked.

"Sure," said Flip, and they started forward. "But watch for Conrad. He's a strange one."

"Why?"

"Someone knocked him around a bit." Flip rattled her bucket of peanuts, and Conrad slowly swung his head, his big ears flapping. "It was years ago. Before we got him. But he's got scars on his mouth from a bull-hook, see?"

Harold paused, and Flip went on past him. He

touched his glasses and peered across their tops. The elephant was watching him, the trunk lifting up in a curl.

"The last guy we had for your job quit because of Conrad," said Flip. "I don't know why exactly."

The elephant trumpeted. It was a wonderful, frightening sound. The trunk dropped close to the ground and swayed back and forth. His ears spread wide, Conrad lumbered toward them, until the chain came taut with a clank. The head tilted and shook; it moved as Harold's might, to see something blurred in the distance. And Harold waved his arms. He shouted at the elephant.

"Don't do that!" cried Flip. "Oh, Harold, you'll scare him!"

It was too late. The elephant stomped at the grass. It made that awful rumbling noise, and its ears flapped forward and back. Then, with one pull of its leg, it tore up the stake that held it. And Conrad came thundering forward like a dusty, bellowing engine.

Chapter 23

The elephant roared with its head up high. Its enormous legs hammered at the ground, and it came in a spray of muddy water, dragging its chains behind it.

"Don't run," said Flip.

Harold ran. He bumbled across the lot as fast as his boots would let him. He ran like an ostrich, with high and ungainly steps, his elbows flapping like stubs of wings. He went three miles an hour, and the elephant went thirty.

He looked back once and saw its bulk, the dirt and clumps of grass falling from it. He looked again and saw only a great flat forehead, wicked eyes and dull white stumps of tusks. Then he caught his toe in a gopher hole and tumbled across the ground.

The elephant's feet thumped around him, each toe bigger than his fist, the soles sagging loose as the feet came up, flattening as they thundered down. There was a sound like a rising wind, and the trunk came groping over the grass. It touched his leg and then his back; it crawled across his neck.

The touch was strong and rubbery, a hot, wet suction on his skin. He heard the rumbling from the elephant's chest, and the trunk curled underneath him. It lifted him clear from the ground, so high that his legs dangled down. They looked at each other eye to eye, and then it sat him down but didn't let go.

Flip, who was running, slowed to a walk. She stood beside him and put her hands on the trunk where it wrapped around his chest.

Harold smiled at her. "This is great," he said.

Conrad's ears, as big as tablecloths almost, curled and flapped beside him. Harold saw how the elephant's hair grew in sparse little clumps along the ears and the lips. It made long, shaggy lashes over eyes that were nearly like a person's. The mouth was open, and he saw a tongue that was pink and thick and pointed. He heard the rumble deep behind it, and thought the elephant was purring. And then he saw the scars, the ragged tears in Conrad's lip, and wondered how anyone could do that.

"He could have stomped me if he'd wanted to," said Harold, looking down. "For a minute there, you know, I thought he might. I really thought he might."

"Tell him to let you go," said Flip.

He stroked the trunk, looking up at the elephant's eyes. "You've got to let me go now," he said. "Okay, Conrad?"

Flip laughed. "Not like that. Slap him on the trunk, Harold. Slap him hard. He's not real smart, and you have to *tell* him what to do."

But Harold nearly whispered. "Come on, Conrad," he said. "Please let me go."

And the trunk unwound. It fell away from him in leathery loops, the tip touching his shoulders, moving down his arm, lingering at his fingers. He got up and

Conrad nudged against him, almost toppling him from his feet.

"That's amazing," said Flip. "I've never seen him so gentle."

They started back toward the tent, and Conrad swayed along behind them, swinging his trunk, grunting in his throat. The chains clanked across the ground.

"What do they do?" asked Harold. "In the circus, I mean."

"Not very much," she said, and laughed. "They sort of stomp around and bump into each other. It's meant to be dancing, but it's sure not the jitterbug."

"What else?"

"Well, they work. They raise the big top and help load the trucks. If someone gets stuck, they pull him out."

Flip bent down and picked up the stake. She shoved it back in the hole and stamped the dirt around it. Over the top she dropped the ring on Conrad's chain.

"Is that all that holds him there?" asked Harold.

"It doesn't hold him at all. It's just the thought that keeps him here."

Conrad swaggered in among the other elephants. He bellowed at them and thumped against them. His massive ribs curved high above Harold's head.

Flip shook the bucket, and all three of the elephants came wandering over. They took the peanuts from her palm with the tips of their trunks.

"Can I feed them?" Harold asked.

She held the bucket toward him, and he took out a handful of nuts. With a rumble and a snort, Conrad shoved the others aside to eat from Harold's hand.

He laughed at the delicate touch of the elephant, a tickling at his skin. "Maybe I could teach them some other tricks," he said.

"Don't make me laugh." Flip tipped her bucket onto the ground. Max Graf and Canary Bird groveled at her feet, snuffling up the peanuts. "They're getting old," she said. "They're all worn out, like everything in this stupid little circus."

"It's a great circus," Harold said.

"Yeah? How many times have you watched it?"

"I guess I haven't seen it yet." Harold tossed a peanut. Conrad's trunk snaked up and caught it.

"It's a long-grass outfit," said Flip with a sneer. "It's a crummy, gyppo circus, and I'd do anything to get out of it. I'd marry Wallo the Sausage Man if I had to, and he makes Samuel look like Clark Gable."

Harold tossed another peanut. The elephant missed, then swept it off the ground. "Why don't you quit?" he asked.

"I won't have to quit." She watched as Conrad caught three nuts in a row. "We're going broke so fast it isn't funny. And I can hardly wait until the end. Anything would be better than this, traveling around to every one-horse town with a bunch of freaks and con men."

"Why's it going broke?"

"Because it's a crummy little mud show!"

Harold tossed a nut to Max Graf, but Conrad's trunk shot out and caught it in the air.

"We need something big," said Flip. "Something fantastic. Something that nobody else has ever done."

Harold threw the last peanut high in the air. It tumbled end over end, and Flip turned her head up to watch. Conrad took a lumbering step backward, his trunk stretching up. The peanut slowed and started down.

"Like elephants playing baseball?" asked Harold.

And Conrad reached out and snatched the peanut as it fell.

Chapter
24

Flip told him it would never work. "Elephants can't play ball," she said. "No one's *ever* taught them that."

"Maybe no one's ever tried," said Harold.

"Yeah," she scoffed. "Because it can't be done."

But it seemed to Harold that if *he* could learn to hit a ball, then anybody could, and certainly an elephant, with its two enormous eyes. "Let's just try," he said.

She shrugged. "Well, suit yourself."

Harold brought his glove, his bat, the gaudy painted ball. He said, "I guess I'll start with batting," and Flip squatted down to watch him.

He stood under Conrad's chin, and the trunk draped across him like an enormous snake. Its tip was almost like a pair of fingers, and they groped along the bat as the elephant sniffed at the wood.

"Hold it like this," said Harold, arranging the trunk with his hands. "You swing it back, and you swing it forward. See?" He held on to Conrad's trunk. "Back and forward. Back and forward." He looked at Flip. "Okay. Throw us the ball."

She groaned and got up. "It's not going to work," she said.

"Just try it."

She threw underhanded, in a long and gentle arc. Harold saw the ball come spinning from her hand. And then he closed his eyes.

"Just try it," his brother had told him. "Watch the ball as long as you can, then close your eyes and swing." And after that, Harold had never missed. It was as though he *knew* where the ball was, though if he tried to see it rushing past he couldn't. A moving ball was just a blur, and he always batted with his eyes closed.

"Swing!" he shouted now, and pushed against the trunk. He heard the crack of the ball against the bat and felt the tremor of it through Conrad's trunk.

"That was you," said Flip.

"Well, he's got to learn," he said.

They tried it again, and then again, until Flip panted from running back and forth. Harold never missed. Every time he swung, he felt the thud through Conrad's trunk, then opened his eyes to see Flip hurrying after the ball, to see Max and Canary Bird watching the game. They trumpeted and shook on their feet like fat, excited fans.

"See?" said Harold. "I think it's going to work."

"But it's you that's hitting it," said Flip. "Not him."

And they let the elephant try it by himself.

Flip tossed the ball to Conrad; Harold stood behind him. "Swing!" he shouted, but the elephant didn't move.

"Try to hit the bat," said Harold.

"Geez!" said Flip. "I'm not Dazzy Vance!"

They pitched and caught, and pitched and caught, as though the elephant wasn't there between them. Conrad never moved until the ball thumped against his shoulder. Then he hurled the bat across the field and wandered off, grumbling in his throat.

"Forget it," said Flip. She gave the ball and glove to Harold and left him there alone. "If you think they can learn this, you're as dumb as they are."

But Harold kept practicing. He arranged the bat in Conrad's trunk and pitched the ball from seven feet away. He tossed and shouted, "Swing!" and got the ball and pitched again. He played as patiently and happily as David once had played with him.

The broken clouds filled and darkened. The afternoon went by. But Harold didn't give up. He went on and on in his lonely corner of the circus lot. And on the three hundred and thirty-first pitch, Conrad swung the bat and hit the ball.

The sound it made was like a fence rail breaking. The ball whizzed past Harold's head. It bounced with a squirt of mud from the ground behind him, and when he spun around to look he saw Max trundling along, dragging his chain, chasing the ball with his trunk.

But no one was there to see it.

Harold ran to Conrad. He threw his arms around his trunk and pressed his cheek against the warm and leathery skin. "You did it," he said. "You did it."

The elephant dropped the bat and held him. The trunk coiled around his shoulders, squeezing hard but not too hard, and once again Conrad purred like a cat.

Chapter

25

Princess Minikin wouldn't come very close to the elephants. She shouted at Harold from the corner of the tent, waving her arms to get his attention.

"Supper's starting," she said. "Didn't you hear the bell?"

Harold shook his head.

"You have to come and eat," said Tina.

"Now?" Under the elephant's shoulder she looked like a small, frightened mouse. "I think they're starting to—"

"It's not a restaurant," she said. "Come on."

He dropped the rings over the stakes, and the elephants straightened their chains. They followed him as far as they could, until the stakes wavered in the ground. Standing at the edge of their worn-away circle, they made sounds he hadn't heard before, that reminded him of Honey and how she had cried when he left.

"I'm coming back," he told them, and remembered with a shock that he'd said the same thing to Honey. "Don't worry," he said. "You bet I will." Then he put the bat over his shoulder, slipped the glove on the handle and hurried after Tina.

They went together to the cook tent, where a metal triangle hung at the entrance.

135

"That's the dinner bell," said Tina. "When you hear it, you've got to come."

She took him past it, through the flap to rows of white tables and benches. There was room for fifty people, but in the middle, all alone, sat only Samuel and the Gypsy Magda. They were eating from trays, Samuel's hairy arms sprawled across the table.

Tina led him to the counter, and they each took a tray from a stack at the end. A cook in a greasy apron, strands of cabbage in his teeth, ladled sauerkraut into battered metal bowls.

"Say, that looks delicious, Wicks," said Tina, though the smell was just awful. "You'd better give lots to my friend here."

Wicks didn't talk; he served the food in a glum silence, never looking farther than his bowls and plates.

Samuel made a place for Harold, pulling his elbows in. "Hello, stranger," he said, and smiled a gruesome smile. "You got a job, did you, Harold?"

"Yes," he said. "It's great. I'm working with the elephants."

"Good for you." Samuel clapped him on the shoulder. "We knew you would. You're one of us; didn't we tell you that?" And then he got clumsily to his feet, stepping backward over the bench. "Excuse me," he said. "But I have to squeeze this geezer."

He was delighted, as pleased for Harold as Harold was himself. He wrapped his big arms around the boy's chest and rocked him on the bench.

Harold felt the furry jowls scrape against his cheek and looked across at the Gypsy Magda, who sat stone-

136

faced, watching, a fire burning in her eyes. "Aren't you happy for me?" he asked.

"You get a job, that's good it makes you happy," said the Gypsy Magda. "But do you remember what I told you?"

He nodded.

"Say it," she said.

He remembered the words exactly, even the sound of her voice on the prairie. " 'Beware the ones with unnatural charm. And the beast that feeds with its tail. A wild man's meek and a dark one's pale. And there comes a monstrous harm.' "

"Good," said the Gypsy Magda. "Now eat. We keep the others waiting."

"Where are they?" Harold asked.

"They wait, I said!" she snapped. Then her face softened, and her hand jingled as it reached across the table. "I'm sorry; the rules, they are strange to you."

Harold looked around the empty tent, at the cook with his back toward them. "What are they waiting for?"

Tina smiled at him over the edge of the table. Only her face could be seen. "They eat later," she said. "It's the same at every circus. The freaks eat first."

She said it so simply, as such a matter of fact, that Harold laughed with surprise.

"You think it is funny?" asked the Gypsy Magda.

"No," he said. "I just don't see why."

"Tradition," said Samuel, climbing back in his place. "It's the way it's always been, and circuses don't change."

The Gypsy Magda snorted. She pushed her plates

away. "Power," she said. "That is the reason. It is the same as you feeding your dog, but in the circus, the dogs—they eat first."

"My dog eats when I do," said Harold.

"I bet she does," said Tina. "That's a lucky dog."

Harold ate quickly, eager to get back to the elephants. He shoveled the sauerkraut into his mouth and barely bothered to chew it. Then he heard the scrape of benches and looked up to see a lady settling in at the next table.

He saw her from the back, nylon stockings rising to a yellow skirt belted tight at her waist. She held a tray in her left hand, and in her right a baby. Just the crown of its head poked above her shoulder; its hand clung to her blouse. She put down the tray, and her hand went up to take the baby.

"Hi, Esther," said Tina.

The lady turned her head, and Harold felt his eyebrows jump. Esther had a beard, a great black beard that covered her cheeks nearly to her eyes. "How's it going?" she asked in a man's deep voice. Then she sat, and the baby crawled down to the table.

And Harold's fork fell from his hand.

It wasn't a baby at all. It was a man, with wrinkles on his face, with red and wiry hair. He had no legs and no arms; miniature hands grew straight from his shoulders, tiny feet—like flippers—directly from his hips. He lay on his stomach, pushing forward on his fingers and toes, crawling over the table to the tray full of food.

"Hi, Wallo," said Tina. She leaned sideways. "You look happy today."

"Sauerkraut." Wallo tipped up his head. It was

wider than his shoulders, and nearly half of all he was. "I love sauerkraut," he said.

Harold shuddered. He remembered how Flip had said she'd marry Wallo the Sausage Man if she had to. He tried to imagine that, Flip in her wedding dress, Wallo beside her . . . But he couldn't.

Wallo ate straight from the tray, slurping up the shreds of cabbage. He said between mouthfuls, "Is that the elephant boy you've got with you?"

Tina nodded. "This is Harold."

"Welcome to Hunter and Green's," said Wallo. He burped. "Excuse me."

"Harold's come to meet the Cannibal King," said Tina.

"Good luck," said Wallo. "The King's miles from here, scouting a path toward the mountains."

Samuel picked up Harold's fork and put it back in the boy's hand. "Eat," he said softly. "You'll make him uncomfortable if you stare."

Harold looked down at his dinner, at the strands of pale yellow on his plate. The fork felt as heavy as a shovel, but he forced himself to eat. He saw Wallo just in the corner of his eye, a bizarre shape like a turtle without its shell. He said, as though to his cabbage, "Is he coming back?"

"Naw, not the King." Wallo slurped and grunted. "Right now he'll be sleeping. At the side of the road, in a field or a forest. When the sun goes down, so does the King. Then he rises with the moon and travels on, and he never goes back, only ahead. At night he's a wild man."

Harold smiled to himself. It was just as he'd pictured the Cannibal King, dancing in moonlit jungles with his strange tribe of Stone People. He even heard the drums, or thought he did, and saw Wicks beating on the counter with the handle of his spatula.

"Come on," said Wicks. "Come on. There's people waiting now."

Wallo looked up. "We'd better hurry," he said.

The moment they were done, Wicks chased them from the tent. "You can't sit around all day," he shouted at Harold. "It ain't a restaurant."

Harold got up. "Samuel?" he asked. "Does the Cannibal King ever eat here?"

"Take your talk outside," shouted Wicks.

Tina levered up on her arms, her shoulders rising to the table. "It's okay," she said. "We can tell you about him later, Harold. Say, you're coming to the trailer, aren't you?"

"Sure," said Harold. He watched Esther take Wallo in her arms and carry him toward the door. He put his bat over his shoulder and followed Samuel down the rows of tables, past the counter where Wicks picked at his teeth with the spatula blade.

"About time," said the cook. "Show some consideration, for crying out loud."

Harold didn't answer. He followed Samuel through the door, past a line of people who stood along the canvas or leaned against the guy ropes. He squinted at faces that were blurred and indistinct, and spotted Flip in a group of four, her yellow hair shining. But she turned away as though she hadn't seen him, and suddenly he felt ashamed to be coming from the tent with Samuel and the others. He ran a hand through his black hair and heard the voices asking, "Who's that kid?" and, "What's he doing here?"

He tightened his fingers around the bat. Someone laughed and said, "It's the Babe." And another voice said, "Look at his hair! Maybe it's Jackie Robinson."

Harold blushed. As dark as his hair was, no one could mistake him for Jackie, the Dodgers' Negro infielder. He shrank inside himself, bewildered by the teasing. Didn't he look the same as everyone else?

Tina hurried to his side. "Come on," she said. "We're all going back to the trailer."

Harold tried to look away, but she circled around before him, her little legs, her little shoes, flashing through the grass. "Don't you want to come?"

"Later," he said. "Okay?" He veered off and broke into a run, heading for the elephants.

Chapter
26

"Swing!" shouted Harold. "Now you've got it!"

The elephant was catching on. Conrad nearly always swung the bat, though often wildly, and rarely hit the ball. He swung it like a golf club as the ball passed overhead, like a tennis racket as it skittered on the ground. And sometimes he just let go and sent the bat spinning in the most frightening directions. Then it bounced past Harold's feet, and Canary Bird picked it up and held it in his trunk.

"You want to try?" asked Harold. "You want to have a turn?"

He tossed the ball. "Swing!" he shouted. And Canary Bird hit a long and sizzling drive that ricocheted off Conrad's head with a wooden-sounding thunk.

Conrad looked so shocked, so startled, that Harold had to laugh. Then the big brown eyes blinked, and the trunk hung down like a wilted mustache. Harold ran to touch him. "I'm sorry," he said, stroking the trunk. "I shouldn't have laughed. You're trying your best, and I shouldn't have done that."

He gave the bat to Conrad, and Canary Bird pouted like a child; he kicked at the ground and whimpered. "Oh, gosh," said Harold. He couldn't keep all of them happy. "You want to be the catcher? Huh? You want to try that out?"

He maneuvered the elephants into position, amazed by their grace, amused by their strange, rolling gait and the skin that drooped like sagging diapers from their haunches. He pitched and fetched, tossed the ball and ran to get it; Canary Bird was a better backstop than a catcher. But the elephants were learning, and he kept at the game with the patience he had used to teach Honey all her tricks.

It started to rain, but he kept on practicing. He never got angry when the elephants missed, when they stood accidentally on the ball and buried it deep in the mud. Sprinkles turned to showers, to short and heavy bursts.

Canary Bird was hitting one ball out of every ten, almost, when Flip came by. She stood in the shelter of the tent, and watched with her hands in her pockets.

"He's not Pee Wee Reese," she said.

"He's batting nearly a hundred," said Harold.

She laughed. "Gee, Harold, what if it works? You know something? People would come for hundreds of miles to watch elephants playing baseball."

He took the ball in his glove and walked across to Flip. "I was thinking," he said. "They should wear little caps. Little socks, maybe. A clown can be the bat boy, and you can wear an umpire's shirt. Maybe the band could play 'Take Me Out to the Ball Game.'"

She was staring at him.

"What's the matter?" he asked.

"Your hair." She touched her face. "It's leaking."

He didn't understand.

She touched Harold's face, stroking down his cheek, and her fingertips came away black.

Harold gawked at them. He rubbed his cheeks, his forehead, smearing black across his face. He squeezed a hand through his hair and saw the water dribble black as mud down across his shirt.

"The dye!" he said. "The dye!"

"The what?" asked Flip. She giggled. "Harold, your hair's going white."

Harold panicked. He clamped a hand across his head; he covered it with the baseball glove. Flip laughed, and Harold turned to dash away. He ran into the tent rope and stumbled back, and Flip doubled up with laughter.

He ducked his head and dashed away again, under the rope, around the tent, across the field to the trailer.

He burst through the door, into the sitting room, and Tina looked up from the armchair; Samuel too. They laughed to see him, and he whirled down the corridor with the trailer rocking on its wheels, ripped open the door to the bathroom and locked himself inside. For only a moment he saw his face in the small mirror, and he was shocked by the streaks of black that dribbled down his cheeks. Then he tore his glasses off and twisted the faucets as far as he could. He shoved his head down in the sink, into the stream of water, and it poured and splashed around him, swirling down the drain in a black and inky stream.

He cried for himself, for his shame. He could never be anything better, he thought, and he was stupid to have tried.

Someone knocked at the door. Harold didn't answer.

The knocks came again, not loud but gentle.

"Go away," said Harold. "Leave me alone. Please leave me alone."

The door swung open. "That lock doesn't work anyway," said Tina. "It hasn't ever worked."

She came in and closed the door; she climbed up onto the frilly cover of the toilet seat and leaned across to take Harold's glasses from the corner of the sink. She folded them neatly and balanced them on the cushion of a toilet-paper roll.

"I should have known," she said. "I should have guessed this would happen."

Harold sniffled in the stream of water. He kept hearing Flip's laughter, and imagined the joy she must have taken in his black-streaked face.

"I'm sorry I laughed." Tina picked up a bar of soap that was twice the size of her hands and worked a froth into Harold's hair. "I shouldn't have laughed. But you looked so funny. All that black dripping off you. You looked so darned surprised."

The bar of soap squirted from her fingers. She was laughing again, tears in her eyes. "I'm sorry," she said. "But you'd be laughing yourself if it was someone else you saw."

Harold shook his head. He would never laugh at anyone.

"Say," she said. "You're not angry with me, are you?"

"She knows," said Harold.

"What do you mean?" asked Tina, busy with the soap again. "Who?"

"Flip," he said. It was like being back in Liberty, but even worse. She would tease him now not only for what he always had been, but for what he'd tried to be as well. "She knows all about me."

"Well, of *course* she knows." Tina turned off the faucets and squeezed the water from Harold's hair. "She knew right away, Harold. You don't see a lady walking down the street in a rabbit-skin coat and say, 'Oh, look! There goes a rabbit,' do you?"

"Then she *pretended* she didn't," said Harold.

"That's Flip. She was just having a bit of fun and sort of leading you on." Tina patted his neck. "Head up."

Harold lifted his head from the sink. He took the towel Tina held toward him. "She'll hate me now," he said.

"Oh, gracious sakes, she won't. Not Flip."

He covered his head, rubbing with the towel. It muffled the sound of Tina talking, and the tremendous crash that followed—that shook the trailer—seemed all the louder for it.

"What on earth!" said Tina.

Harold tore off the towel.

"Something hit us," she said.

They ran down the hall and out through the door. Samuel was already there, standing on the grass under the small bathroom window. He scratched his head as he stared up at a dent in the metal, a crater perfectly round. But no one else was near; the circus lot was empty.

"It must have been one of those disks," said Samuel. He turned around, looking up at the sky. "Everyone's seeing them now, those flying disks."

"Oh, they've got to be bigger than that," said Tina.

146

"They're from outer space," he said knowingly.

She stooped, tipping her head to see under the trailer. "You lug, it's just a baseball."

A figure came running over the lot, shooting out from the tents, skidding on the wet grass. Only a blur for Harold, it stopped, then started again, sprinting straight toward them.

"It's Flip," said Tina.

Harold gasped. He fumbled through his clothes, feeling at his pockets. "My glasses," he said.

"You don't need them," she said. "You don't see any better with them."

"But I *look* a lot better."

She stopped his hand as it groped frantically across his hip. "Oh, Harold," she said. "Don't you ever learn?"

Flip came running, jumping, toward the trailer. "He did it!" she cried. "Harold, he did it!"

He turned to face her; there was nothing else to do. He faced her white from head to toe, his hair rubbed into standing tufts, his eyes like drops of water. He felt like a criminal turning to face a judge.

"It was Max Graf!" she shouted, fifty yards away. "I gave Max a turn, and he hit it clear across the lot."

She ran straight to Harold and bowled into him. She spun him around and carried him along, and they slammed their shoulders on the trailer. "They can do it," she said. "You were right, Harold. It's going to be the greatest show that ever was."

Then she leaned back, her hands on his arms. She looked at his hair, his eyes, his face as white as flour. "Well, that looks better," she said, and hugged him tightly. "That looks a *whole* lot better now."

Elephants chased Harold through his sleep on the Airstream's narrow sofa. Feet trampled around him, and he jolted awake, slamming his hand on the trailer's wall. He heard a far-off bugling that frightened him for a moment, then the rasping rumble of Samuel's snores.

He closed his eyes and felt as though he was back in Liberty. Almost every night he'd been lulled to sleep after troubling dreams by the sound of his father snoring. Then he put his hand on the metal wall and felt it shake very slightly as Samuel breathed, and he wriggled down into the cushions feeling safe and happy.

But it wasn't Samuel that he thought of, nor his father, as he drifted back to sleep. He thought of Flip, of how she'd hugged him and danced him in a circle. He could still feel her arms around him, the sparks her fingers made. And Harold the Ghost, for the first time in years, fell asleep smiling.

In the morning they went back to work, the two of them together. Flip showed him how to feed and groom the horses, how to clean the stables. But all the time it was the elephants she talked about.

"They're hard to teach, but once you've taught them something they remember it forever. They *like* to

learn. Sometimes I've seen them dancing by themselves." She laughed. "Or sorta dancing."

She talked to him across the stables, leaning her
head now and then past General Sherman to catch his
eye as he worked.

"They cry, you know that? Elephants cry," she said.
"And tricky? Oh, you gotta watch them all the time,
'cause they're always up to something."

Flip showed him how to comb the horses' manes,
standing beside him as they worked on General Boggs.
"Like this," she said, and put her hand on his to show
him how, her tanned fingers holding his, whiter than
the horse's mane. He grinned a stupid grin, feeling
giddy and sort of sick.

He loved her more than ever now. She hadn't said
another word about the way he really looked, and he
felt as though they shared a secret. He watched their
hands moving together and thought he could spend
the rest of his life combing horses with Flip. But then
she said, "It's just like brushing your dog," and that
made him sad to think of Honey. His clear, pale eyes
filled with tears, and he thought he had to wipe his
nose but didn't want to take his hand away. And he
stood there crying, thinking of Honey and then his
mother, seeing them both staring out the big front
window of his house.

Flip stopped brushing. "What's the matter?" she
asked.

"I don't know." He sniffed. "I feel sort of squirly
inside."

She frowned, then giggled, and that made him
smile. "You know, you're kinda cute," she said.

They combed all six horses, going from stall to stall.

They brought in hay and water, and the chores were nearly done when Tina came by to tell him that breakfast was ready.

Flip was pitching hay through the open gate to General Jackson's stall. "We're not quite finished," she said.

"But he's got to eat," said Tina. "The kid's done a day's work already."

"He'll eat," said Flip. "Don't worry."

"When?"

"With me." Flip closed the gate. "He works with me, I guess he'll eat with me."

"Well, okay," said Tina. But she sounded doubtful, even sad. "And you'll make sure he gets two eggs?"

Flip laughed. "Geez, you're not his mom."

"I wish I was," she said.

Harold felt a twinge inside as the little princess wandered off. But it didn't last very long. He shook it off and went back to work, until the second bell rang for breakfast. Then he walked with Flip toward the cook tent and was surprised to see Mr. Hunter lining up for his breakfast like everyone else, waiting for the freaks to finish theirs. He looked so thin in his waistcoat, the watch chain looping down, that he might have been a nail that had snagged a bit of thread.

"He's the stingiest man in the world," said Flip. She chewed on a stem of hay as she matched her steps to Harold's. "And he doesn't like to argue, so whatever he tells you, just nod and say, 'Yes, sir.'"

Harold nodded and bumbled along beside her. And Mr. Hunter smiled to see them. He shook Harold's hand with fingers that felt like pipe cleaners. "Ah, we meet again," he said. "I'm hearing a prodigious lot about you, son."

Harold nodded. "Yes, sir."

"I understand that you're practicing with the pachyderms, are you not? Batting baseballs, I believe?"

"Yes, sir," said Harold.

"I should like to observe that. After breakfast, perhaps." The thin fingers touched the waistcoat buttons. "Ah, the prodigies have done."

From the tent came the bearded lady, carrying poor Wallo in her arms. Behind them walked Samuel, then Princess Minikin, then the Gypsy Magda. They passed through the door in a silent line, watched by everyone there. Harold squinted and thought—as though for the first time—that his friends were very strange, the first so huge and the second so tiny and the third so odd in her scarves and flowing shawls. He had never seen them like that, as a group from a distance, and felt a terrible happiness that he wasn't among them, that he wasn't a freak himself. Then his thought embarrassed him, and he tried to hide behind Mr. Hunter's pencil legs. But the Gypsy Magda turned her head, and her gaze went burning through the knots of people, as though it hunted for him. Her hand went up to shield her eyes from the sun, and her scarves fell in darkened folds to show the numbers on her arm. And the eyes came around and found him in the sun.

She didn't call to him; she didn't slow in her steady, jingling walk. But she watched him, and Harold was ashamed.

"Come on," said Flip, and pulled him into the tent.

Harold got his tray and started down the counter. But the cook, too, was staring at him. He held stringy bits of bacon in a pair of metal tongs, shreds as dark as the eyebrows that made a straight line across his brow.

Harold blushed; he couldn't help it. He wondered if the cook had recognized him, if he wondered why his hair had gone from black to white.

Wicks let Mr. Hunter pass, then glared at Harold. "What are you doing here? Didn't I tell you?"

"Tell him what?" asked Mr. Hunter, turning back.

Wicks seemed suddenly startled. "Yesterday he came in with the freaks. I mean, I thought he—"

"The boy's with me," said Mr. Hunter. "Is there a reason that he shouldn't be here?"

"No, sir," said Wicks.

"Serve him, then."

The cook did, but grudgingly. He picked the hardest bits of bacon and the blackest slices of toast, and plopped a mound of pale eggs on top. Then he pushed the plate across the counter.

Harold took it up. "Thank you," he said. "It looks very good."

He sat at the closest corner of the nearest bench, with Flip beside him and Mr. Hunter straight across.

"Tell me about this baseball scheme," said Mr. Hunter.

Harold swallowed. He started to talk, but Flip interrupted.

"It's great," she said. "I wasn't sure it would work at first, with only three elephants. But it only has to *look* like a game, after all, and the roses are catching on like lightning. Picture this, Mr. Hunter." She leaned forward, her arms spreading out to make grand designs in the air. "The band is playing 'Take Me Out to the Ball Game.' The spotlights swing to the entrance, and the elephants come trotting into the ring. They're wearing

152

baseball caps and little socks. Little red socks, see. A clown carries the bats."

Harold chewed his eggs and listened as she described the game as he had imagined it. He could almost see it, she made it so exciting. He was glad she'd spoken for him.

"But can they *play?*" said Mr. Hunter.

Harold nodded. "Yes, sir. They—"

"Well, they're not the Dodgers," said Flip. "But I saw Max hit a ball right across the lot." She laughed. "It put a dent in the freaks' trailer."

"Gracious!" Mr. Hunter touched his fingers to his mouth. "Do you think it's safe? I mean, what if he were to put a dent in a child? Or in a lawyer, say?" The fingers dabbed at his lips, down to his chin. "I don't know. There's a potential there for catastrophe and litigation, don't you think? A possible parcel of perils."

Harold shook his head. "No, sir," he said.

"No?" Mr. Hunter touched his throat. "No, you say?" He looked surprised, as though he'd never heard the word before.

"They could use a rubber ball," said Harold. "It wouldn't be any harder than a sponge."

Mr. Hunter's hand, so thin, was like a cricket perching on his Adam's apple.

"No one would mind being hit by a sponge," said Harold. "Not if an elephant did it."

"But then they'll go trampling madly about," said Mr. Hunter. "The elephants, I mean. They'll be rushing around in wild abandon. And *that's* a dangerous game in a crowded circus tent. That's a harbinger of hazards, Harold."

"I guess you're right," said Flip. She looked down at her plate, poking at the eggs. "It would sure be crowded, all right. I bet a *thousand* people would come every night to see elephants playing baseball."

Mr. Hunter's fingers twitched against his throat. "A thousand people? That many?"

"Or more," said Flip. "They'd come from everywhere."

"Hmmm." Mr. Hunter leaned back, looking up at the roof of the tent. "Does Ringling have it?"

"No one does," said Flip. "But Harold's thinking of taking it to Barnum and Bailey."

Harold raised his head. He hadn't thought of that at all. He looked at Flip and felt her hand, beneath the table, briefly squeeze his knee.

She smiled at him. "Harold doesn't really care where he goes. He just wants to teach elephants how to play baseball."

"Then better it should be here," said Mr. Hunter. He stood up and pulled his watch from his pocket. He opened the case and closed it again. "Find someone else to clean the stables, Flip. I want this boy to work with the elephants every chance he has. I want them playing baseball before we get to Salem."

"Massachusetts?" asked Harold.

"Oregon!" said Mr. Hunter. "Son, we're going to Oregon." Then he stepped over the bench and left the tent, swinging his watch by the chain.

Flip winked at Harold.

"You lied to him," he said.

"Just a little bit." She smiled coquettishly. "You have to know how to handle Mr. Hunter. The only sense of the circus he's got is *dollars* and cents."

154

Chapter

28

Harold went straight to work when breakfast was
done. He laid out lines in the drying grass and
carried stones from the riverbank, one at a time, to act
as bases. Conrad lumbered back and forth behind
him, as far as the chain would let him. But on the last
trip, the elephant nudged Harold with his trunk, then
took the stone that Harold lugged along and carried it
himself.

Harold and Flip laid the bases just twenty feet apart
and got the roses running around the circle. The
ground shook from the thunder of elephants' feet, and
their trumpeting brought people to watch. The band
came, carrying bugles and drums. The calliope player
lit a corncob pipe. The juggling clown rolled his wheel
of rings across the grass and sat cross-legged, stony-
faced and grim. Someone shouted at him: "Hey, Mr.
Happy." But he answered with only a sour smile.

All afternoon the people came and went. They
cheered when the elephants fielded the ball, and they
laughed when Canary Bird ran the bases counterclock-
wise by mistake. But no one laughed at Harold, no
one shouted "Whitey" or "Maggot," and as the hours
passed, Harold almost forgot they were there. He
watched for Samuel and Tina and the Gypsy Magda;

155

he wished they would come, but they didn't. It seemed sad to him. They were a part of the circus, but *apart* from it too.

Harold stood on the pitcher's mound with the ball in his hand, watching the elephants practice. He heard them trumpet and saw them crash together at home plate. A roar of laughter rose from the circus people, and as it died away the clang of Wicks' dinner bell echoed from the tents.

Nobody moved. The roustabouts lounged on the slope to his left, propped on beefy arms. Mr. Happy lay flat on his back, scowling at the sky.

Harold squeezed the ball in his hand. He wondered if no one else had heard the bell, then realized they probably had. *The freaks eat first.* There wasn't any hurry.

"Throw the ball," said Flip. She waited at home plate, holding the bat in Conrad's trunk. The huge gray mass above her jiggled in Harold's glasses, but it seemed the elephant was watching him. Everyone was.

He heard the bell again and imagined Wicks ringing it, his big belly shaking as he bashed at the rusted triangle. Somewhere among the tents Samuel and Tina were heading off to dinner; the Gypsy Magda was jingling beside them. And Harold could join them, or not.

"What's the matter?" shouted Flip.

He shrugged. He bounced the ball in his palm, the big red-and-yellow ball. Then Flip came toward him. She looked like Yogi Berra marching across the grass, her head down and her arms swinging. And everyone watched her. The little corner of the circus lot buzzed with voices.

"What's wrong with you?" she asked, coming up beside him.

She shimmered in his glasses. Conrad seemed to sway behind her as he shifted his weight on his feet.

"Huh?" she said. "You look kinda dumb just standing here, you know."

He smiled his ghostly smile. "The dinner bell," he said. "It's time for dinner."

"For the *freaks*," she said. "We've got another half an hour. Maybe more, 'cause Wicks has to scrub the table first."

"I have to eat," he said.

"But not with *them*."

"Yes, I do." He blinked. "They're my friends," he said.

She laughed. "You like them more than me?"

"Well, no," he said. "But . . ." It wasn't fair that he had to choose.

"You've got work to do," she said. "We'll be in Salem soon, and you know what this means to Mr. Hunter. Besides—" She slithered up against him. "I thought you *liked* to eat with me."

He smelled the soap in her hair, the sunburn on her skin. It made him dizzy to be so close to her.

"They're not *natural*," she said, and a little shiver shook him. "You don't belong with them."

But he did, he thought. They had brought him to the circus. Samuel had been almost like a father, Tina like a mother. If they didn't look so *strange* . . .

"Please stay," said Flip. She whispered in his ear. "I hate it when you're not around."

It felt as though something was stuck in his throat; he had to swallow hard. Her arms squeezed him. Then an elephant bugled, and all the people laughed, and Flip pulled away.

At home plate, Conrad held the bat high in the air. He tickled its end on his spine, then swept it down and tapped his toes. Leaning left, then right, he swayed his enormous head, and he looked in every way like a batter waiting for a pitch.

"Come on," said Flip. "Let's play."

"I can't," he said. "I'm sorry, but I can't."

He turned and ran. He ran in his bumbly way, up the slope in his big boots, past the roustabouts with the sun glinting on his glasses. He didn't look down at their faces, he didn't listen to their voices. And he didn't stop running until he reached the tent.

Wicks filled a bowl with thick brown stew. Harold nodded as he passed Wallo and Esther, then took his seat beside Samuel.

"Hey, kiddo," said Tina. "We were starting to think you weren't coming."

The Gypsy Magda looked up at him and smiled. It didn't matter to Harold that she had no teeth; it was a lovely smile, he thought.

"I am proud of you," she said. "It must have been hard."

"What must have been hard?" said Tina. But Harold didn't answer; he knew the Gypsy Magda understood.

"Jolly jam," said Samuel, his little eyes gleaming. "Come on, everyone. Squeeze the little geezer."

They wrapped him up and rocked him on the bench. And he closed his eyes and knew by touch alone who held him closest. He felt the Gypsy Magda's bracelets, Tina's tiny hands and Samuel's hairy arms.

Then benches creaked and others joined him; he felt Esther's beard against his neck, and the awful hands of Wallo pressing at his ribs. They all held him so closely that he couldn't hug them back. And Harold the Ghost, his arms pinned at his sides, tilted stiffly on his seat like a small white toy, a teddy bear.

He let them pull him to the left, then push him to the right; he was very close to tears. They made him feel warm and safe but mixed up inside, that squirly feeling coming back. It wasn't right, he thought, to think of Flip and wish *she* was holding him. It wasn't right that he was glad she wasn't there to see him.

Then they moved away and went back to their dinners. Samuel's huge hands squeezed his shoulders one more time; then only Tina was left, her arms around his neck.

"You make me so happy," she said. "I don't think I've ever been this happy in my whole life." She squeezed him as hard as she could. "You're such a swell guy, Harold."

He didn't feel like a swell guy. He ate without tasting his food, so quickly that he was the first to finish.

But he was the last to leave the tent. He dreaded going out in the sunshine and shuffled along behind Esther, with Wallo's strange face looking at him over her shoulder.

Harold couldn't possibly walk any slower. He let his fingers drag along the tables, his feet scuff along the ground.

"I know how you feel," said Wallo. "It's like going into a lions' den out there, isn't it?"

Harold sighed. It was bad enough, he thought, that Flip and all the rest would see him coming from the tent among the freaks. But now they would see him talking with Wallo, the strangest of them all. They might even think they were friends.

He wondered again if the Cannibal King ate with the freaks. He wished he did, and he wished he was there. The Cannibal King would keep him safe; it would be like walking with David again.

"Head up," said Wallo. "Nothing to fear but fear itself." Then he passed through the door as Esther carried him out.

Harold felt the heat on his shoulders; the light made him blind. He stumbled along behind Esther, his palms suddenly sweating. But no one laughed, and no one teased him. There might have been no one there at all, for the silence. Then he looked up and saw shadows of people, only three or four shadows, and Mr. Hunter's voice called his name.

He didn't know where to look; he stopped and gazed around.

"The pachyderms are catching on. They've got the spirit of the game," said Mr. Hunter. "What a pity— what a palpable pity—that you weren't there yourself."

"What happened?" asked Harold. He found Mr. Hunter's gaunt shape and tried to steady his eyes.

"They performed what I believe is called a double play."

"Gosh," said Harold.

"No one cared to come to dinner," said Mr. Hunter. "If you hurry, son, you might see the sight repeated."

Harold went off at a trot, squinting against the light. He met people coming the other way, ragged groups of circus folk who laughed and stepped aside.

They said, "You missed it, Harold. You should have stayed." And they clapped him on the back as he sprinted past, on toward the elephants.

Only Flip was left when he got there. She was holding Canary Bird, her arms around his trunk. "Oh, there you are," she said, and grinned. "Harold, I wish you'd seen it."

"They really made a double play?" he asked.

"Who told you that?" she said.

"Mr. Hunter."

She laughed. "He *would*. It was just an accident, really. But I think they're learning, Harold. I think they know what they're *supposed* to do."

"What happened?" He stood beside her, stroking the elephant's trunk. It twisted between them, the tip reaching up to his shoulder.

"Max hit the ball," she said. "He did it by himself. It went shooting out like a rocket, and Canary Bird caught it."

Harold looked up at the elephant's eyes. "Did you?" he asked. "Did you catch it?"

"He looked kinda shocked," said Flip. "I'm sure he didn't *mean* to catch it. And then . . ." She giggled. "He went staggering back and crashed into Conrad. *He* was running around the bases; you can hardly stop him now. And they hit right there at second base. A great big thud and all this dust." Her arms went up, drawing balloons of dust. "Oh, it was great. Just so great."

Harold smiled. He felt as though he really *had* been there; he could see it better in his mind than he would have seen it in his eyes. "I bet he did try to catch it," he said. "I just bet he did."

161

He stroked Canary Bird's trunk, up and down the bulges and the wrinkles. His hands touched Flip's, and then she leaned across and kissed him on the cheek. He had to hold on to the trunk to keep from fainting, and he barely heard Conrad's high-pitched trumpet. Then Conrad barged up between them and pried him away.

Flip laughed. She shook her finger under the elephant's enormous head. "Now, you stop that, Conrad Ferdinand Meyer. You jealous thing."

They practiced until the sun went down, then walked the elephants to a high-roofed tent of plain brown canvas. The door was enormous, and the elephants strolled right through it, into a vast circle of straw-covered ground. The roses collapsed on top of it like gray blimps with their air let out.

"I'll walk you to your tent," said Flip.

Harold frowned. "I don't have a tent."

"Then where do you sleep?" asked Flip.

He nodded toward the door. "In the trailer. In the Airstream."

"With the *freaks*?" She sounded shocked.

"I don't mind," said Harold. He thought of the little room they'd made for him and wondered why he didn't want to tell Flip about it.

She said, "You don't have to sleep with the freaks."

"I like them," he told her.

"Oh, so do I," she said quickly. "They're funny freaks. That Tina, she's like a great big bug. But you don't really want to sleep there, do you?"

Harold shrugged. He hadn't imagined sleeping anywhere else.

"Gosh, I'd be afraid to even go inside that trailer."

She shivered and held herself. "What if you catch something? What if you turn all hairy like Samuel?"

He hadn't thought of that. He looked at his hands. He rubbed one on the other, as smooth and white as china. He wondered: Had his fingers always curled like that? When he straightened them, then relaxed his muscles, the fingers curled right back. Were they already turning into claws?

"You could sleep in Roman's tent," she said. "It's empty now."

"Who's Roman?" he asked.

"Oh, just a rigger." She tossed up her hand, as though riggers were nothing. "He's gone with the canvas boss to have the big top fixed. He won't be back tonight."

She took him there, to an orange tent beyond the row of trucks, at the edge of a grove of leafy trees. There was a cot inside, and nothing else, and she left him by himself.

Harold lay on his side, staring out through the open flap at a spot of yellow in the darkness, the window of the Airstream. It surprised him that the light was still on, that Samuel and Princess Minikin were sitting up so late. He remembered promising to go and see them. He couldn't remember when that was, but they were going to talk about the Cannibal King.

He rolled onto his back. He could reach up and touch the tent's low roof. Then he sighed and spilled himself out of the cot. He crawled outside and walked toward the light.

The trailer seemed empty when he got there, just the one light burning to show his way in. His bed was made; a chocolate chip cookie had been left for him on the table. Then Tina called to him from her room in the back: "Is that you, Harold?"

"Yes," he said.

"Have you got everything you need?"

"Yes," he said again.

"We left a cookie for you."

"I found it," he said.

"I love you, Harold." There was a long pause. "Harold?"

He didn't answer. Suddenly he was crying.

Chapter
29

By morning the skies were clear. Harold stepped out into the day's first, pale light, the trailer still shaking with Samuel's snores. He found the elephants awake, stirring their trunks through the straw, and he led them across the field to the place that was beaten down by their feet, and practiced with them there.

Flip joined him when her chores were done. She lingered at the corner of the tent, her hands in her pockets, watching as Max Graf came around to home and took his place again. She applauded and, smiling, came up to Harold's side.

"You're doing just great," she said.

"I can't get them to drop the bat," said Harold. "They can't drop the bat or throw the ball, and I don't know how to teach them that."

"You'll figure it out. You've got more than a week."

"Is that all?" said Harold. "It's not enough."

"It has to be, 'cause then we'll be in Salem. And if we don't make money there, it's finished, Harold. The circus is finished."

Harold groaned. "I don't think I can do it."

"Oh, sure you can," said Flip. She licked her fingers and wiped dust from Harold's cheeks.

They stood close together, nearly chest to chest.

Harold closed his eyes and let her fingers rub along his chin. He felt as though he might keel over in a faint.

"Don't you think you can?" she purred. "It's so important to Mr. Hunter."

He had never kissed a girl, and he thought he might just then. He got his hands all ready; he opened them and closed them. He thought he would put them around her waist. He stood so close to Flip that he could feel her breath against his cheek.

But Conrad nudged her aside. Harold was annoyed, almost angry. But Flip only laughed.

"He *is* jealous," she said. "Well, I won't have to worry about the other girls when *he's* around."

They practiced batting, giving each of the roses a turn. Conrad was Harold's favorite; he'd hoped he'd be the best. But Max Graf was as close to a natural as an elephant could be. "I guess he'll have to be the batter," Harold said. "Now let's see who's best at pitching."

"How?" asked Flip.

Harold had seen the elephants throwing pebbles and dirt, but always over their backs, and that wouldn't do for pitching. "I guess I'll have to show them," he said.

He tried to move his arm like a trunk, the ball between his fingers. "Look," he told them. "Watch." And his arm snaked around behind his back, above his shoulder. In his mind he looked like an elephant, but he was more like a mad orchestra conductor, like a rubber man, his arm a twisting noodle. Then he gave the ball to Conrad, who popped it into his mouth.

Flip giggled. "It's going to take a bit of work."

"They'll learn," he said. "I know they will."

She stood twenty feet away and caught the ball for

166

Harold. She tossed it back and he pitched again, though it hurt his arm to swing it around like that. He kept on going—thirty times, fifty—until Conrad raised his trunk and made the same strange motion himself.

And right then the dinner gong sounded, a tingle of metal, as though the elephant had rung a magical bell.

Harold pitched again, more slowly, and the elephant's trunk moved the very same way, like a giant shadow of his arm. "He knows what he's doing," said Harold. "I'm sure he knows."

"Let him try by himself," said Flip.

Harold held out the ball. Conrad's trunk reached toward him, the round nostrils opening and closing. It snatched the ball and swept it down across the ground.

"Like this," said Harold, moving his arm. The trunk moved with it. "Now throw!" He opened his fingers, but the ball stayed in Conrad's trunk.

Flip groaned. "He's *almost* got it."

"He will," said Harold. "He still doesn't know what I want him to do."

"Huh?" said Flip. She wasn't listening; she wasn't even *looking*. She stood staring off toward the tents, and then she said, "Oh, geez."

"What?"

"Look who's coming now."

Harold turned and squinted across the field. He could barely see the person wading through the grass, but it could only be Tina; there was no one else as small as that.

"I wish she wouldn't keep coming here," said Flip. "I wish she'd let us work."

Harold watched the little princess push through a

clump of tall grass, coming with her funny waddle. Conrad tapped his shoulder with the baseball, but Harold ignored it.

"She doesn't understand that you've got work to do." Flip stood at his side. "She doesn't think anything's so important as breakfast."

Conrad banged the ball a little harder. Harold stroked his chin, surprised to feel a short hair where he'd never felt one before.

"If you quit now, Conrad might *never* learn." She touched his arm. "Besides, I like it when you eat with me. I miss you when you aren't there."

"Really?" Harold said. Then Conrad nearly toppled him with a sudden push against his back. He stumbled forward and caught his balance. Tina wouldn't come any closer.

"Didn't you hear the bell?" she shouted. "It's time for breakfast, Harold."

He looked at Flip, at Conrad; he plucked at the hair with his fingernail.

"Tell her," said Flip. "You'll eat later; tell her that."

Tina waved at him. "Come on," she said.

"I can't," said Harold, not loud enough that she would hear. He coughed and shouted back, "I'm really sort of busy."

He regretted the words right away. They made him think of the girl at the restaurant, bent over her coloring book. It seemed far away and long ago, but he remembered the sound of her voice, and how they had fled from there.

Tina cupped her hands around her mouth. "Okay, Harold. I'll catch you later, kiddo."

She raised a little arm in a wave, then turned and walked away. In a moment she was just a speck to Harold, a blur retreating toward the tents. She looked like a child, like Harold himself. She looked the way he'd felt so many times, fleeing all alone from people who'd told him to go.

"She should stay away from here," said Flip. "You gotta tell her that."

Harold nodded.

"She makes the elephants jumpy. They can't figure it out, how small she is."

"Okay," said Harold.

They practiced until the second bell rang, and then a little more. Flip went off for breakfast, but Harold lingered even longer, in case he met the freaks coming from the tent. He crept like a spy through the circus lot, listening for the jingle of the Gypsy Magda's bracelets. And he arrived so late that the second breakfast was nearly finished.

Wicks gave him the last scoop of eggs, the scrapings of fried potatoes from the griddle. "You should have come sooner," he said.

Harold nodded. "I know," he said, "it's not a restaurant."

He carried his tray to the closest bench, to his corner by Flip and Mr. Hunter. They had both finished eating. She was talking about the elephants, about Conrad learning to pitch, and he was leaning forward, smiling.

Harold put down his tray. Then, the moment he sat, Mr. Hunter popped to his feet. It gave Harold a little start, as though by sitting he had lifted Mr.

Hunter, as though they were partners on a teeter-totter. Mr. Hunter picked up his fork and rang it on his water glass.

"Friends," he said in his ringmaster's stirring voice. "Ladies and gentlemen." The buzz of voices stopped. "For those of you who haven't met him, I'd like to introduce the newest member of our family. He's got the roses running ragged, he's got the pachyderms playing proficiently, he's the one who'll turn our fortunes around; he's . . ." His arm swept up in a grand gesture, and Harold felt Flip's hands on his arm, pushing him to his feet. "Harold Kline."

Harold stood up, blushing like a beet. He stared at the table, at his white hand still holding a knife. Someone clapped and someone whistled, and the tent filled with a squeaky rumble as everyone swiveled around on their benches.

"Harold hails from Liberty," said Mr. Hunter. "Where the great Hunter and Green's Traveling Circus performed not a fortnight past. Now he works under my direction, to do what no one else has ever done. He will tell you himself what fabulous feats he has formed."

The tent fell silent. Harold blinked down at his plate.

"Say something," said Flip.

"I—I—I, uh . . ." He stammered badly. "I'm, uh, teaching them how to play baseball." Well, they knew that already, but he couldn't think of anything else. Then he saw his hand turn scarlet, and knew that all of him was that same bright color. He sat down as quickly as a jack-in-the-box with its lid slammed shut.

The tent seemed to shake with laughter, with cheers

and applause. Mr. Hunter grinned. "And better words were never spoken," he said, reaching across to put his hand on Harold's shoulder.

The Ghost felt huge. He felt as warm as the stones on the bank of the Rattlesnake. He could hardly believe he could be so happy, and he shook his head at the thought of it, his white hair flying in a puff. Here he sat at the best seat in the cook tent, with the prettiest girl at his elbow. What a long way he'd come, the saddest boy in Liberty. It seemed so far that there was no going back.

Chapter 30

Conrad proved to be a terrible pitcher. He waved the ball just as Harold had shown him, and he looked majestic doing it, like an enormous magician, almost like a dancer. But he looked nothing like a pitcher.

"Why can't he throw the ball?" asked Flip. "Oh, Harold, this is *never* going to work."

"It has to," he said. "You can't play baseball without a pitcher."

"Then how about Canary Bird?"

He'd thought of that but wouldn't admit it. He had set his heart on Conrad pitching, the grandest of the elephants standing in the center of the ring.

"Just give Canary Bird a try," said Flip.

Harold took the ball from Conrad. He saw the elephant's eyes droop in their masses of wrinkles, the trunk sag pathetically. Harold understood; he knew what it felt like to be sent to the outfield. "I'm sorry," he said. "Oh, gosh, don't cry."

But there were tears in the elephant's eyes. They filled each wrinkle and dribbled down to the next, then ran in dusty streams across his cheeks.

"Look how sad he is," said Harold. It almost broke his heart.

"He's only sad because you're sad yourself," said Flip. "He knows how you feel, and he's crying because of that."

That didn't make it any easier. Conrad wailed as Harold took the ball away and gave it to Canary Bird. His cry was so low and so deep that it shook the bones in Harold's head.

"Just watch," Harold told him. "And maybe you'll learn." But Conrad turned away and sulked. He went with his toes dragging, his tail and his head hanging down. He went straight to the edge of the fresh, tall grass and tore it up in enormous clumps. He ripped them from the ground, not to eat and not to throw across his back, but just to fling in every direction in a little rage, a tantrum.

"Sure. You can throw *grass* around," cried Harold. He was amazed at the animal's strength. "Why can't you do that with a baseball?"

"Come on," said Flip. "Just leave him."

Harold showed Canary Bird how to pitch. He moved his arm, and Canary Bird moved his trunk, and Harold shouted, "Throw!" And the ball went soaring off across the field.

No one was more surprised than Harold. He watched the red-and-yellow blur arc up and down, to land so far away he couldn't see it. Inside a tent, it would have reached the very roof, or gone smashing through the bleachers.

Flip went running off to get the ball. She threw it back, but it bounced in the mud only halfway toward him, and she had to run and throw again to get it to Harold.

He stuffed it into the elephant's trunk. He felt as

though he was loading a cannon. Then Canary Bird wound up; he didn't wait for Harold's signal. He snaked his trunk above his head, snapped it straight and fired the ball in the other direction.

Flip was panting as she passed. "At least he's got the right idea," she said.

For an hour they let Canary Bird pitch. The ball flew to the south and then to the east; it flew fifty yards or just ten feet. Once it ricocheted off Conrad's back, and the giant elephant—still in his fury—let out a startled shriek and barreled, bugling, across the field. He was halfway to his sleeping tent before Harold could bring him back again.

"This isn't working," said Flip. She'd turned a stunning red from all her running.

Harold grinned. "What would Mr. Hunter say?"

"Geez." Her eyes opened wide. "Don't let him know," she said.

He sat down in the shade of the roses, watching them blow puffs of dust across their backs. "I've got to think of something else."

"Well, think fast," she said. "'Cause there isn't a lot of time." She settled beside him, then stood again; she shuffled her feet in the dirt. "I hate just waiting. It's driving everyone nuts, sitting around like this."

Harold gazed at her. He marveled at the way the sun made her skin so brown, her hair such a silvery gold. He didn't mind waiting; he wished he could wait forever.

"Listen," she said. "I'm going to work with the horses. I'll see you at dinner, okay?"

"Yes," he said.

"And tonight maybe I'll come to your tent. If you get the roses pitching, I'll come to your tent and we can look at the stars; we can count the stars. Wouldn't that be nice?"

Harold nodded very quickly. He found he couldn't speak.

"So just keep working, and I'll see you later, huh?"

He watched her go, her hair shining like a sun. He didn't tell her that stars were a blur to him, that he couldn't hope to count a blur. He didn't tell her that he hadn't slept in the tent but he would tonight. He might even pack up his clothes, he thought, and move them there.

Grinning, giddy, he tried to keep pitching, but he couldn't. He wasn't thinking at all about baseball. And finally he sat, his hand on his chin. His finger stroked the little bristle, and he thought about the night ahead.

In his mind it was already dark, and he saw Flip beside him in the starlight. She would put her head on his shoulder and look at the stars. Already he could feel her leaning against him; he could smell her soap and sunburn. They would hold hands, and he would tell her then how much he loved her. His lips moved as he thought of what he'd say. *I get sick when I think about you.*

He rubbed his thumb in circles. Then suddenly he stopped.

There was another hair beside the first, and he *knew* it hadn't been there long ago. A cold chill ran through him to think that Flip had been right. *What if you turn all hairy like Samuel?* He felt along his jaw, and down his throat, but there weren't any more little hairs. Then he felt a great relief to think that maybe more would never grow if it was soon enough to stop them.

He got to his feet and ran toward the Airstream. And in the shadow of the Diamond T, he came across the Gypsy Magda.

She sat in the sun, in a folding chair. Her eyes were shut, and she didn't open them. "Hello, Harold," she said.

"Hi," he said.

"Have you lived your dream?" she asked.

"What dream?" said Harold.

"Then you have not lived it yet." She rolled her head toward him but still didn't open her eyes. "You will live your dream, and then you will begin to learn the truth of what I have told you."

Suddenly her eye slid open, only the one that the sun fell upon. Its darkness and its depth disturbed him. She said, "If you do not hurry, you will meet them."

He knew what she meant by that. It was the *only* thing he understood, and he went on his way without another word. He ran to the trailer and found it empty, just as she'd said it would be. He cleared the shelves behind his bed, stuffing all his things into the same white pillow slip he'd brought from Liberty. Then he folded his blankets and piled them neatly on the end of the sofa. He took down the cloth wall of his room and put it on top of the pile.

Harold carried his bag across the field, to the orange tent at the edge of the trees. He didn't stop; he tossed the bag through the door and went back to work with the elephants. For an hour, they practiced pitching,

176

but it wasn't any good. The elephants, he thought, would never learn to throw a ball.

"Maybe you *can't* be pitchers," he said. "Maybe you just can't do it."

Conrad murmured at him.

"It's all right," said Harold. "Maybe it was dumb to even try." He patted Conrad's leg hard enough to hear the slaps, to shake the dust away. Then he sighed and went to fetch the roses water, bringing bucket after bucket, and each was emptied the moment he set it down. The elephants plunged their trunks inside and drained the buckets as though through straws, then curled them up and squirted the water into their mouths. When they'd had enough to drink they squirted it over their backs, great blasts of water that shimmered in the sun.

"I have to figure this out," he told the elephants. "I have to teach you how to pitch."

But instead he thought of Flip. It seemed that no matter where he started, he always thought of her. If he hadn't taught the elephants to pitch by dinnertime, would she still come and see him at the tent? Would they still hold hands and count the stars?

The bell startled him. Surely Wicks had made a mistake and rung it hours early. Then Harold saw how far the sun had moved toward the west, and he got to his feet with a terrible feeling of hopelessness. He kicked through the grass until he found the ball, then called to Conrad. "Just try," he said. "Really try, okay?"

But no matter what he did, he couldn't teach Conrad to pitch. The elephant only waved the ball around, and Harold felt like crying. "It's no good," he said. "It just won't work."

For ten minutes he stood there, staring at Conrad. Then he heard the plod of a horse's hooves coming up behind him. It was a steady sound, soft on the grass, hard on the dirt. And Harold turned slowly, expecting to see the old Indian, but instead seeing Flip, riding bareback on General Sherman.

The horse shied away from the elephants, but Flip held it there, twenty feet away, as it pranced and skittered sideways. "So, how's it going?" she asked.

Harold wanted to lie, to say, "It's great." But he couldn't; he only shook his head.

High above him, she leapt forward and back as the horse stamped its feet. Her face was a blur; he didn't know if she was smiling or angry.

"But it's *going* to work," she said. "You're getting *somewhere,* aren't you?"

"It's pretty hard," he said.

"Well, sure it is." The horse jostled backward. "All they've ever done is their stupid little dance. You've got to teach them things they've never even *thought* of. And I think you're doing great, Harold. You're doing just fine."

He gazed up at her. His hand, by itself, went to his chin.

"So don't think of quitting, okay? Don't even *think* of that."

"No," he said, and shook his head.

"And you'd better come to dinner now. You've been out all day in the sun."

"Okay," he said, and started to go, bumbling across the dirt.

Flip laughed. "Well, don't you want a ride?"

She helped him up. She held his hand for a moment

as he ran in a clumsy circle beside the spinning horse. Then she pulled him up, and he settled down behind her.

"Hold on," she said.

He put his hands on her hips, on the ridges of her bones. "Tighter," she said, and he pressed as hard as he dared. Then she took his wrist and wrapped it around her waist, and he could feel the hardness of her ribs and the softness of her stomach. He shook, and she laughed. Then General Sherman went off at a canter, and Harold held on far more tightly than he'd ever held to the old Indian. He banged against the horse's back so hard it knocked his teeth together. But he felt as though he rode on clouds, that he dashed with an angel through heaven.

They took the horse to the stable and went on to the cook tent. Side by side they walked around the corner and met a line of people waiting. Harold gasped; they'd come too soon. In the darkness of the tent the freaks were moving, coming to the door. He tried to step away, back behind the canvas wall, but Mr. Hunter saw him.

"Ah, there you are," said Mr. Hunter. "Speak of the devil, what? We were just pondering the pachyderms' progress."

"Huh?" said Harold.

"The roses, son. Are you making headway?"

"Yes, sir. A bit." He looked wildly for somewhere to hide. The Gypsy Magda's bells tinkled in the tent.

"All set for Salem?"

"I hope so." Harold maneuvered around behind Flip. He wished Mr. Hunter would leave him alone, at least until the Gypsy Magda passed. She was the one he worried about, the one who could shame him with just a look of those black eyes.

"Have they learned to pitch and toss?" asked Mr. Hunter.

Harold shrugged. Everyone was looking at him as he squeezed himself thin behind Flip, as he trembled and sweated. They watched him with curious frowns, and he put his hand up to his chin, to hide the little hair that he imagined they were staring at. He crouched on the ground.

Flip looked back. "What are you doing?" she said. Then Esther came out of the tent with Wallo on her hip, those bizarre little feet making dents in her clothes, his head resting on her beard.

"Hello, Wallo," said Mr. Hunter. "Why, Esther, what a pretty dress."

"Gee, thanks," said Esther in her strange, manly voice. Then she passed, and the Gypsy Magda came behind her, dark and huddled in her scarves, staring fixedly at Esther's back. Samuel and Tina stepped together from the tent, and Harold lowered his head, suddenly busy with the laces on his boots.

Tina said, "Oh, there he is! Hey, Harold. Hi, kiddo."

He lifted only his eyes, looking at her over the round darkness of his glasses.

"You took your things," she said. "All your things."

He nodded, too embarrassed to talk.

"We'll miss you something awful." She was smiling, but Samuel only glowered. "We don't know what to do with all the space," she said. "Do we, Samuel?"

His little eyes were half shut. "Maybe we'll sit there like we used to."

"Oh, you lug." She laughed. "But you'll come and see us, won't you, Harold? You'll come when you're not so busy."

He nodded too quickly, everything blurring together, as though he peered through pebbled glass. He had to turn his head away to find her again. And by then she was gone.

Chapter 31

From dinner till darkness, Harold worked with the elephants. Flip stayed at his side, and together they worked first with Canary Bird and then with Conrad. But one elephant threw the ball too wildly, and the other wouldn't throw it at all. And when the first stars came out, the roses were led to their tent, where they tossed the straw into nests and settled down on their sides.

Flip was disappointed. "Maybe they'll do better tomorrow."

"I hope so," said Harold. He wanted to get away from there, to walk with Flip to his little tent.

"I wish you could teach them."

"I wish there was another one," said Harold. And then, to show he meant it as a joke, he laughed. But Flip was very quiet.

"There used to be," she said.

She had her back toward him, fiddling with the harnesses. He could hardly see her at all.

"He was my favorite," she said. "Even bigger than Conrad, smart as a person almost."

"What happened to him?" asked Harold.

"He died in a wreck."

She talked softly, without turning around. Harold had to lean forward to hear her.

"My dad was driving. My mom was beside him. They went over a cliff, and all three of them died."

"Gosh," said Harold.

"I was in the next truck. Me and—one of the riggers. I saw it happen. Right in front of me."

"How long ago?"

"Oh, ages. A year, I guess. A bit more than a year."

Harold heard her sniff. The harnesses clattered in the darkness.

"I loved them so much," she said. "My mom and my dad. I could never have run away like you. I would have missed my mom like crazy."

The elephants made chuckling sounds as they fell asleep. The straw crackled when they moved their legs or trunks.

"Don't you miss your mom?" asked Flip.

"A bit." He missed her a lot when he thought about her, but not at all when he didn't. The truth was, he missed his dog more than his ma. A little part of him was *always* thinking of Honey, a tiny part that never stopped feeling rotten—like a toothache—about leaving her behind.

"See?" said Flip. "I would have missed my mom like crazy if I'd ever run away. I couldn't have gone a mile without running back again."

She was making him sad, as though misery was a germ that could spread like a cold.

"I wish I was a bit like you," she said. "I wish I *could* have run away, you know? I wish I was that sort of person."

It made him love her even more. Harold had spent his whole life wishing he was like other people. No one had *ever* wanted to be like him.

Conrad started snoring. A faint rumble at first, it built to a roar. It sounded as though a diesel truck was racing through the tent. Flip giggled. "Let's get out of here."

Harold squinted and turned his head, looking for the patch of starlight at the door. He reached out to grope at the darkness and saw his hands like pale blobs, and nothing beyond them. Flip came and led him out. She didn't say anything; she just guided him like a blind man. He felt the canvas brush against his shoulder, then felt a breeze on his face. He took off his glasses, and his skin shivered.

Flip started him walking, her arm around his. He saw the silver smudge of the Milky Way, blotches of light from tents and trailer windows. He squeezed his glasses, frightened he would lose them.

"Mom would have loved this," she said. "Everyone camped under the stars. She hated traveling. It scared her, driving at night."

"My dad told me stars are souls," said Harold, surprising even himself. He thought he'd forgotten everything his dad had said. "Whenever a person dies, a star gets put in the sky. That's what he said."

Flip bumped against him. "That's nice," she said.

It seemed funny that he'd forgotten about the stars. Even when his dad had died, he'd forgotten to look for the new one. If it had been off by itself, not mixed in with the smear of others, he might have even seen it.

He looked up, and there were black holes blotting out the Milky Way. He thought for an instant that the stars were dying, until he realized that Flip had led him

184

up to the trees, and their leafy tops covered the sky. Then he stood at the door of the orange tent, and Flip let go of his arm.

"Listen," she said. "I'm sorta sad now. My mom and everything. If I stayed here with you, I'd just start bawling on your shoulder, so I think I'd better go."

He didn't mind if she started bawling on his shoulder. "Just for a bit?" he said.

"No, Harold. I'm sorry." She eased away, vanishing among the shadows. "Tomorrow, okay? We'll sit out here tomorrow night. *All* night, maybe. Cross my heart; I promise."

She left him alone, and he'd never felt more lonely. He could have kicked himself for asking about the other elephant, for making her too sad to stay.

Harold sat by the door of the tent, imagining she sat there too. With the stars above him, the enormous blotch of stars that he couldn't possibly have hoped to count, he put his hand on the ground and pretended that hers was there below it. But the stars made him feel tiny and scared; there were so many that he couldn't imagine the number of people who had died to make them. He wondered which was his father's, and then if maybe there was one for David. Then he thought of his mother; he pictured her out on the steps, tonight and last night and the night before, each time furiously counting, trying to make sure there wasn't one for him.

An owl hooted from the trees. A little tinkle of laughter came from a tent in the distance, and a trailer's squeaky door slammed shut on its spring. And Harold the Ghost sat all alone, wishing he wasn't. It was the first night in his life he had spent all alone.

Chapter
32

The elephants burst from their tent the moment Harold opened it in the morning. They almost bowled him over as they bugled past, trampling off to their corner of the lot. His glasses on, his shirt buttoned so high that the collar hid his chin, he followed them across the grass to the trodden diamond. He found them waiting there, the bat laid neatly across home plate, as though one of the roses had set it down for him.

"Where's the ball?" he said. They stood in a line, their ears flapping slowly. They rumbled and purred.

"We can't play without the ball," said Harold. "Come on, who's got it?"

Conrad swayed his head, and Harold saw the red-and-yellow ball nestled in the tip of his trunk. He laughed. "You're scared I'm going to make you pitch," he said. "Aren't you, Conrad?"

The elephant grumbled.

"Okay. We'll do some fielding first. Is that what you want?" It was dumb, he thought, to expect the elephant to know what he was saying. But he stretched out his hand. "Throw me the ball and we'll play five hundred."

Conrad's head tossed back.

"Just throw me the ball." Harold flexed his fingers. "Come on, Conrad."

The trunk swung close to the grass. The ball came out, bouncing and tumbling, then rolling to Harold.

"Gosh, that's better." He had only to stoop to pick it up. "You've been thinking, I bet. You've probably been playing in your sleep."

He batted the ball and the elephants chased it. They ran it down, kicked it forward and ran it down again. Then Conrad swept it up and threw it back—or *bowled* it back—with the same lazy swing of his trunk that seemed the best he could do. And Harold praised him so highly that the other elephants stole the trick themselves.

By the time Flip arrived, the roses were bowling back each ball Harold batted. She watched as they thundered across the field in a dusty heap of trunks and flapping ears. Then out from that mass of elephants came the ball, bouncing straight toward Harold.

Flip shrieked. "I don't believe it," she said. "You've done it!"

"Not really." He picked up the ball and batted again. The roses went running.

"What do you mean?" she said. "They can bat and field and run the bases. And now—"

"But they don't play *baseball.*" Harold leaned on the bat. "They have to put it all together. And they *still* have to learn to pitch."

The ball dribbled toward him. He picked it up but only held it in his hand.

"What's wrong?" asked Flip.

To the west, at the summit of the hills, a cloud of

dust floated on the skyline. It moved toward them down the slope. And then a truck appeared, dragging the dust behind it like the tail of a speeding comet. It crossed the river and slowed as it neared the circus.

"Who's that?" asked Harold.

"I don't know," said Flip.

He swiveled as he watched the truck. Max Graf bellowed at him from the edge of the grass. The truck tilted up from the road to the field and vanished past the tents. "Do you think it's him?"

"Who?" said Flip.

"The Cannibal King."

"I don't think so," she said.

"It might be the Cannibal King." Harold let his arm drop at his side. The ball fell to the ground, and—yards away—the elephants lunged sideways.

Harold waited for the truck to appear from behind the tents. His hand shook, and he slid it up his clothes and into his pocket. He wasn't sure now that he *wanted* to meet the Cannibal King.

"Harold!" shouted Flip. "We don't have time to look at stupid trucks."

"Is it him?" he asked.

"No!" she said, sounding terribly angry. Then she sighed and walked up beside him. "Look. I'll go and see, and you can stay here with the elephants."

Harold smiled. "Okay."

"And listen," she said. "You don't have to stop for breakfast; you don't have to walk all that way. I'll bring you something. Just tell me what you want, and I'll ask Wicks to make it special."

"He wouldn't do *that*," said Harold.

"He might if I ask him," said Flip. "I think he sorta

likes me." She touched his arm. "Okay? I'll bring your breakfast here."

He felt light-headed again, her face jiggling in front of him. "You don't have to do that," he said. "I can—"

"Oh, I'd *like* to." She stood even closer. "We'll have a little picnic."

"Okay." He nodded, his chin inside his shirt.

He went back to work when she left, batting the ball for the elephants. But they tired of the game before the first bell rang for breakfast. They moved like slugs across the field, stopping to graze at the grass. And by the time the second bell sounded, Conrad was lying on the ground, his long ribs heaving.

"You're worn out," said Harold.

He dropped the bat and the ball and walked down to the cook tent. He hoped that Flip would be surprised to see him, and by the look on her face he was right. She stared at him as he carried his tray from the counter, her eyes as big as the hard-boiled eggs that rolled around and around on his plate.

"What are you doing here?" she said.

He grinned. "Surprised?"

"You shouldn't have come," she said.

"I couldn't wait." He sat beside her, pleased to see that she made a space for him, though much bigger than he needed. Mr. Hunter nodded, and Harold nodded back.

"What about the roses?" said Flip. She leaned past him, peering out toward the door, as though she thought he'd brought them to the tent.

Harold laughed. "I'm giving them a rest." Her head leaned very close, and he looked at her hair tumbling down across her cheek. He couldn't help touching it.

She jerked away. "Don't do that!"

Harold blinked. Even Mr. Hunter looked up from his eggs.

"And don't sit so close," said Flip. She pushed her plate along the table, then moved in front of it. "Don't even talk to me."

He sat, bewildered, in his place. He poked at one of his eggs and felt like crying. "I'm sorry," he said. The egg bounced and rocked. "Whatever I did, I'm sorry." Then he lifted his head, and she was smiling.

Harold smiled back, but she didn't seem to see it. She was looking past him, toward the door, and Harold swiveled slowly around.

The sun came in through the door of the tent. It made a silhouette of the person there, a young man—a boy— with broad shoulders and muscles on his arms. He was waving. He was waving straight at Harold, it seemed.

Harold waved back. Then he saw that it wasn't him the boy was waving at; it was Flip.

"Who's that?" asked Harold.

Flip didn't answer.

He said it again, a little louder in case she hadn't heard. Then Mr. Hunter turned in his seat. He said, "Oh, Roman's here. That's splendid. We can be on our way tomorrow."

The boy took a tray and went down the counter, then brought it across to the table. He stood behind Harold. "Shove over, Whitey," he said, and squeezed between Harold and Flip.

Suddenly she was laughing again, as happy as she'd ever been. And Harold felt his heart plummet to his stomach. He kept eating, though he didn't want to. He felt hollow inside. He kept reaching for things—for the salt shaker, for the pepper, for anything he could think of that would let him lean forward and glance across at Flip.

Roman was strong and dark and tanned. He was exactly the person Harold was in his dream—the old dream—before he woke to see his white arms and his white fingers.

Flip laughed at everything Roman said. She touched him the way, just that morning, she had touched Harold.

Soon the table was covered with things and there was nothing else to reach for. And Harold hadn't eaten half his breakfast before the boy and Flip stood up together and headed for the door. Harold followed them, dismayed to see them walking so close they almost touched. He followed them out of the tent, and only then did Flip turn around.

"Oh, Harold," she said, as though surprised to see him. "Listen. You go back to the elephants, and I'll come by in a bit. When I can."

CONRAD WAS STILL on the ground when Harold came back, feeling sad and puzzled. The elephant had eaten every blade of grass that he could reach but was too lazy—or too tired—to shift himself farther. The huge head lifted as Harold neared, then fell again with only the smallest toot of a bugle.

Harold sat in the curve of Conrad's neck, leaning against the elephant. "She'll come in a minute," he told himself. "She'll come and say she's sorry." The trunk snuffled around, and Harold held it. "I bet she's on her way right now," he said.

Huge black flies buzzed near the elephant's hide. Harold lolled in the shade of Conrad's head, trying to figure out what he'd done, how things had gone so wrong.

The elephant made a sputtery, sleepy sound that was very much like Honey's. Harold stroked the trunk, thinking how he'd used to wish he could make himself a tiny thing and nestle in his dog's thick coat. His hand ran up the trunk, around its curve to the elephant's chin, where a clump of bristles grew in a sparse and wiry bush. And he took it away, quickly, not liking the feel of the hairs that reminded him of his own. He worked his fingers inside his collar, the backs of them touching his skin. He wondered if that was why Flip had acted strangely—because she knew he was becoming a fossil.

"I bet she's telling that guy all about me," he said to Conrad.

His spot of shade shrank away as the day turned into noon. The sun touched his feet and crept up to his knees, burning on his trousers. It seemed to set his chest on fire, then went blazing through his hair. But Harold stayed where he was, watching Canary Bird and Max Graf showering themselves in dust.

And when the sun had crawled across the elephant's back and put him in the shade again, he realized that Flip wasn't coming. He felt exactly as he had every Saturday morning when the train blew past him at the Liberty station. And now, like then, he sighed a little breath and got to his feet.

"Up trunk," he said. "Come on, you lazy thing."

It was just like calling to Honey. The elephant twitched and raised his head. He rolled onto his belly and pried himself up. His great ears flapped like sheets on a clothesline.

Harold got the bat. He gave it to Max Graf and herded the other two elephants down the slope. "You're fielders now," he told them. "You chase the balls and throw them to me. Understand?"

He pitched to Max Graf, who batted to Conrad, who bowled the ball to Harold. The Ghost couldn't stop himself from grinning, though he didn't feel happy at all. He pitched again, and the ball whistled past his head. Still rising, it soared in a curve above the scattered tents and on across the field.

"Gosh," said Harold.

He went after the ball, down the slope and around the tents, past the row of trucks and on toward the silver shape of the Airstream.

He heard the voices before he saw the people, Tina's first: "Say, look who's coming."

Harold slowed and glanced around, hoping he would find the ball before he reached the trailer. He heard Samuel grunt. "Yeah. Isn't that the boy we used to know?"

They sat in wood-and-canvas chairs. Tina, in her doll-sized one, wore a funny hat of artificial flowers. The Gypsy Magda was bundled in a gray blanket, and Samuel—his legs crossed—held a glass of lemonade.

"Yes, I *think* it's him," he said. "He looks familiar, doesn't he?"

Harold stopped. He could feel a coldness there. He said, "I lost the ball."

"Underneath the trailer," Samuel said. "You didn't quite dent it this time."

Harold tried to smile but couldn't. It was hard for him to stand there, so close but far apart.

"Can't you hear?" said Samuel.

"Samuel, don't," said Tina.

"Why not? It's not like he's a friend or something."

"Please," she said, but Samuel ignored her. "It's underneath the trailer," he said again. "You don't think I'm going to get it for you, do you?"

"No," said Harold. He felt like crying.

Samuel got up first. He tipped the glass and spilled his lemonade across the ground. Then he turned his back and went inside the trailer, and Tina followed with just a glance at Harold.

The Gypsy Magda's fingers tightened on her chair. The skin shrank around the bones, and her rings stood up above her fingers, leaving tunnels underneath. "You are like the stray kitten," she said. "You let others care for you. Wherever you go, someone cares for you." She pushed herself to her feet, dark shawls swirling around her as the blanket fell away. "The stray kitten, it is much loved and never forgotten."

Her bracelets jangled. The bells at her ankles tolled her off toward the trailer door.

"Wait," said Harold.

The Gypsy Magda shrugged her scarves around her shoulders. "But the stray *cat*," she said, still walking. "The stray *cat*, it spends its nights alone, howling at the shadows."

The door closed behind her, and the sun glinted off a solid surface. Harold squeezed his hands together. He felt as though he didn't have a friend in the world.

For a while he just stood there, glowering at the trailer. Then he crawled underneath it to fetch his ball.

194

It had rolled impossibly far, as though someone had kicked it under there. He had to squirm on his belly to get out again, then started back across the field, past the orange tent.

His pillowcase lay on the ground, the top open and his clothes spilling out. It looked as though it had been tossed there, thrown from the tent in a fury. Harold collected everything slowly, then carried the bag, slung over his shoulder, up the slope to the elephants.

They stood in a group, staring at him with their nearly human eyes. Conrad swept his trunk along the ground, then curled it up and blew a cloud of dust across his back. He looked as sad as sadness.

"What's the matter?" Harold asked.

The elephant swayed toward him. The trunk stretched out and suctioned at Harold's arm, at his shoulder. The tip squeezed him as a hand would, and the elephant made a sound that Harold had never heard before. He rubbed the trunk and leaned against it. He looked up and saw that Conrad was crying; tears as big as his thumbnail trickled down the enormous, dusty cheeks.

"How do you know?" asked Harold. "How do you know how I feel?"

Chapter

33

Flip never came to see him. The dinner bell rang, and rang again, but Harold didn't leave the diamond. He was too ashamed to go the first time, too frightened the second. He practiced half heartedly, or simply sat, for hours, until the sun was going down and he knew she wasn't coming.

He led Conrad toward the straw-filled tent, and the other roses followed, in a chain from tails to trunks. They plodded along, as though in Harold's sadness. Their ears and trunks drooped. He watched them settle in the straw, their front legs bending and then their back ones, and the whole tent quivered as Max Graf rolled up against the canvas. Then Harold patted their heads, each in turn, and wandered out by himself.

The night was warm and calm. From hilltop to hilltop, stars stretched across the valley, and a little quarter moon gave a silver glow to the huddled town of circus tents.

Harold carried his pillowcase through them, past the Airstream trailer, down to the banks of the river. It was slow and flat, a ribbon of melted stars flowing south between shrinking banks of muddied grass. And he sat there all alone, with nowhere else to go. He fell asleep in darkness and woke beside a fire.

196

It was a small and smoky fire, and the old Indian squatted over it, on a blanket of white and red wool. He was roasting strips of meat on the point of a gleaming knife blade.

"Are you hungry?" asked Thunder Wakes Him.

Harold sat upright on the grass. His back was stiff; his clothes were wet from dew.

"Where did you come from?" Harold asked.

"From here." The old Indian patted the ground through his blanket. "Right here where you sleep I was born."

Harold rubbed his eyes. He could hardly believe he wasn't dreaming. But he could smell the meat and the burning grass; he could just make out the chestnut horse nibbling grass by the riverbank.

"At that time there were a hundred lodges here," said the old Indian. "A hundred lodges, and the snow was fresh and as high as a horse's belly." He turned the knife. Fat sizzled down into the fire. "The soldiers came from there. Behind you. Out of the morning sun they came like ghosts, riding on the snow on horses that had no legs. Their bugle notes were beautiful to hear. Terrible, but beautiful. The soldiers came over the snow, their horses snorting white breaths, running in snow up to their bellies—I thought they slithered on the top like snakes. It was powder snow, rising in a mist, and the soldiers came and drove us to the river."

The old Indian drew his knife from the fire. He touched the bits of meat, squeezing with his fingers.

"They set the lodges burning," he said. "The flames were tall and narrow. A hundred lodges burning, and the smoke went out across the snow and turned the sun to a little brown shadow." He put the knife back in the flames, turning it over and over. "All around, my people lay twisted up like bugs. They froze like that, their legs and arms all stiff and pointing up. Only five of us were left."

"How old were you?" asked Harold.

"Three weeks old. It is the first thing I remember, the sound of the bugles that morning." The old Indian tossed grass on the fire. It smoked and smoldered, then burned with yellow flames. "My mother hid me in the snow. She tunneled deep in the snow by the river. And when the soldiers were gone, when the smell of the fires was gone, she came out. And others came out. And we started walking; our horses were gone. For days and days they carried me, until only three of us were left, and we came to the village of Crazy Horse."

The old Indian toasted the meat on the fire. Yellow flames shone along the knife blade. Harold looked at the chestnut horse and tried to imagine the snow up to its belly, imagine walking for days through that. He thought of the Gypsy Magda and how she, too, had walked through the snow with soldiers behind her.

Harold watched the flames shimmer on the knife. He couldn't understand how Thunder Wakes Him had done all the things in his stories.

"They hated us for living under stars and not under roofs," said the old Indian. "Even today you are thought strange if you carry your home wherever you go. You must have found that, my friend, for you have traveled far."

"Well, sort of," said Harold. "But they thought I was strange before I left."

The old Indian smiled. He pulled a strip of meat from the knife, then held the blade across the fire.

Harold took a strip. It was hot and black on the outside, pale and cold in the middle. "Gosh, that's good," he said.

"Gopher." The old Indian pushed the knife forward again. Harold looked at the dangling bits of meat and shook his head. "A car got him. I found him by the road. By the tracks, I think it was a Studebaker."

The old Indian looked through the fire, through its flames at Harold. He leaned forward, then rose and walked to his chestnut horse. He rummaged through the bundle on its back.

Harold peered and squinted; he would have loved to see what Thunder Wakes Him carried there. He heard a clinking sound, a rattle.

"I will give this to you," said Thunder Wakes Him. He dug deeper in the bundle, then threw the hides back into place. When he came back to the fire, there was a silver cross in his hand. "You must be careful with this. Very careful, every time you use it."

Harold nodded gravely. He put his hand out to take this thing, this amulet. It would give him strength, he thought, and courage.

The old Indian covered Harold's hand with his enormous fist. "You are crossing the great divide that every boy must cross, with manhood on the other side. The slope beyond is so long and so steep that you can never come back. This will take you there."

Smoke eddied around them. The old Indian's hand slid away, and Harold looked at his palm. He saw what Thunder Wakes Him had left there, and he was disappointed. "It's a razor," he said.

"But not just any razor. It's a *safety* razor," said the

199

old Indian. "In the morning you will shave for the first time. And you will start your way across."

Harold stared at it, then laughed. He wasn't becoming a fossil; he was growing a beard, that was all. He laughed from relief but right away regretted it. The old Indian looked wounded.

On his blanket, in the darkness, Thunder Wakes Him pouted. "I don't know why you laughed," he said. "It's a good razor. It cost me two dollars."

"I'm just happy," said Harold. "That's all."

"The blade will last you a year. And it's guaranteed not to rust."

"I like it," said Harold. "Thank you."

But the old Indian still sounded sad. "That's all you need to become a man: a good razor. In all other ways, a man is just a boy in bigger clothes."

Harold nodded. He studied the razor from every angle; he thought it would seem rude if he just put it down.

"You might be a doctor someday," said Thunder Wakes Him, stretching out on the ground. "You might sell shoes or argue in a courtroom. You might build houses or travel with a circus." He gathered the blanket around his shoulders. "But whatever you do, you will need a razor."

Harold moved closer to the fire. He put on another handful of grass and watched the flames run up the stems. "I would like to be like you," he said.

"You would be surprised. Underneath, we're the same already." The old Indian tightened his blanket. "Good night," he said. "When you wake, I'll be gone."

Chapter
34

In the morning, Thunder Wakes Him was gone. There were only marks in the grass to show he had been there at all: a circle burned by the fire; a patch clipped short by his chestnut horse. Harold walked down to the river and washed himself in water as brown as the Rattlesnake. He splashed it across his neck and into his hair. He dipped his razor in the stream and scraped away the two small hairs on his chin. And then he put on his glasses and looked up to see the elephants coming.

They marched in a line abreast, with Conrad in the middle and Flip riding high on his back. With flapping ears and twisting trunks, they swayed across the grass. Then Conrad trumpeted, and the sound was clear as a bugle in the morning air. Harold thought of Thunder Wakes Him, three weeks old, seeing the soldiers riding over the same bit of ground.

Flip shouted and banged her fists on the elephant's back. And they came faster then, pounding over the grass, through the mud, into the water with a great burst of froth and spray.

"Down trunk!" shouted Flip, and Conrad knelt in the river. She slid down from his back. "Hi, Harold," she said.

The elephants frolicked like children. They waded in and out of the current; they blew fountains from their trunks, squirting themselves, squirting each other. Conrad squirted water at Harold and seemed to laugh at his joke.

But Harold didn't even smile. He glowered at the elephants.

"You're not mad at me, are you?" said Flip.

He shrugged. "You said you'd come by and you didn't."

"I had things to do," she said, suddenly angry. "Some people have to *work,* you know, to keep a circus running."

Harold turned away. He walked up from the water, past the round, deep holes stamped in the mud by the elephants' feet.

"Where are you going?" said Flip.

"Nowhere."

"You're not quitting, are you?" Flip followed behind him, but he didn't look back. "You're not going home, are you, Harold?"

He heard her running through the mud. She caught his sleeve and stopped him. "I'm sorry," she said. "I didn't know we had to work. But the canvas came and we had to get it ready because we're moving on today."

Harold pulled away. He trudged back to the scorched bit of ground where he'd slept. His pillowcase was damp and spotted by the dew, and he shifted it to a higher place already warmed by the sun. He unfolded the top and put his razor inside. "Is he your boyfriend?" he asked.

"Who?"

"Roman," he said.

"Oh, he'd like to be. He *thinks* he is, I guess."

"But he's not?"

"Oh, maybe once," she said, standing right in front of Harold. "But I hardly like him anymore."

She smiled at him, then reached out and smoothed his collar down. "He's just a rigger, that's all he is. He puts up tents and takes them down. Not like you." She patted the wrinkles from his shoulders. "You teach elephants how to play baseball. And he's *scared* of them, believe it or not."

Harold closed his eyes as her hands tingled across his chest.

"Look," she said. "We've only got an hour—just an hour—before we start packing up the tents. Can't we practice with the roses?"

He swayed on his feet, that same squirly feeling coming back. He'd been foolish, he thought, to get angry when all she'd been doing was working. He opened his eyes, and they were level with hers on the sloping bank.

"Please?"

He thought that if he tried to talk, only a squeak would come out. He nodded instead.

"Gee, thanks," she said. "You're a sweetheart, Harold. You really are."

Harold fetched the bat and ball, and they practiced by the river, above the banks where the ground was hard and dry. Harold worked with Conrad, trying to show him how to pitch. Max Graf batted, and Canary Bird fielded, trumpeting up and down the riverbank with his great bulk shaking like jelly.

Flip was the catcher. "Max misses more than he hits," she said.

"Well, so does Dixie Walker," said Harold.

"But it's sort of boring."

They shouted back and forth across the diamond. "I thought you'd be standing there," said Harold. "Where you are. You could do all sorts of funny things."

"Like what?"

"Crank his tail," said Harold. "Like you're trying to start a car."

He came and showed her. He leapt up to spin the tail, then laughed. "What if the drummer makes a sound like a car backfiring?" He held his nose, pretending he'd smelled something awful.

"Yeah," said Flip. "Okay."

He kicked dust at the elephant's foot; he dragged down the corner of an enormous ear to whisper something in it. He cavorted like a clown, and Conrad—with an angry trumpet—stomped down to the river, into the water.

"If he misses a pitch," said Harold, "you make the batting box bigger." He sketched it into the ground with his heel, then a bigger one, and a bigger one still. He pretended to sweep it with a tiny brush, then grabbed Max Graf's trunk and used it like a vacuum hose.

Flip laughed until she cried. "That's great," she said, her cheeks streaming. "Oh, Harold, that's terrific. I'll have the greatest act that ever was. Or we will, I mean. The circus will."

"But the pitching," Harold said. "That's the problem. If they can't learn that, it's useless."

He watched as Conrad stomped through the shallows, spraying water through his trunk. "He's having another fit," he said.

"Maybe a clown could pitch," said Flip.

"No. Then you'd just have people playing baseball. It has to be the elephants."

"There isn't time," she said.

Conrad raged through the river, squirting water so far that it misted on Harold's glasses. He wiped them dry, then his hand stopped in midair. "I've got it!" he cried. "A bucket. We need a bucket."

"What?" said Flip. "He's going to throw a bucket?"

"No." He took her hand and pulled her along. "I'll show you what I mean."

Harold dragged her to the ball, picked it up and carried on, pulling Flip behind him. They splashed through the mud and into the river, and he whistled for Conrad to come. He grabbed the elephant's trunk and plunged it under water. "Take a drink," he said.

The trunk pulsed as it filled. Then Harold pulled it up and corked it with the ball. "Blow!" he shouted.

Conrad had no choice, his nose was so full of water. With a blast of spray, with a popping sound, he snorted out the ball. It soared above the river, the red stripe spinning on the yellow, a straight and perfect pitch. It plopped onto the grass beyond the bank, and Harold grinned. "Strike one."

"That's it," said Flip. "That's it; you've got it." She took Harold by the hands and twirled him in a circle. She spun him around and around, until the river and the elephants blurred across his glasses, until Conrad pried them apart with his trunk.

"Hey!" said Flip, but she was laughing. She pushed at Conrad's trunk. "What are you, his bodyguard?" And then her laughter stopped. Someone else was standing there.

Chapter
35

Roman Pinski was only fifteen. But he was bigger than most men twice his age, made strong and taut by the swinging of sledges and the labors of a circus lot. He held the baseball bat in three fingers, by the bulge at the end of the handle.

"What's all the giggling about?" he asked. The bat swung in his hand like a bell clapper.

Flip was disheveled. Wet from the river, spotted with mud, she stood breathing hard from her laughing. She brushed a hand through her hair. "Hello, Roman," she said.

He stood just above the mud, looking down at Harold. "What are you doing here?" he asked. "Huh? What are you doing here, Whitey?"

Harold hung his head so far that the glasses nearly fell from his nose. It seemed to him, right then, that Liberty had come after him, that it always would come after him, like a pack of dogs, no matter where he went.

"I asked you a question." Roman leered at Harold. "What are you doing here, Whitey?"

Flip laughed. "What do you *think* he's doing here, you goof? He's got a baseball and a bat and a buncha elephants. What does it *look* like he's doing?"

"Making time," said Roman. "That's what. It looks like Maggot's making time with you."

"His name's not Maggot, and it's not Whitey. It's Harold." She stood between them, facing Roman. "And what does it matter to you what he's doing?"

"I don't like freaks," said Roman.

"Harold's not a freak."

"He looks like one." Roman swung the bat against his boot. It made a steady thudding like a drum. "Hey, Maggot. Why are you so white?"

Harold's shoulders tightened; his arms crossed against his stomach. He only had to wait, he knew, and Roman would just go away.

"Are you sick or something?" The bat thumped against Roman's boot. "You look half dead."

Harold could see him only as a blur in the arc at the top of his glasses. All around him the ground shivered and shook, and Canary Bird was a gray jelly looming over Roman's shoulder.

"Hey, Flip," said Roman. "Don't you think Maggot looks half dead?"

She stood close beside Harold, the river up to their ankles. "Just go and do your stupid rigging. Just leave us alone, okay?"

"Who's going to make me?" Roman grinned. "You going to make me, Whitey?"

Harold felt himself shriveling, tightening, like a spider poked by a stick. His legs wanted to run, but the rest of him couldn't. *He'll stop,* he thought. *He'll go away.*

"Look at him. Those dumb little glasses. Take them off, Whitey. I want to see your eyes. I bet they're pink, huh? Little pink eyes like a rat."

"They're blue," said Flip. "Now leave him alone."

208

There was an angry tremble in her voice. "Give him the bat and leave him alone."

"This bat?" Roman held it up. He took a step closer, from the grass to the mud. "Is this your bat, Whitey?"

Harold's fingers stiffened into fists. The nails pressed into his palm. It was David's bat, not his, and he was frightened that Roman would break it in two just for the pleasure of that, or suddenly hurl the thing into the river, laughing.

"You want your bat?" Roman held it out as he took another step, and another, crossing the mud to stand at the edge of the water. The river crept in behind him, filling the hollows his boots had made. "Go on; take it. I got better things to do than stand around and look at the freak show."

Harold stretched out his hand. He knew what would happen, and it did. Roman pulled the bat away.

"Take it, Whitey."

He'd played the game a thousand times—ten thousand times, perhaps—with his schoolbooks and his winter hats, his mittens and his fishing poles. He'd played it with the tears rolling down his face. And he decided now, with Liberty five hundred miles behind him, that he just wouldn't play it anymore. The bat dangled before him.

"Take it, Maggot."

He didn't move—not a muscle. The bat was just inches from his chest.

"You dumb white freak."

Conrad's ears flapped behind Harold, throwing shadows over Roman and the river. From his throat came the low rumble that could set Harold's hair tingling if he heard it from a distance.

Roman glanced up. He took a step back, then—grinning—came forward again. "Don't you want your bat, Whitey?"

Roman's fingers, curved around the top, nudged against Harold's chest. "Take it," he said, and pushed again.

It wasn't hard enough to topple him, but Harold stepped back.

"I could bust you in two," said Roman. "I could punch right through you if I wanted." He prodded Harold's breast with his fingers, each time a little harder.

Conrad's rumbling sounds deepened. His trunk thrashed at the river.

"You'd better stop," said Harold.

Roman sneered. He mimicked the Ghost's soft voice: "You'd better stop." Then he poked again, harder than before. "Come and make me, Whitey."

Harold moved backward. His heel caught on the river bottom, and he staggered and fell, sitting down in the water. He heard Conrad roar a terrible roar, a wail like a siren, that started low and ended with a shriek. He felt the trunk thrash at the water, and he saw Roman's eyes swell huge with fright.

Conrad came surging past Harold, right *over* Harold, with the water coursing around his legs. The elephant's belly covered him like a thick gray cloud. Flip screamed, and Roman dropped the bat; he turned and ran. He slipped on the bank and clawed with his fingers; he pulled himself up to the top. The mud on his hands grew as thick as boxing gloves. Then he stood on the grass and shouted back, "You keep that thing away from me. You stinking freak."

Conrad trumpeted. His trunk curled high above him. Roman was shaking his hands, spraying mud across the grass. And all the time he kept retreating, until only his head showed over the bank. "I'll get you, Whitey," he shouted. "I'll smash your stupid white face."

Harold didn't move. Roman's shouts faded away, and then he saw Flip wading toward him, her legs splashing through the water, her body hidden by the elephant. She stooped and looked under Conrad's belly. "Are you all right?" she asked.

He nodded. He crawled out, and the trunk snaked down to help him. Then he stood by Conrad's shoulder, and he didn't think he'd ever move from there.

"Take him up to the tent," she said. "Get his harness ready, and I'll meet you there in a minute. And whatever you do, don't leave the roses alone."

"Where are you going?" he asked.

"I gotta talk to Roman." She wiped a clot of mud from Harold's cheek. "I gotta set things straight."

Harold watched her cross the mud and climb the bank. He waved to her, but she didn't look back. Then he put his hand on Conrad's trunk. "Come on," he said, and started walking.

He stayed in the elephant's shadow. With Conrad beside him, and the other two roses plodding behind, he felt safer than he ever had. For the first time in his life he crossed an empty field without a twinge of fear. He walked into the elephants' tent, took a harness from its peg and dragged it back to the sunlight.

On the grass he stretched it out. But no matter how he pulled at the pieces, he could see no sense in all its chains and buckles. The breakfast bells rang, but he kept at work, frowning to see the tangles he was making, each one bigger than the last. And he was down on his haunches, still puzzling it out, when Flip walked up behind him. She had changed her wet and dirty clothes for clean ones, and she carried a tray in her hands.

"I brought you some breakfast," she said.

He took the plate of eggs and blackened toast, and he sat on the grass to eat it. Conrad stood above him, leaning left, then right, his ears flapping slowly.

"I guess Roman's pretty mad at me," Harold said.

"Good guess." She dragged a chain through a loop of leather, and it clattered into a heap. "He wanted Mr. Hunter to get his gun and go shoot Conrad."

"What?" said Harold. "Why?"

"'Cause he turned so mean."

Harold squinted at her. "Conrad didn't turn mean."

"No." She laughed. "Roman did."

"So nothing's going to happen, right?" Harold held a bit of toast above his head. Conrad took it in his trunk. "Mr. Hunter isn't going to shoot him, is he?"

"No," she said, shaking her head. "You've got to help me now."

Harold held the plate up and let Conrad take the last of his toast and eggs. Then he stood and helped Flip put the harness on the elephant.

It went quickly once he saw how it was done. With Conrad kneeling, they stretched the leather in place. Then Flip made him stand and tightened the buckles under his belly. "Down trunk!" she said.

Again Conrad knelt before her, with the clumsy grace Harold thought he would never get tired of seeing. The knees bent; the great bulk of the elephant's

212

head came down to rest on the ground; the trunk spread across the grass.

Flip stepped up it, over the forehead, onto the ridge of the elephant's spine. She sat facing Harold. "Okay. Climb on."

"Me?" asked Harold.

"Sure," she said. "Someone has to drive him."

He grinned and followed Flip, sprawling up across the hardness of the skull, crawling to the spine. It seemed much higher than he'd thought, and he clung to the harness as he turned himself around.

"Shove your feet under the strap," said Flip. "You're going to steer him with your feet, like a bobsled."

She pressed against his back, reaching past to show him what to do. Then her arms circled his stomach. "Tell him, 'Up trunk.'"

"Up trunk," said Harold, and felt himself soaring higher, backward, floating up above the ground. And he laughed from the feeling of it, the giddy sense of flying.

She showed him how to start the elephant going, how to turn him and how to stop him, how to step him backward. Clinging to the harness, Harold circled the tent, then turned and circled the other way, with Flip holding so fiercely to him that he felt every part of her pressing at his back. But she *had* to hold him; he teetered on Conrad's bony spine like a drunken man.

"Tighten your legs," said Flip, laughing. "Let go of the harness."

"I'll fall off."

"You won't," she said. "Put your hands on your hips."

He sat straighter then, rocked to and fro by the

elephant's odd, lopsided gait. He settled into it as the ground blurred past below him. But still Flip hugged him from behind, leaning on his back with her chin resting on his shoulder.

"Are you ready to work him alone?" she asked.

"Alone? Gosh, I don't know," he said. "I—"

"Don't worry so much!" She squeezed him. "It's easy. Go where people tell you and leave the work to Conrad. He's done it so often you'll just be along for the ride."

"Okay," he said.

"Now let me off."

He made the elephant kneel, and Flip slid down to the grass.

"Up trunk!" said Harold, and felt himself soaring, giddy again. He looked down at her from an incredible height, feeling enormous himself, as though the strength and the size of the elephant were now his own.

He went off to his job feeling that nothing could hurt him.

Chapter

36

Sidewalls were stripped from the tents, rigging wires and quarter poles removed, and the great buildings of canvas came tumbling down. Center poles were taken out, the canvas sections separated. Then men lined up along their edges and ran the canvas across, folding it into squares and strips, into bulky rolls that weighed two thousand pounds or more.

The elephant was the machinery of the circus. Now a tractor, now a skidder, now a donkey engine, Conrad dragged the canvas and the bundled poles across to waiting trucks. Chains were connected and disconnected, derricks and pulleys rigged. And the elephant—with Harold on his back—strained at his harness, kicking gouges in the field, to load the circus a ton at a time onto the backs of Fords and Chevrolets, until the trucks sagged on groaning springs.

And the last thing loaded was the elephant. Harold drove him up a ramp at the back of the Diamond T, into a stall with long, slatted windows cut in the side. He chained him there, then clambered out, and saw that the convoy was already moving.

The trucks started one by one, lurching over the field, joining in a column streaming to the west. The Airstream trailer passed in a flash of sun, and the

215

Gypsy Magda drove behind it. A quarter mile of trucks and trailers and huge black cars stretched along the road in a growing cloud of dust.

Then the yellow jeep came bouncing across the field, its wheels spraying dirt as it turned in a tight circle. It stopped behind the Diamond T, and Mr. Hunter leaned across the gearshift. He was wearing a pair of big goggles. "Harold," he said. "Jump in."

Harold clambered up through the low open door. He dropped into a seat that surprised him with its hardness, then clung to the windshield frame as the jeep leapt forward. It hurtled across the field, climbed to the road and sped along through the dust from the convoy. It passed the trucks one by one, with little toots of the horn as each cab went by. Gravel banged from the fender, and the dust went by in clouds, and Harold looked up at the drivers.

He saw the Gypsy Magda standing as she drove, but she didn't look down. Then he passed the Airstream, and Samuel's truck was swaying beside him. Harold pulled himself up by the windshield; he raised his head above it, and gritty air blasted hard against his face. Dust spewed from the truck's front wheel, boiling like smoke beside him. Then he waved to Samuel, the wind snatching his hand and pulling it back.

Samuel glanced down. His lips moved behind the bush of beard, and Tina suddenly appeared in the window, grinning and waving back. But Samuel neither waved nor smiled, and his hands stayed tight on the steering wheel. Then he fell away behind the jeep, and the other trucks passed in dust and gravel, until the jeep shivered on the road and zoomed ahead, through air that was clear and warm.

Harold dropped into his seat. He wiped the dust from his glasses and watched the road twist and open ahead. It seemed to leap toward him, to throw itself under the wheels, and the fence posts skidded past beside him; the dust filled in behind.

Mr. Hunter pulled off his goggles. The lenses were gray with dust. He tossed them into the little backseat as the air whistled past the windshield. "So," he said. "You had a run-in with Roman."

"Yes, sir," said Harold. They had to shout above the sounds of wind and engine.

"Don't let him intimidate you," said Mr. Hunter. "He's a bully; that's his job."

"I thought he was a rigger," Harold shouted.

"Yes. But that's a mindless means of making money." Mr. Hunter smiled. "When the show starts, he prowls around the big top. He chases off the boys who endeavor to crawl beneath the tent. I pay Roman to run them off. Rapidly," he added.

Harold nodded. He imagined it was the sort of job Roman would love.

"Any more trouble, you tell me," said Mr. Hunter.

"Yes, sir."

"We don't stand for trouble at Hunter and Green's."

Harold watched the fences pass. Behind them were forests of corn, and now and then a farmhouse. Then a man passed, standing close beside the road, and Mr. Hunter laughed to see Harold's hand come up to wave. Harold blushed. It was just a scarecrow, though he could tell that for sure only when he saw the birds perching on its stiffened arms.

The jeep drove west all afternoon and into twilight. Harold and Mr. Hunter stared ahead, rarely looking at each other. Talking took such an effort that they did it only in bursts, then sat back, panting, for another dozen miles. And then Harold would become uncomfortable, thinking it was his turn to talk, and he'd lean sideways and shout across the jeep.

"When will I meet Mr. Green?" he asked.

Mr. Hunter frowned. Harold thought he hadn't heard him and shouted again, louder.

"Soon enough, soon enough," said Mr. Hunter. "I don't see any hurry." Then he tilted across the gearshift. "But you shall meet him, as you say. Don't worry about that."

It sounded to Harold as though he *should* be worried, but he didn't know why. And he rode along at a slant, knowing it was his turn again.

But Mr. Hunter spoke first. "I feel fortunate for finding you," he said. "It's been a difficult season; you know that. My best clown deserted me a month ago, a sad and somber separation. Then the lion tamer left with his lions. Took his tiger, too."

"Gee, that's a shame," said Harold.

"Problems at every turn. The great Hunter and Green's shrinking away. Slipping slowly, steadily, sorrowfully . . ." He moved his hand, searching for another word that started with an *S*. "Away," he finished lamely.

"Gosh," said Harold, because he couldn't think of anything else.

"But the elephants. Ah, there's our hope. You're our baseball benefactor, boy. You're our saving grace, the foundation for a firmer future." His head bobbed at the end of his thin neck. "Yes, Harold, I have great trust in you."

Then he straightened in his seat, and the wind eddied between them. Harold leaned back, watching telephone wires curve up and down from passing poles. He fell asleep, and woke, and fell asleep again. And the next thing he knew, the sun was streaming through the windshield and Mr. Hunter was shaking him by the arm.

"Wake up," said Mr. Hunter. "We're here."

"Where?" asked Harold.

"Trickle Creek."

It was a tiny little town. The main street was only half as wide as Liberty's, but the stores that lined it shone and sparkled. Trees grew from planters on the sidewalk, and every window sported a bright box of flowers. The road was paved, and the jeep hummed along it at seven miles an hour.

Harold looked back. The convoy was bunched behind him, the trucks nearly bumper to bumper. They crawled down the street as people ran out from the stores, from their houses and their cars, lining the curb to watch the circus pass. They waved and cheered, and Mr. Hunter grinned.

"You feel like a soldier, don't you?" he said. "You feel as though you're liberating something. It's just like Holland, Harold."

"You were there?" asked Harold.

"I saw the newsreels," said Mr. Hunter, and he waved at the crowd. He shouted, "Evening show at six! Wave, Harold."

Harold waved. He was frightened at first, and he wished the jeep was moving faster. But no one laughed at him; they hardly seemed to see him. One by one, as Harold drew beside them, they tipped back on their

219

feet, trying to look at every truck at once. It made him think of a row of sunflowers rocking in the wind, of the wheat that had nodded in the convoy's rush of wind. Then he stood up, his hands on the windshield, his head above the glass, and he did feel like a soldier. He felt like a hero.

The people kept cheering. A boy looked down from a treehouse. And then, already, the town was behind them, and Mr. Hunter pressed the gas pedal. The jeep jolted forward, speeding past scattered houses. It turned to the left, at a pole hung with three of the crimson arrows, then left again to a big football field stretching out to vacant lots. And there, parked at its edge, was the home of the Cannibal King.

It was an Airstream trailer, smaller than Samuel's, hitched to a huge black car. Painted all across its surface, covering every inch, was a jungle scene in bright enamel, the grass along the bottom browned by dust and chipped by gravel roads. Coconut trees swept up the sides and met at the top in a tangle of fronds where monkeys played on swinging vines. Gaudy parrots flitted past the trees. In the grass lay heaps of grinning skulls.

"He's here," said Harold, holding his breath. "The Cannibal King."

"He's been waiting for us," said Mr. Hunter. He bent a wiry leg out of the jeep. "Now hurry, son. We've got a circus to build, and not a moment to lose."

Chapter

37

The children came like bees, in a swarm from every side. Sunburned, scruffy boys followed Mr. Hunter as he paced across the field with a paint can and a brush. They bent down when he bent down, and watched openmouthed as he dabbed the grass with whitewash. But they left him when the roustabouts came, naked to the waist with their hammers on their shoulders, and formed circles around *their* circles, around Mr. Hunter's gleaming marks. The boys chanted the roustabouts' chant as the sledges rose and fell to drive the stakes to hold the tent.

Girls in grass-stained white dresses watched the horses stepping from the truck. They watched Flip Pharaoh lead them down the ramp, two abreast with white manes flashing, and wished they were her.

But every child in Trickle Creek, every boy and girl, came running to the bugle call of Conrad.

Harold, high on the elephant's back, hauling poles across the field, saw them coming from every side. He heard their voices; he saw how they raced each other, and fear tingled through him to see an army of boys running at him.

Conrad always knew how he felt. The big, floppy ears grew wide and stiff. The trunk curled up and blasted out an angry, frightened sound. And the chains clanked taut, pulling harder at the bundled poles.

Harold saw the children mob around him. Twenty, thirty children, they moved in a mass as the elephant moved, coming forward behind him, going backward ahead. Conrad's ears were as big and wide as doors. His head lowered and swayed, and the trunk slashed back and forth. It was only the poles that held him back; he ran in slow motion at a redheaded boy the way he had hurtled at Roman.

But Harold found he wasn't frightened anymore. He was part of the elephant, a little white growth on its back, the brains of a creature nearly twenty feet high. He swaggered through the children, his hands on his hips, rocking with the elephant's roll.

They called him "mister." "What's his name, mister?" they shouted. "How much does he eat?" "Mister, how much does he weigh?"

But Harold didn't answer. He bullied through the group of children, then steered Conrad toward a blur of people and the fuzzy shapes of elephants. Max Graf was there, and he called to Conrad; they bugled back and forth.

Harold knew people by their voices as much as by their faces. He knew Roman's right away.

"Hey, Whitey! Bring those poles over here."

He nudged the elephant with his foot. The poles slid and rattled behind him. He steered straight for Roman Pinski.

"Okay, Maggot. That's good."

But he went a little farther, until he towered over Roman, and still he kept going.

"Stop, you freak!"

Harold smiled inside himself to see how Roman leapt away, how he cowered from the elephant. The boy ran a dozen yards before he stopped, quivering, as laughing men unhooked the chains and sent Harold off again.

He went in a dead straight line no matter who was in his way, seeing with a sort of pleasure how people scampered from his path. He brought the side poles and the quarter poles and then the rolls of canvas. And he saw, in snapshots, the big top going up; the center pole standing in its rigging, the tallest thing in sight; the canvas spread around it like a rippled, colored sea as men waded in to lace the parts together; the side poles like a forest of dead trees; the elephants hauling on ropes, and the canvas rising, swelling into shape.

The tent was smaller than he'd thought, all worn and faded by the sun. The new section of canvas was bright and clean, and all the rest looked sadder for it, so often patched that there were patches on the patches. But still it impressed him, and it swallowed whole a huge flatbed truck loaded with ring banks and bleachers.

He brought the pieces of the sideshow tent, the pieces of the cook tent. And the canvas city grew around him, until he rode the elephant down narrow lanes where—an hour before—there had been nothing but an empty field.

Through the afternoon, people came from miles around as news of the circus reached them. They wandered through the lot, around the tents and down the line of trucks. And Harold bullied through them. He knocked aside a farmer and his children, turned a corner, and came upon the painted trailer.

He hadn't planned to go there, or didn't think he had. But he leaned forward, his elbows on Conrad's back, and stared at the home of the Cannibal King. When the trailer started to shake, he thought it was only his eyes. But the trees broke apart as he watched, and a black hole appeared between two trunks, growing wider as the door swung open. Harold straightened.

Out through the door came the Cannibal King, as though he had stepped right from the jungles of Oola Boola Mambo.

He wore a leopard skin that draped to his knees and left one shoulder bare. And underneath he was white as bones, just as white as Harold was. His hair had that color that had no color, like sunlight on the water. But it ballooned from his head in a tremendous bush that shook as he walked on legs like springs from the trailer to his car.

"An albino," said Harold, half aloud. He breathed the word atop the elephant. He had never seen one before, except himself—the mirror boy he'd always found so white and freakish. But the Cannibal King was handsome, almost beautiful, and graceful as a cougar. He *stalked* toward the car.

Behind him came a group of children, creeping around the trailer, dashing from there to the shadows of another truck. They giggled with their hands over their mouths, stealing from shadow to shadow, from wheel to wheel. But the Cannibal King turned on them suddenly, spreading his arms, shouting at them in what must have been the grunted words of the Stone People.

"Bunga!" he roared, his enormous arms shaking. "Unga dooloo makena!"

The children scattered, and he walked on. He opened the car's rear door and pulled out a huge cardboard box, which he dropped to the ground with a rattle and a thud. He pushed it along with his foot.

The children came back, like birds frightened briefly from a feeder. They peered around fenders and bumpers and wheels as the Cannibal King shunted his box toward the trailer. Then he bent and reached inside it. He pulled out a bone, another bone, an arm with fingers at the end. He waved them at the children, roaring at the top of his voice, "Pago pago manihiki!" And the children shrieked and darted away.

The Cannibal King laughed deeply. He hoisted the box through the trailer door and closed himself inside. The door vanished, overgrown by the painted jungle.

Harold stared at the trailer, at the parrots and the monkeys. He wished he lived in a place like that, in the land of the Stone People. He'd be normal there, the same as everyone else, and the freaks would be people like Roman Pinski and Dusty Kearns. He longed for the door to open again, for the Cannibal King to appear.

"Go and meet him," a voice told Harold. It might have been his conscience, but it came from down below. He looked past the elephant's shoulder and saw Tina staring up, the Fossil Man beside her.

"Go on," she said. "You've come all this way to meet him, and it's just a few more feet you have to go."

"Can I do that?" Harold asked. "Can I just go up and talk to him?"

"Sure." Her little hands rose in a shrug. "Why not?"

"He's a king. You can't just go and talk to a king."

"Oh, nuts," she said. "I talk to him all the time, and he's just the same as me."

225

"But you're a princess," Harold said.

"Don't be silly," she said, and laughed. "You want to meet him, go ahead."

Samuel never raised his head. "Forget it," he said. "You're wasting your time. Look at him up there, bigger and better than anyone else. You'll never get him down to our level again."

Harold blushed on the elephant's back. He wished Samuel would at least lift his head.

"Come on, Tina. We'd better go before he tramples us."

"Not Harold," she said. But she wasn't much taller than the elephant's ankle, and she did step away from the enormous front leg. "Harold would never turn on his friends."

"His friends?" said Samuel. "I don't see anyone like that around." He bent down and took Tina in his arms. "If we had our little house, I bet he wouldn't come near it. Not even to hear the cuckoo sing."

Tina looked over his shoulder as he carried her off. Her arms around his thick, hair-covered neck, she looked back at Harold.

"He'll be welcome at my house," she said. "He'll always be welcome there."

Samuel said something that Harold couldn't hear. Then he passed the next truck, hidden for a moment by its khaki hood, and when he came out on the other side the Gypsy Magda was walking beside him, as if she'd been waiting there for them. Samuel knelt, and Tina slipped down to the ground, and they walked away, three in a line.

It felt to Harold as though they had left him

behind, as surely as he'd fled from Liberty. It felt as though he would never talk to them again.

"Well, who needs you?" he muttered. "Bunch of freaks; who needs you?" He *was* better than them now. He had a job; he had a girlfriend, didn't he? He certainly had the best seat in the cook tent, and he couldn't even move without everyone saying hello. He wasn't the same boy who had left Liberty. That was for sure.

He watched them until they were gone, then turned again to the painted trailer. But the jungles of Oola Boola Mambo shimmered now in his eyes, and that feeling was gone, that urge to meet the Cannibal King. In a way, he was frightened to meet him.

Chapter

38

Conrad hurried along as he came closer to the other elephants. His feet hammered on the ground as his plodding walk quickened to a trot. Women pulled their children out of his path; men whirled aside with angry shouts. Even Harold was nervous; the elephant felt out of control. It trumpeted, another bugled back, and Conrad hurtled around the big top with his ears pinned back.

In the shadow of the tent Flip was dressing Max Graf in a feathered crimson headpiece. The elephant was kneeling, and she stood atop his forehead as Conrad pounded up beside her, scattering the people who had gathered to watch her work.

"Stop showing off," she said. "Don't run him like that."

"He ran himself," said Harold.

"Then at least *he* knows he should have been here."

Conrad growled. "You shouldn't get angry at me," Harold warned. "Conrad doesn't like it."

Flip's face was nearly as red as the feathers. "Then where have you been?" she demanded.

"I thought I'd walk him for a while," said Harold. "I thought—"

"No, you didn't." The long feathers ruffled across her face. "You didn't think at all. The circus starts in an hour, and there's a million things to do. So get offa there and help me."

Harold pulled his feet from the strap. "Down trunk," he said, but Conrad didn't move. "Down trunk!" He kicked against the hide.

Conrad stood facing Flip, huffing breaths that shook his chest. He stepped forward.

"Back!" shouted Harold, pulling at the leather. With a sudden rush of fear he thought the elephant would go after Flip. But Roman Pinski raised his head over Max Graf's rippled trunk and slowly edged away.

"You white creep," he said. "I told you, keep that thing away from me."

Conrad lashed at the ground with his trunk. Harold laughed. "You'd better go," he said, and laughed again as Roman turned and sprinted off toward the tent, through the doorway in its back. "Yeah, you'd better run, you bet." He was glad there were people to see it.

"Proud of yourself?" asked Flip.

The elephant knelt, and Harold clambered down. Instantly he felt smaller. He stayed close by Conrad.

"You'll ruin that elephant like this," said Flip. "You know that? You're making him mean and ugly."

"I am not," said Harold, patting Conrad's trunk. "Roman shouldn't have been here."

"*Someone* had to help me," said Flip.

"Well, I don't want him here."

She rolled her eyes. "You sound like Roman."

"Good," said Harold, but he blushed. He could

hear his voice like an echo in his mind. He had sounded *exactly* like Roman.

"Now please come and help me," she said.

Together they fixed the feathers onto Max Graf. As more people came to watch, they placed a saddle blanket of tasseled velvet on his back, shining collars on his feet. And Harold grinned to see how proud Max was, bending up his trunk to preen the feathers on his head.

"I gotta get ready, so you'll have to do the others by yourself," said Flip. "Give Conrad a wash before you dress him, and when you've finished they can each have two oranges. There's six in the harness box."

"Wait," said Harold. There was quite a crowd by then. "Can't you stay and help?"

"I would," she said, with a brilliant smile. "But you came so late there isn't any time. I'm gonna dress the horses and come right back to get you."

"Can you make these people go away?"

"Oh, I wish I could," she said. "But everything is part of the show in a little town like this. They've maybe never seen a circus, let alone an elephant."

His eyes jiggled. He had to tilt his head to see her.

"I'm sorry," she said. "You'll just have to get used to it. If this was Barnum and Bailey, there'd be *thousands* here to watch you."

She touched his shoulder and stepped away, and Harold groaned inside. He fumbled with the bucket as he set it down by Conrad's head. He fumbled with the brush so badly that it popped from his hands like a bar of soap. And when he bent to pick it up, he stepped on it by mistake. The people laughed behind him; they screamed with laughter. Harold whirled around to see that Conrad had drained the bucket and sprayed the

water across the crowd. A little man with stringy hair—
an important-looking man—was dripping from his
nose and chin. But he was laughing harder than anyone.

Harold smiled. It was the elephants they were
watching, not him. And he went to his work with a
feeling of pride, knowing how strange the animals
looked to people who had never seen an elephant.
Conrad reveled in all the attention that he got. Once
more he sprayed the crowd. Then he tipped the bucket
upside down, picked it up and set it on his head.

"What's his name?" a woman asked.

"Conrad," said Harold.

"He's a monkey, isn't he?"

"Gosh, ma'am," said Harold, feeling awfully sorry
for the woman. "He's an elephant."

He washed Conrad down, put on the feathers and
the blanket and the collars. He dressed Canary Bird as
well. Then he got out the bag of oranges, and the elephants twitched and murmured. He put on a show,
tossing the oranges to Canary Bird, who plucked two
in a row from the air. He fed two to Max, seeing how
the people craned forward to watch, seeing for himself
how strangely an elephant ate, the trunk curling back
to stuff each orange into a tiny slit of a mouth.

As he fed Conrad, he heard a little boy shouting,
"Mom! Look at that. Mom, the elephant's taking
oranges in its tail and sticking them up its bum!"

There was a burst of laughter. Everyone laughed,
except for Harold. He heard, in his mind, the Gypsy
Magda's voice raised eerily high on the prairie. *Beware
of the beast that feeds with its tail.*

He felt as though he had to see her, that he couldn't
wait another minute. But already the calliope was

playing, its music growing louder. Already Flip was coming to get him.

She pushed through the crowd in a white robe that was tied at her waist by a gleaming black ribbon. "Okay," she said. "Let's go."

Chapter

39

The band played a brassy, jangling song, and Flip led the parade on Conrad's back. The three elephants linked trunk to tail, a pair of clowns and the six gleaming horses marched around the hippodrome, and more came after that. Mr. Hunter, in a morning coat of red and gold, in the center of the ring, called out names as people entered through the huge rear door. As the elephants went marching out, others were marching in to join a circle without an end, right around the tent. And last of all the elephants were sent around again, to make the show seem that much bigger and grander than it was.

Harold watched from the assembly hall, a vast square of canvas at the back of the big top. There were five hundred people in the bleachers, but he would have guessed five thousand by their cheering and the stomping of their feet. The sound made Conrad nervous; he came bellowing from the ring with his trunk swinging wildly.

"Hold him!" Flip shouted. She pushed her horse against the elephant. "Harold, grab on to his harness."

"I can't stay," said Harold. He had seen the beast that feeds with its tail. "I have to—"

"You have to *hold* him," said Flip. "You have to hold him every second."

Harold groaned, but he did as he was told. He slid his hand through Conrad's harness, and the performers swirled around him, passing in and out of the big top as Mr. Hunter announced each act in turn.

"The Fearless Flying Frizzles!" he shouted. And out past Harold ran a man and a woman dressed in white. The woman was chubby, the man very short, and both so old that their hair was gray. A drum beat a slow roll as they climbed up dangling ropes to platforms at the top of the tent, where the sun made dappled patches on the canvas. The crowd went silent as the Frizzles stood there. Then a trumpet squeaked, and the band burst into "The Daring Young Man on the Flying Trapeze." The Frizzles swung out in the air. For nearly five minutes they soared from trapezes, back and forth, crossing in the air. Harold watched through the entrance, glad in a way that he had one hand stuck in Conrad's harness. The Frizzles weren't good enough to make him want to clap.

The music changed to "Waltzing Matilda," and a tightrope walker came on, but he trembled like a leaf. The audience stopped cheering, and the tent seemed hollow and empty. The clowns barely got a laugh; the woman with the dogs got booed. Harold blushed, embarrassed for them all. Then Flip was standing beside him, her white robe nearly touching the ground. "Pretty sad," she said. "Isn't it?"

Harold didn't answer.

"Well, it's gonna get worse right now."

Mr. Hunter's voice echoed from the tent. "They dance, they waltz, they do the tango. They weigh sev-

234

enteen tons, but they're as light on their feet as Ginger Rogers. Ladies and gentlemen, the pachyderms!"

Flip took Conrad's harness. "You gotta see this."

She led the elephants into the big top, and Harold couldn't leave, not then. He stood right in the doorway as the roses went dancing to the swing of "Mairzy Doats." They bumbled around like pigs in a sty, lurching backward and sideways as the tune bounced merrily on.

Harold was glad when it ended. He rubbed Conrad's trunk and said, "That was pretty good," to make him feel a little better.

The tumblers passed him, dashing out and puffing back. And just as Harold thought he might sneak away, he saw Flip leading her horses in a snorting row through the assembly hall.

"And now!" shouted Mr. Hunter. "She's amazing, she's astounding, she's ab-so-lute-ly beautiful!"

Flip untied the black ribbon at her waist. She pulled off her robe and gave it to Harold. "Hold on to this," she said. "Okay?"

"S-Sure." He stammered and blushed. Underneath the robe she wore nothing but spangles, just a tiny suit that gleamed and glistened as she climbed onto General Sherman.

"Wish me luck," she said. But Harold couldn't speak.

The crowd had fallen deathly quiet; they'd long ago stopped clapping. Mr. Hunter's voice was the only sound in the tent. "She's a fearless, fabulous fabricator of wonder. She's the one you've always heard about, the girl on six white horses. She's . . ." A drumroll started. "Filipina Pharaoh!"

235

"Filipina?" said Harold.

"Don't laugh." She nudged the horse, and it leapt forward.

Into the ring she went at a gallop, leaping the bank to the sawdust-covered ring. The band played "She'll Be Comin' Round the Mountain" as she galloped around and around the ring, the five other generals falling into line behind her, as perfectly spaced as cogs on a wheel. Light sparkled on her spangles; sawdust flew at the horses' hooves. But there was just a spattering of applause, a feeble sound.

Then Flip stood up. She teetered and caught her balance, then leapt from the horse, somersaulting backward. She landed on General Grant, and leapt again to General Lee as he passed. The horses ran, their tails sweeping back, and she somersaulted from one to another without seeming to move at all.

The applause grew louder, then louder still when she turned and ran from horse to horse as they thundered by below her. Then half the horses turned and raced the other way, and she rode two at once, switching as they crossed paths. The crowd whistled and applauded loudly enough to drown out the band.

Harold took his glasses off. His eyes were blinking as fast as insect wings. The horses were a blur of white and Flip a streak of blue, but he had never seen a thing even half as great as that.

A hand fell on his shoulder. Big red fingers squeezed him. "She's good, for a white girl," said Thunder Wakes Him.

The old Indian stood in his headdress and his leggings, his chestnut horse behind him. He held his lance upright, with the feathers hanging at the top. "You sleep well," he said. "I told you so."

"Told me what?" asked Harold.

"That when you woke, I'd be gone."

Flip rode General Grant out from the ring to the hippodrome. She circled the track twice and came through the door at a gallop, to a deafening din of applause. She was glowing with pleasure and pride, her face as bright as her spangles.

"Oh, hi, Bob," she said to Thunder Wakes Him. She took her robe from Harold.

"You did well, little rider," said the old Indian.

"Boogie Woogie Bugle Boy" boomed from the tent, and another tumbler went somersaulting out and nearly sprained his ankle. He came limping back as Mr. Happy passed him, his welded rings spinning. The voice of a child carried through the silent tent: "I bet they're stuck together." And then Mr. Hunter held up his hands, as though to call for a quiet that was already there.

"Our grand finale," he said. "A sight you will never forget."

The old Indian tugged at his buckskin. "That's me," he said, and pulled his horse toward him. From its back he took his roll of leather and hides and placed them on the ground. "Will you keep this safe?" he asked. "My medicine bundle's in there."

Mr. Hunter stood alone in the ring in his top hat and tails. "From the untamed West!" he cried. "From the battlefield of the Little Bighorn! The last of a tribe of red men! The most daring, the most dashing, the most death-defying rider you will ever see! The man who counted coup on Custer! The man who rode with Sitting Bull! We are proud to present Thunder Wakes Him!"

The old Indian rode out from the assembly hall at a slow, sedate walk. He circled the hippodrome, and the only sound was the hooves of the chestnut horse beating at the hardened ground. The tail of his headdress hung behind him; the feathers on his lance rippled back. Then, with a whoop, he threw down the lance and flung off the headdress, and put his heels to the big brown horse. It broke into a run, but a very slow run that wasn't much faster than its walk.

The band played a war dance full of drums and bugle shrieks, and Thunder Wakes Him did tricks on the horse's back. But the music was fast, and Thunder Wakes Him as slow as molasses. He was like a mechanical toy at the end of its clockwork, creaking from one side of the horse to the other, now sitting frontward, now backward, all the time moving as though surrounded by water. The crowd started to laugh.

The old horse came panting around the track, and a clown stepped out with a rifle. He held it up for the old Indian to grab, and he stood there for a long, long time—checking his watch, pretending to yawn—until the horse went plodding by. Thunder Wakes Him reached out and snatched the gun, and he made it seem—somehow—as though he'd done it on the fly. He spun the rifle end over end in such a slow and laborious way that the crowd cheered when he'd finished, and laughed all the harder.

He stretched out along the horse's back, and it seemed that he might have gone to sleep. Then the gun poked out under the horse's neck, and he fired blanks toward the bleachers as the horse plodded on.

The clown turned and chased the horse. In his baggy pants and enormous shoes, it took him twenty yards to catch it. He hung on to the tail and sledded on his shoes as Thunder Wakes Him did his slow, pathetic tricks. And the audience laughed hysterically. Then the clown's pants fell down and he tumbled along the hippodrome, leapt up and overtook the horse, and raced it from the ring. He beat it by a dozen yards.

The old Indian came a minute later. He reined the horse and patted the side of its head. "Did you hear them out there?" he asked.

"Yes," said Harold.

"They cheered me, didn't they?" He grinned down from the horse's back. "Didn't they cheer me, Harold?"

"Yes, they did," said Harold.

"They cheered me more than Flip, I think." His ancient face cracked across the wrinkles. "Did you hear them laughing at the clown?"

"Sure I did," said Harold.

The old Indian smiled. "Where is my bundle? My medicine bundle?"

"There," said Harold. "Where you left it."

Thunder Wakes Him took the bundle and tossed it on the horse's back. "I'll carry it now," he said. "In the closing parade."

"It's over?" asked Harold. "The whole circus?"

The old Indian nodded. He was lashing his bundle in place.

Harold gazed all around him. The band began to

play the jazzy song that had opened the circus. Flip, in her spangles, was hauling Conrad down to his knees.

The music swelled inside the tent and then grew soft as Mr. Hunter announced the closing parade.

"Ladies and gentlemen, boys and girls," he said. "For one last time, in all its entirety, I present to you the great Hunter and Green's Traveling Circus."

Cymbals clashed and drums beat fast and loud. It was a wave of music that crashed through the big top.

"At the head of our parade," said Mr. Hunter, "is the paragon of pachyderms, the largest living thing that ever walked in Trickle Creek."

Harold turned to leave, but hands grabbed him, pulling him sideways. There were many hands, a sudden blur of faces. Only by their voices did he know the people there. The Frizzles shouted at him, "Come on, Harold."

Mr. Happy grumbled. "Just pull him over."

"Stop," cried Harold. "I have to go."

He heard Flip laugh. She was right in front of him, pushing him back toward Conrad. "You can't," she said. "Not yet."

A trombone whooped; a piccolo shrilled. "And on his back," said Mr. Hunter, "is a boy called Harold Kline!"

Then all those hands were lifting him up, hoisting him onto Conrad's velvet blanket. He scrambled for a handhold as he felt the elephant rise.

"He's the pachyderms' pal," said Mr. Hunter. "He's the mentor of the monstrous mammals."

Conrad went forward at a high-stepping trot. Harold swept through the entrance and into the ring. The music seemed to crash around him like waves, and he saw a crowd of faces on his left, a blur of hands applauding. And on his right was Mr. Hunter, turning in the center of the ring.

"He will bring to Salem, for those with means to see it, a feat never before accomplished in the known universe. Drive to Salem in your motor cars; take the bus or catch the train; walk there if you have to, and if you cannot walk, then crawl. But take yourselves to Salem or forever rue the day you did not see . . . pachyderms playing baseball!"

The bleachers shook, and voices cheered. Conrad trumpeted as he circled through the tent with Harold clinging to his back. Every spotlight was aimed at the Ghost, and they glinted off his little black glasses; they shone in his colorless hair. And he raised one hand, one small white hand, in the tiniest little wave.

He blinked at all the people, though he couldn't tell the men from boys, or the boys from girls, the way his eyes were shaking. But Conrad trotted on, his head so high and his trumpeting so loud that he might have thought the cheering was all for him. Behind him came Max Graf and Canary Bird, the Frizzles and the high-wire men. When Harold was halfway around the ring he could see the performers still coming out, Mr. Happy rolling his rings like a wheel, Flip with her six white horses. They spaced themselves so perfectly that Harold passed the old Indian right in the entrance. He steered through the flaps to the assembly hall.

And waiting there was Roman Pinski. He stood in the shadows, close against the canvas. His voice came up through the din of noise, through a clatter of bleachers as the audience flooded from the big top.

"You think you're really something, don't you, Whitey?"

Harold didn't stop. He urged Conrad into a faster walk, into a trot through the rear door. Roman shouted after him. "Come back here, Maggot." But the elephant pounded from the tent, and Harold nudged him to the right, past a startled man who fell away like a toppled chair. Conrad hurtled along as Harold bounced on his back, steering always to the right, until he reached the elephants' tent. The hose was still running, the patch of mud now wide and deep. Conrad splashed through it and stopped on dry grass.

"Down trunk!" shouted Harold. "Conrad, down!" He slid too soon from Conrad's back and fell four feet to the ground. A little girl standing there looked in amazement as he sprawled in the grass.

She was holding a pen and a piece of paper. "Can I get your autograph, mister?" she asked.

Harold struggled up. "I can't," he said. "Not now." And he went off at a run, straight for the sideshow tents.

THEY FORMED A STREET, a narrow lane that stretched before him. A stream of people flowed along it, making eddies at a ring-toss booth, around the men who sold balloons and birds, at a cart where popcorn popped in a glass box that glowed yellow like butter.

He waded into the stream and let it sweep him off to the side. He was the Ghost again, flitting along.

On a platform draped in bunting, a man in a black-tailed coat shouted at him—at everyone—"Step right up and see the freaks of nature!" He held a cane, which he swung to his right and then to his left, toward enormous painted banners of Samuel and Tina. They made Samuel seem twice as monstrous as he really was, while Tina stood atop his palm, no bigger than his thumb. "You'll never see the likes of this again," the caller shouted. "A living fossil from the jungles of deepest Africa. A full-grown princess smaller than a baby."

From the tent, through the canvas, Harold heard a roar and a clang of metal, then a woman's startled shriek.

"We've got him caged!" The caller rapped his cane on the platform. "Bars of steel between you and the Missing Link."

On another platform, another man in another black-tailed coat shouted about the Cannibal King. "He's fierce, he's frightening, he's right inside this tent." And Harold stopped below the stage, in a backwater in the stream of people. Jostled by the crowd, he stared at the banner behind the caller, the same picture of the Cannibal King he had seen for the first time in Liberty. The shrunken head that dangled from a white fist was now the size of a dog. The Cannibal King's eyes glared straight at Harold and followed him down the midway as the crowd caught him again in its stream.

He flowed along with it, down to the foot of the midway, where the calliope shrieked and whistled. Then he turned to his left, into a small striped tent, under a banner that said, Fortunes Told, Secrets Revealed. He swept aside the flap and let it close behind him.

The Gypsy Magda sat at a little table, behind a crystal ball. The scarves she wore were red and gold; from her ears hung hoops of silver.

"It happened!" cried Harold. "I saw it. The beast that feeds with its tail."

She looked up at him. "Sit," she said, and waved him to a chair.

There was only one. It stood away from the table, turned aside, as though someone had suddenly pushed it back to go running from the tent. Harold pulled it closer. He dropped to the seat. "It happened," he said again.

"And this surprises you?" The lamplight flashed around her hoops. "Didn't I tell you it was so?"

"Yes," said Harold. He rhymed it off, what she had told him. "Beware the ones with unnatural charm, and the beast that feeds with its tail. A wild man's meek and a dark one's pale, and there comes a monstrous harm."

The Gypsy Magda smiled. "You know all that I know," she said.

"But not what happens next." He rubbed his hands together. "Won't you tell me that?"

"I can't," she said.

"Look in the ball."

"It won't be there."

"Just look," he said.

She reached out, her bracelets jangling, and cupped her hands around the ball. Her rings clinked against its surface. "You may not like it," she said. "What I see."

Harold leaned forward. He heard the whistle of the calliope, the shouting of the callers on the midway. And then he heard the little silvery tinkles of the Gypsy Magda's rings as she moved her hands along the crystal, and that was all he heard.

She swayed in her chair. Her golden scarves glistened in the lamplight.

"I see a boy," she said. "He is angry, I think; he is

244

like a storm inside himself. Others, they are scared of him. But he likes this fear, this boy."

"Yes," said Harold. "That's Roman; I know him."

"Shhh! Don't speak." The Gypsy Magda rubbed the crystal ball. Her hands fondled it the way Thunder Wakes Him coaxed his fires from little embers. She peered down at the glass. "This boy, he will bring about the harm, the monstrous harm. There is nothing now to stop him."

"What will happen?" Harold asked. "The death you smelled, is that the harm?"

"Ach, it's gone." The Gypsy Magda took her hands away. "I told you not to speak."

"Look again," said Harold.

She shook her head. "You cannot look twice."

"Then guess!" he said, more sharply than he meant. "Tell me what you saw."

She leaned back. The hoops in her ears turned in sparkling light. "I'll tell you what I *see*," she said, staring at him. "I see one who's changing. A boy who's growing up. I see a boy who's stronger than he was, but one who will not learn from what he's done."

"I don't understand," said Harold.

"The soldiers," she said. "They were boys like you. They came from farms and villages—from cities, some. It does not matter; they were only boys, not good or bad. What was it, do you think, that made those white, blond boys the way they were?"

"I don't know," said Harold.

The Gypsy Magda pointed at him with a gaunt finger. "I told you once never to think that you are less than other people. I should have told you too never to think that you are better."

Chapter 40

The crowd was thinning when Harold left the tent. He pushed his way easily against the stream, to the enormous billboards of the Cannibal King. And he stood there, staring up. He had to meet him now. Now or never meet him. He wanted to throw himself at the feet of the King and say, "I'm Harold the Ghost. I'm scared and I don't know what to do."

There was no one waiting at the door. He could go straight inside if he wanted.

But suddenly he found himself thinking of the grassy schoolyard with its rusted swings, and the time he'd played Five Hundred with Samuel and Tina and the Gypsy Magda. It was more than thinking; he was *there*. He smelled the grass again and felt the hot sun that had fallen on him. But he didn't know why, until he realized the calliope was playing the same music that had carried to him so faintly that day, the tune that Samuel had called the breaking-down song. Then he heard the roar of truck engines and saw that one end of the big top was already sagging, the canvas coming down.

Flip would be furious that he wasn't there. Mr. Hunter would be angry too. "I told you to stay with the pachyderms," he would say. If Harold wasn't there, Flip would do his job; Flip would work with Roman.

He didn't know what to do. The doorway gaped at him, wide open and empty. The big top towered up at the end of the sideshow. He took a step in one direction, a step the other way. And those eyes of the Cannibal King watched his every move. But in the end, he couldn't go past the door; it sucked him in like a whirlpool.

A roustabout stood on a ladder, taking down the panels of a metal grate. Behind it was a huge stage built of many steps, a velvet carpet climbing to the very top, to an enormous throne of wood and crimson leather. All around that majestic chair stood coconut trees that bent toward each other, their fronds meeting, making a giant parasol.

Harold moved closer. He was looking at the scene from Tina's postcard, at the very same thing she had shown him as they drove west chasing the Cannibal King. He remembered that she'd laughed. *They're just such funny trees.*

He bumped against a wooden bench. The roustabout heard him but didn't look down. "Show's over," he said. "Get outta here."

"Where's the Cannibal King?" asked Harold.

"You missed him."

"Already?" But it only made sense. The Cannibal King would always be the first to leave, he thought. He'd be driving west right then, marking a trail for the circus to follow.

The roustabout pulled off a panel. He dropped it behind the grate, and it clanged against the stage. The coconut trees swayed as though in a hurricane. Then one of them fell against another and—like dominos—they tumbled from the stage.

Harold couldn't believe it—they barely made a sound. They sort of scratched against each other, then landed with just the faintest bumps. They were only paper trees.

"Hey," said the roustabout. "I told you to go."

Harold stumbled out. And Harold started running. His elbows pumping, his boots flailing, he ran to the elephants' tent.

He groaned to see Conrad. The huge elephant was rolling in the puddle, his collars and feathers and blanket all coated with mud. Max and Canary Bird were splattered with round clots. Their feathers drooped like bedraggled crows.

"Oh, gosh," said Harold. "Look at you. Just look what you've done to your clothes."

He laughed to hear himself; it might have been his mother's voice. "I sound just like my ma," he said. "But I better wash you down, I guess."

He pulled the hose out of the mud. He found the bucket but not the brush. "Where's the brush?" he asked.

And Roman Pinski came out from the darkness. "Looking for this, Maggot?" he asked. The brush was in his hand.

Harold stopped. He held the hose, and it dribbled water on his boots. Behind him, Conrad growled as he thrashed on his side, kicking at the mud.

"Whitey thinks he's really something," said Roman, as though to the elephants. "But Whitey's just a piece of dirt."

248

"Leave me alone," said Harold.

"Leave me alone," whined Roman. "Yeah, he's right. He sounds just like his ma."

Harold squinted. Flip was there, behind Roman. She stepped out of the same shadows, tugging at her little spangled suit. The fear he'd felt changed into something worse. He wondered what they were doing just before he got there.

Roman put the brush on his shoulder. "Whitey's getting too big for his britches."

"Quit it," said Flip. "Just quit it, okay?"

"Whitey's got to learn a lesson."

Harold dropped the hose and started backward. "Don't let him push you around," Mr. Hunter had said. But Mr. Hunter wasn't here.

"Where's your ma now? Where's your ma, you little freak?"

Harold stumbled back. Roman came after him.

"Whitey, don't you want your brush?" He held it out.

Harold tried to pluck it away. He ran at it, but his hand touched nothing but air. He staggered and straightened, turning again to face Roman.

"Close," said Roman. "You had me scared. Ooh, you had me shaking there."

"Oh, stop it!" said Flip.

Conrad rolled onto his chest. His legs were still bent below him, and his body heaved as he struggled in the mud. He roared, and Roman looked back.

"He's stuck." Roman laughed. "Too bad. Eh, Whitey? Isn't that too bad?"

The brush rose in Roman's hands. It stood above his shoulder, then came swinging down. Harold covered his head.

But the blow never came. Conrad's trunk shot out and looped around Roman's ankles. It pulled him back, dragging him down. Roman dropped like a falling tree.

"No!" screamed Flip.

But Conrad hauled the boy into the mud. Roman writhed in the elephant's grasp, twisting like a snake until his back was on the ground. His hands left long ruts in the ground. The trunk curled inward, and Roman's legs, and then his hips, and then his shoulders slithered through the mud.

"Help!" he shouted.

"Up trunk!" cried Flip. She ran forward and grabbed Roman's hands. She pulled as hard as she could but only skidded forward. Feet as thick as stumps pounded down by Roman's shoulders. "Up trunk! Harold, stop him."

Harold was too surprised to move. He saw the trunk come loose, then rise in a long curve.

Conrad trumpeted with that awful, blood-chilling howl. He rose from the ground, towering in a shimmering coat of mud. Then he tipped forward and pressed his great, broad forehead onto Roman's chest. Mud squirted around the boy's shoulders, around his ribs and hips. Flip was still screaming. "Up trunk! Conrad, up trunk."

She threw herself at the elephant. She battered her fists at Conrad's head. Underneath it, mud welled around Roman's ears; the boy was being pushed right into the ground. And beside him, Flip hammered her fists on the elephant's cheek.

It had all happened in seconds, in the time it had taken Harold to cover his head, to close and open his eyes. And it seemed that those seconds lasted for minutes, and the minutes forever. It occurred to Harold in that strange, extended time that he could leave the elephant to its fierce revenge. He saw, vanishing into the mud, every boy who had ever taunted him, every bully and giggling girl who had made his life a misery.

"Help!" said Roman. His arms clawed up from the mud, his hands pushing at the trunk. "He's going to kill me!"

Harold ran forward. He slipped and fell and ran again. He grabbed big flaps of the elephant's ear, and he shouted, "Stop it, Conrad! Let him up. Let him go!" The elephant's forelegs were bent, all his weight on his knees and his head; he would crush the boy in the mud.

"Please," said Harold, "Oh, please let him up."

He pushed, straining with his arms: ninety pounds of skinny boy and seven tons of elephant. "Conrad, up," he said. "Up trunk!"

And slowly Conrad stood up. His legs straightened; his head lifted from the ground. He snorted, and he nuzzled Harold with his stump of a tusk.

Roman squirmed through the mud. Flip grabbed on to his shirt and pulled him all the faster. He didn't stop until he was twenty feet away. And then it was Harold he shouted at.

"You stinking freak!" he screamed. "You lousy, stinking freak!"

Conrad's trunk was dripping mud. He raised it high and trumpeted.

"Get him away from me!" screamed Roman.

Flip scraped gobs of mud from his hair and his cheeks. Then she helped him to his feet and led him away from the river.

"You see what you've done?" she said, glaring at Harold. "Are you happy now?"

Harold didn't answer.

"Stay here," she told him. "You just stay right here and wait for me."

Chapter

41

Harold used the hose to wash the mud from Conrad. The water sprayed off the elephant's hide and flowed in rivers down the ribs.

"You've done it now," he said. "Oh, gosh, you've done it now."

He heard a coughing sound as a generator started. Then the night was dazzled by electric lights. They glinted faintly off Conrad and shone in the huge and growing puddle. The calliope wheezed the breaking-down song.

Harold expected Flip to come right back, but it seemed as though ages passed before anyone arrived. And then it wasn't Flip at all. It was Mr. Hunter, and he carried a shotgun with the barrel broken open. It pointed down, as thin and stiff as an extra arm hanging from his shoulder.

Harold dropped the hose. He stood under the elephant's chin.

"There's no reason you have to witness this," said Mr. Hunter. "It would be better that you left."

"You're going to shoot him?" Harold hugged the trunk as it drooped across his chest. "You're not going to shoot him, are you?"

"Yes, I am." Mr. Hunter balanced the gun under his

arm and took a shell from his pocket. "I don't like that boy, that Roman Pinski. He's hotheaded and far too full of himself. But if it wasn't Roman that Conrad trampled, it would have been someone else."

Harold rubbed his hand along the ripples of the trunk. "He didn't trample anyone," he said.

"Don't play word games," said Mr. Hunter. "From what I gather, he nearly killed the boy."

Harold hung his head.

"I'm sorry, son. But pachyderms get a taste for this. They see how big they are, how small a person is, and they just decide that they won't be pushed around. Conrad's crazy, boy. He's mean."

"He's not," said Harold. "You're standing there with a gun. He's going to let you put the barrel up against his head and pull the trigger, that's how mean he is."

"You don't understand." Mr. Hunter pushed the shell into the breech of his gun. "Next time he could turn on you, or on me, or on a bleacherful of children. And there won't be any warning; he'll just do it."

He swung the barrel up, and the gun cocked with a click that seemed terribly loud and final. He hoisted it up to his shoulder.

"Don't," said Harold. "Please don't."

The calliope paused, and a different song started. Conrad's ears flapped sadly. Then he made his funny chirping sound and tottered up on his two left feet. He swayed, fell flat, and tipped to his right. Then his front feet started moving, shuffling in the mud. He was dancing—such a pathetic effort, such a clumsy dance, that Harold began to cry. The tears dribbled out from under his glasses, and he looked up and saw that the elephant too was crying.

Even Mr. Hunter seemed to pause, his cheek lifting from the gun.

Conrad rocked and shuffled in the mud. Then he slowed, his huge head falling, and he stopped.

"Aw, gosh," said Harold.

Mr. Hunter sighed. "You're just prolonging this. I have to do it, though Lord knows I wish I didn't." His finger slid around the trigger, and he brought the shotgun up to his shoulder.

"No!" shouted Harold. "It isn't fair. It wasn't even his fault."

"Not his fault?" Mr. Hunter sighted down the barrel. "He nearly killed a boy."

"Who came at me with a stick!" said Harold.

"Is that a fact?" Mr. Hunter let the gun point down. "Roman threatened you with a stick?"

"A brush; yes, sir. He was going to hit me with it."

"And Conrad came to your rescue?"

Harold nodded. "And you can't shoot him for that. You just can't."

"I might have known," said Mr. Hunter. "That part of the story was omitted in its telling." He looked at the gun with a hopeless frown, then up at Conrad. "Tell me: Can two elephants play baseball?"

"No," said Harold, shaking his head. "No, it's just impossible."

Mr. Hunter licked his lips. "You say Roman came at you with a stick?"

"Yes, sir," said Harold.

"Did he mean to strike you?"

Harold sniffed. "I'm pretty sure he did."

"Then I'll tell you what. Due to these extenuating circumstances, I'll suspend the sentence here." Mr.

Hunter opened the gun and shook out the shell in his hand. "But from now on you won't let this pachyderm out of your sight. You will sleep with him and eat with him and ride in his truck. You will spend every hour of the day and night at his side."

"Yes, sir," said Harold. He hugged the trunk fiercely, and the tip curled up and touched his hand with its rubbery suction.

"And I want him in chains every moment that he isn't working. Every moment; is that clear?"

"Yes, sir."

"Now get him harnessed. A bit of work might drive this madness from him."

HAROLD UNFASTENED Conrad's collars. He took off the muddied blanket and the headdress made of feathers. In their place he put the harness, fussing with the straps, whispering into Conrad's ear. He was fastening the last buckle when he heard Flip coming toward him.

"Roman's okay," she said. "He's going to be fine."

Harold shrugged. He found that he didn't care too much one way or the other.

"That wasn't the first time he's been knocked in the mud." She put her weight on the harness, pulling out the slack. "Most times, though, it's people that do it."

It annoyed him that she was thinking of Roman when Conrad was nearly dead. "Well, Conrad's fine too," he said. "Mr. Hunter didn't quite shoot him."

She laughed. "Of course not. What makes you think he would?"

"Oh, the bullets," said Harold sarcastically. "The gun. He had it all loaded and everything."

"But he never woulda done it." She cinched the strap tighter. "He looks at elephants and all he sees is a great big heap of dollar bills. He might have liked to shoot him, but he couldn't."

"I don't know," said Harold.

"Sure. He just wanted to scare you."

Harold frowned. Nothing at the circus was the way it seemed to be. Like Mr. Happy's welded rings, the false-fronted tents and the banners that made Samuel too big and Tina too small, everything was fake if he looked closely enough to see it. Even Flip, he thought, could sometimes be two different people.

He pulled Conrad's trunk. It curled down and made a step for his boot. He stood there in the curve and let the elephant hoist him up.

"Anyway," said Flip, "Roman won't be working tonight. So you don't have to be scared of seeing him."

Harold settled in at the harness. "I'm not," he said, and started the elephant walking.

Chapter
42

In an hour the big top was just a pool of canvas at the foot of the center pole. And an hour after that, there was only a circle of sawdust in a patch of beaten grass, in a field littered with paper wrappings. Harold drove Conrad up the ramp to the back of the Diamond T. He fastened chains to the elephant's feet, then walked around the truck to the passenger's door.

It was high above him. He had to climb to a little step and balance there to reach the handle. Then the door swung out so fast that it almost knocked him off. And he stared into a cab that was dirty and warm, foul with a smell of sweat. The seat was torn in a hundred places, each one patched with cellophane tape that long ago had come unstuck, that crinkled now as Harold settled there. An old pillow, blotched with yellow stains, covered the driver's side. A little plastic doll, a naked woman, dangled from the mirror.

Harold stuffed his bag behind the seat. He dropped his ball and bat on top and sat down to wait for the driver. He tried to think who drove the Diamond T.

On either side the trucks went by. With the yellow jeep in the front, they started down the road, the tents and balloons and celluloid birds moving away in a convoy. Then the lot was empty, and at last the driver's door creaked open. Hands groped up at the wheel, thick fingers and dirt-caked nails. Harold stared across the seat. *Don't let it be Roman,* he thought. *Please, not Roman Pinski.* And into the cab came Wicks, the cook.

"What a day. What a frigging day," he said, settling into his seat. He *splattered* into his seat in his dirty clothes and bulge of fat. "When's this outfit going to start making some real money? Eh? Tell me that, kid. Are we going to have a bigger crowd tomorrow?"

Harold frowned. "Maybe," he said.

"Shoot! Just tell me yes or no."

"I hope so," said Harold, puzzled. "I guess we'll have to wait and see what happens."

Wicks glowered at him. "So that's the way you're going to be, is it?" He jammed the truck into gear, jammed it up to second, spun the wheel and brought it jolting to the road. He jammed it into third, into fourth, and wriggled down in the squealing springs of the bench. "You don't want to tell me, that's fine. But let's get this straight," he said. "I don't like talking, I don't like singing, I don't like wise guys driving with me."

Harold turned his head to the side window. He leaned against the door, watching fence posts pass. The cab was filled with the nauseating smells of grease and sweat. Harold rolled his window down.

"And I don't like wind, okay?" said Wicks. "So roll that window up."

They drove for thirty miles without a word, through darkness and a swirl of brown dust in the headlights. The road twisted through low brown hills, and Harold stared at the little plastic doll that swung, spinning slowly, in the middle of the windshield. He wished he was riding with Mr. Hunter again. Even more, he wished he was back with Samuel and Tina. They'd be playing their game of grocery stores, he thought, imagining Tina on her apple box. They'd be laughing as the miles went by, talking of the little house they'd have someday.

Harold watched at each curve for a gleam of headlights on the Airstream trailer.

"I guess you're rich," said Wicks, so suddenly that it startled him.

"Why?" he asked.

"Come on!" said Wicks. "I hear you albinos can sniff out gold like horses sniff out water. Ain't that right?"

"I don't know," said Harold. "What does gold smell like?"

"I told you, don't be a wise guy. You do it with sticks," said the cook. "Albinos dowse for gold, and ain't that the truth?"

"Not me," said Harold.

"Why not?"

Harold shrugged. "I never thought of it, I guess."

"Say," said the cook, his brows all wrinkled. "When it's dark, when it's pitch-black dark, can you see stuff?"

"No," said Harold. He could hardly see stuff in the daylight.

"But you can tell the future, can't you?"

"I can guess," said Harold.

"Aw, shoot!" The cook shrugged. He was sweating. "Then you're not a real albino. *Real* albinos, they dowse for gold. They live in darkness—in caves and stuff—and never come out except when it's dark. And they can see the future like nobody's business."

260

"Gosh," said Harold. "Can the Cannibal King do all of that?"

"Shoot, no. He's not a real albino either."

The big Diamond T rolled along, following the convoy. Bugs splattered on the windshield, and Wicks turned the wipers on. Yellow goo smeared across the glass.

"What is he?" asked Harold.

"The Cannibal King?" said Wicks. "He's just a frigging white guy, a sugar-cookie guy, same as you." He stomped on the clutch and wrenched at the gearshift. "Shoot! I bet you're no different than a regular fella except for your skin and your hair and stuff."

"Why are you angry?" asked Harold.

"There's nothing special about you!" Wicks shook his head fiercely. "Shoot! I guess there's nothing in this world that's better than anything else."

"I never said I was," said Harold.

The cook wiped his forehead with his fist. "I guess you didn't," he said. "I was only hoping that you were."

The truck dipped toward a creek and rumbled on a wooden bridge. A hawk flew across the headlights' glare. The cook shifted gears. The truck rattled past a crossroad, spitting gravel at the fenders, and followed along behind the convoy.

"How old are you?" asked Wicks.

"Almost fifteen," said Harold.

"Then you're fourteen. You got a family?"

"Not much," said Harold. He was slumped on the seat, his knees on the dashboard.

"What do you mean?" The cook clamped his fist on the gearshift. "You've got a dad, don't you?"

"No," said Harold. "He was killed in the war."

"That right?" The cook turned his head. "Tough break, kid." He squeaked his hands on the steering wheel, and when he spoke again it was a little less harshly. "But you've got a mother, don't you?"

"Sort of," said Harold.

"You do or you don't."

"Well, sure I do. But she's not the same. She used to be really nice, really pretty. And now she's . . . I don't know." He puffed out his cheeks and made himself look fat. "And she married this guy, a banker . . ."

"And you don't like him," said Wicks.

"No."

"So you ran away from home."

"I guess so."

"Was she glad you left?"

Harold hadn't thought of that. The idea made him sad, and then guilty. He hadn't been nice to her lately, not for such a long time that he couldn't remember *ever* being nice.

"You going to go back?" said Wicks, glancing down.

"Oh, I might." Harold picked at a bit of dry mud on his leg. "I don't know."

"Do you even know where you're going?"

"Oregon." Harold sighed. "My great-grandfather went there with nothing but a horse and a wagon, and he made himself rich. You can go to Oregon and start your life all over, and you can be whatever you want in Oregon."

"You're looney tunes," said Wicks. "It's no different than anywhere else."

"Sure it is." Harold picked away the mud and ground it to dust in his fingers. The convoy snaked

262

ahead of them, rising over the crest of a hill. "My brother's going to be there, and we're going to get some horses. We're going to ride up in the forests where it's cool and dark, and we're going to live like mountain men."

The cook laughed. It was a mean, short little laugh that made Harold feel small and childish. It was the sort of laugh his mother would use if he came home late from school. "I guess you've been with your *girl*-friend," she would say, and laugh like that.

The truck slowed, then jolted forward as the cook shifted gears on the hill. "There ain't no mountain men," he said. "Not anymore."

"No?" asked Harold.

"They'd lock them up in nuthouses if there were." Wicks wiped a hand across his mouth. "That sort of freedom's gone. It's finished."

"But Thunder Wakes Him," Harold said. "He—"

"Who?"

"The old Indian. He—"

Wicks laughed. "Big hairy deal. They *shoulda* locked him up, that guy."

"He goes wherever he wants," said Harold, almost to himself.

"Look, kid." Wicks tapped the steering wheel. "I went all the way to Germany fighting for freedom, and you know what? I think I killed it somewhere. The world's too fast now, too crowded up to let anyone go roaming free."

"But you do it," said Harold.

"Don't make me laugh." He shifted gears again, the convoy going ahead. "Let me turn this truck around and go the other way and you'll see how free I am. I wouldn't get to the county line before I was out of gas and out of food, and out of a job to boot."

The truck crawled up the hill, lurching into first. In the back, an elephant bugled. Ahead, with a flash of light, the Airstream passed over the crest and vanished, as though into the sky.

"Well, *they're* free," said Harold. "Samuel and Tina."

The cook laughed again, the same short bark. "A thousand people pay a dime a day to see them. That's a hundred bucks, kid. A hundred bucks a day, and what do they get? Nothing. Mr. Hunter—the nicest guy you'd ever find, but cheap as sin—he takes it all. Then he lets them sell their dumb little postcards, and he takes half of that as well 'cause that's the way a circus works. Free? Kid, they're welded to the circus. They'll die in the circus, and then Mr. Hunter will wrap them up in bandages and charge *two* dimes to see the mummies."

But their house, he wanted to say. *They're going to have a house with curtains and a cuckoo clock.*

"You should be back home," said Wicks. "Wherever that is. You should be doing your learning in school, learning how to work with adams. That's the future, kid: adam bombs and adam plants."

The cellophane crackled as Harold wriggled down in the corner. The sound of the engine, the swinging of the little doll, put him to sleep as the truck rumbled west. He slept until dawn, when he woke with the sun in his eyes.

It was so much like the day before, like so many other days, that he couldn't tell right away *what* day it was, or even which truck he was in. Then he blinked and saw that the cab was empty, and he got a sudden fright before he noticed that the little doll hung stiffly on its thread. The truck wasn't moving.

Harold pulled himself up and looked out the windshield at Oola Boola Mambo. The painted trailer sat right there, with a stubbled field beyond it.

A ticking sound came from under the hood, then a huge bang and a clatter behind him. It was like a puzzle to Harold that he solved half asleep. The engine was still hot, the ramp just falling open; the truck must have stopped only a moment ago. He climbed down from the cab and saw other people coming from other trucks, all rubbing their eyes or scratching their heads.

The work started right away, the building of a city. Harold, up on Conrad's back, watched it rise around him. It was a bit of a disappointment to see they were raising the very same city they had built at Trickle Creek, placing everything so perfectly that they might have moved the holes for the tent pegs too. He hadn't imagined that a circus could ever be the same thing twice. And when the children came, looking like the very same children that had come to Trickle Creek, he felt a little sorry for them at the way they thought it all so new and magical. They made him think of Farmer Hull's children—"dirt poor," his mother said—who got secondhand toys for Christmas and never thought a thing about it.

Harold made a hundred trips from the trucks to the field before the job was done. He watched for Roman but didn't see the boy until he rode Conrad to the elephants' tent. Canary Bird and Max Graf were there, chains at their ankles, tearing at a bale of straw. Other bales lay scattered on the ground, and Roman stood on a broken one, pitching the yellow-green stalks into the tent. He looked up, then jumped behind the bale.

Harold stared down. He had hoped to get off the elephant but now didn't dare.

"Don't come any closer," said Roman. He held the pitchfork like a shield. "I'm busting up the bales, okay? They'll eat a ton of it, a ton of it each."

At the sound of his voice, Conrad's head began to turn.

"Can you keep him there?" asked Roman. "He won't attack me, will he?"

Conrad growled.

"Don't let him come at me," said Roman, his voice shaking.

He suddenly seemed so small and frightened that he made Harold think of himself, of Harold the Ghost. And Harold reached down and patted the elephant's head. "Easy, boy," he said.

Conrad raised his trunk and bugled.

"Okay, I'm leaving," said Roman. He put down the fork and spread his arms apart. "I'm going, okay? But listen, um—Harold. I wanted to . . . I didn't tell you before . . . I . . ." His face looked old and miserable. "Thanks for . . ." He sighed. "Just thanks, okay?"

Harold nodded. He watched Roman leave, and a huge feeling of fright and dismay left him at the same time. It had always been with him, and suddenly it was gone, like a part of him torn away. It gave him that weightless sensation of an elephant rising below him—but made him feel empty in a way he didn't like. He must have been born feeling scared, he thought.

"Down trunk!" he shouted.

Conrad let him off, then attacked his own bale.

266

Soon there was green dust floating through the air, and bits of broken straw covered Conrad's back. Harold put a chain on him and sat down to wait for Flip.

He was sure she would come with his breakfast. She would carry a tray covered with plates, and they would have the picnic they'd missed before. But the bales of straw vanished into the elephant's mouths and she still didn't come. He wondered if she was angry at him, and then if she even knew he wasn't supposed to leave the elephants. He wondered if she was waiting for him, looking around the tent, thinking—maybe—that *he* was mad at *her*.

Harold got up and paced back and forth. The more he thought about it, the more he was sure Flip was waiting for him. He decided he'd better go for his breakfast, and paced a bit that way. But then he looked at Conrad and thought of Mr. Hunter. And he sat down again and waited.

The children came in groups. They stood and stared at the elephants. They stood and stared at Harold.

He pretended not to see them. He turned his back toward them but blushed at every laugh and shout, not sure if they were talking about him or the roses. So he got up and sat in the tent instead. He picked at straws, chewing stems, poking them into his mouth. Once, out of boredom, he poked one into his ear. And there he sat, with a straw sticking out of his head, when Flip finally came.

He heard her laugh and twirled around.

"What are you *doing*?" she asked. "You look like a monkey sitting in here. And Conrad's still got his harness on. Harold, why are you *sitting* here?"

"I was waiting for you," he said.

"Why?" she asked again, frowning.

Because I love you, he wanted to say. But he only blushed and said, "I don't know," and thought he sounded very stupid.

"You should be practicing," she said. "Do you know how close we are to Salem? Didn't you see the mountains?"

"No," he said.

She took him out and showed him. The two of them stood at the tent's front door, looking across the field. The sun was nearly overhead already.

"Look," she said, and pointed.

He put his hands up to his glasses. He held them like binoculars, squinting through the little cracks between his fingers. And he saw the mountains in the distance, a smudge of blue against the sky. They were small, pale, blurry mountains, but they seemed magnificent to Harold. Just looking at them made him feel tiny and huge, sad and happy all at once. It was something like the way he'd felt the first time he saw a Christmas tree, or the day a Flying Fortress thundered over the prairie, right above him, so low he might have touched it. He wanted to shout out loud, and he wanted to whisper too; he'd never seen a thing so wonderful.

"Is that Oregon there?" he asked.

"On the other side it is."

He sighed. "Gosh, they're beautiful mountains."

"Oh, never *mind* the mountains." She pulled his hands down from his eyes. "Can't you see how close we are to Salem? Aren't you worried that the roses won't be ready?"

"They will," he said. "You bet they will."

"I don't see how, if you're sitting here stuffing your head full of straw."

"Why are you angry?" he asked.

"Because you're not *listening*. And I don't think the roses are going to be ready."

"S-sure they will," he said, stammering.

"Then you'd better get to work," she said. "You'd better get your bat and ball and work and work and work."

"But I never had breakfast." His eyes were starting to jiggle. The mountains shimmered like blue fire, and he had to turn his head to see her. "And I'm not supposed to leave the elephants. Not even for a minute. That's what Mr. Hunter said."

"Oh, Harold, that's not what he *meant*, not every single second. You take everything so word for word."

He looked down at his boots.

"Well, go ahead," she said. "Get something to eat, and I'll take the harness off. But then you'd better get to work, 'cause you've let half the day go by."

"Gosh, I'm doing my best," he said.

"I know that, Harold."

Then he bit his lip and added softly, "And I don't think you should be telling me what to do."

"Then think for yourself," she said. "You're not a kid anymore, you know."

He sure felt like a kid. He felt like a stupid little kid as he walked by himself to the cook tent. Just two days ago he'd been so happy. He could remember it exactly, how Flip had danced him around in the river when Conrad learned to pitch. But then everything had fallen apart, and he couldn't get it back together. He didn't know *how* to put it back like that.

269

And then the mountains. He glared at them for a moment. He'd looked forward so much to seeing them, but Flip had hardly let him look. He had to *work,* she'd said. He had to *work, work, work.* If he didn't know better, he thought, he might imagine she cared more about that than she did about him.

His boot dislodged a stone. He stumbled on it, then stopped to kick it away. It skittered ahead across the field.

He felt cheated about the mountains. *There's nothing better than seeing the mountains when all you've seen is prairie,* Tina had told him. And he remembered driving along with her and Samuel, thinking that the first hills he'd seen were mountains. *When you see the mountains you'll know it,* she'd said. *And, say, you know what we'll do? We'll stop and have a party. We'll stop in the middle of the road if we have to, and—jeepers, creepers!—we'll have ourselves a party.*

Yeah, he was having a party all right. Going all by himself to the cook tent.

He booted the stone again, and it bounced along on his path. He almost hoped Tina would be at the tent. But then so would Samuel, and he wasn't sure he could talk to Samuel anymore. And that made him sad; he would have liked a geezer-squeezer. He would have loved a geezer-squeezer, but he couldn't see it ever happening again. Those days when Samuel would fold him in his huge arms seemed as distant as Liberty.

He caught up to the stone and gave it another kick. He kicked it all the way to the big tent with its open door and the wisp of smoke at its roof. And he went in and ate his breakfast, though it was only him and Wicks in there.

Harold sat in his usual seat, and the cook hollered at him from the counter. "There was someone asking after you."

"Flip?" said Harold.

"No." Wicks barked his mean laugh. "The Cannibal King."

Harold looked up. He hadn't thought the King even knew he existed.

"He asked if you were coming for breakfast. I told him you don't sit with the freaks anymore." Wicks came around the counter. He was eating bacon from a bunch of rashers that he held like flowers in his fist. "He got mad."

"He did?"

"He said, 'I'm not a freak, I'm the Cannibal King.' I thought he'd tear up the joint, that's how angry he was. The way I see it, and no offense, anyone who'd eat with Samuel and Wallo has got to be a freak." Wicks took another bite of bacon. "So, anyway, he wants to see you."

"Why?" asked Harold.

Wicks shrugged. "He's seen you walking around; he wants to meet you."

"When?"

"Anytime," said Wicks.

Harold pushed his breakfast away. He stood and stepped over the bench.

"You going now?" asked Wicks.

"I guess so."

The cook nodded. "Good idea. Get him when he's just finished eating."

271

Chapter

43

The door was shut on the painted trailer, and Harold couldn't find it at first. He felt his way down the wall, his hands sweeping over the picture as though pushing aside the jungle trees. Finally he found the hinges, then the handle, and knocked in the space between them.

Nobody answered.

He knocked again. He shouted, "Hello?" Then he twisted the handle, and the door sprang open with a squeak that scared him.

There was no one there; he could see that right away. The trailer had only one room, with a tiny closet for a toilet, but its roundness was hidden by walls that made it square inside. At one end was a table with a single chair pushed against it. There was a small counter with a sink and a hot plate. And most of the rest was taken up by the bed—a big, circular bed heaped with little pillows.

The walls were covered with pictures. There was one of autumn leaves, and one of a red-coated man on a horse, but mostly they were pictures of snow: a village in the snow, a frozen stream, an icy lake ringed by white evergreens. They were huge pictures, but fuzzy, and no matter how fast Harold blinked, he couldn't make himself see them clearly.

Harold closed the door. He felt wrong just looking and didn't even think of going inside. He'd expected a palace and found only a living room. But he wasn't disappointed. It made the Cannibal King seem somehow kind and gentle.

He got his bat and ball from the Diamond T and hurried back to the elephants' tent. It pleased him to find that Flip was there. She lay faceup on the last bale of straw, sunbathing with her hands hanging over its sides, the tails of her shirt pulled up. He could see almost all of her stomach, though he was too embarrassed to look.

She brought her hand up very slowly and put it on top of her eyes. "Where were you?" she asked.

"Just eating." He didn't want to tell her that he'd been in the Cannibal King's Airstream, but it was hard not to. He said, "Have you ever seen inside the Cannibal King's trailer?"

"Who'd want to?" she said.

He ignored that. "What do you think it's like?"

"Gee, I don't know," she said. "Sorta scary, I guess. Sorta creepy."

"Yeah. Full of bones," said Harold.

She looked at him between her fingers. "Not like that. At night you hear him sometimes. He bangs on things. I don't know what, he just sits in there and bangs. Like he's got a great big drum. That's what I bet you'd see, a great big drum."

Harold thought of the huge, round bed. Was it really a drum?

"But who cares?" She sat up, her legs swinging sideways. Harold saw the flash of skin before her shirt fell into place. Its whiteness surprised him. "So let's play baseball," she said.

"You and me?" asked Harold.

"And the elephants, silly."

"But *you* and me?" said Harold. "You'll stay and practice too?"

"Sure."

She smiled at him, and Harold felt the little shiver, the squirly feeling that he'd been frightened that he'd lost.

"I was thinking," she said. "I haven't been around you much. So let's keep going right until the matinee."

He practiced harder with Flip there. He practiced longer, too, without the breaks he took alone. They fielded and batted; they brought buckets of water for pitching practice. Then they set up a little game, and the disappointment started.

Conrad wouldn't pitch to the batter, but only to Harold. Then the fielder wouldn't bring in the ball. He'd only carry it around and around the bases.

"I thought they learned all this," said Flip.

"They did," said Harold. "But not together. They can bat and field and pitch, but it's all been separate games."

"Oh, great." She looked toward the mountains. Now, in early afternoon, they seemed bigger and closer.

"The roses'll learn," said Harold.

"Oh, they've just got to."

She was still gazing at the mountains when Harold walked behind her. His hands trembled as he touched her arms—both at once—above her elbows. Then Flip shook too, as though his hands had made her tingle.

"It means so much to me," she said.

274

Chapter

44

The matinee was over, and Harold practiced in the empty big top. He marked bases in the sawdust, the smallest diamond he'd ever made. Squeezed within the wooden blocks of the ring bank, it measured barely thirty feet from second base to home. The elephants seemed to crowd the space, but they looked enormous pressed together. It would make the game exciting.

He was practicing fielding when Flip came into the tent with a cardboard box that she put beside him on the ring bank.

"I brought you a present," she said. "Take a look at this."

Harold opened the flaps. He reached in and pulled out a mass of cloth and string and cardboard.

"I had the costume ladies make it," said Flip. "They're working on the others."

It was a baseball cap, elephant-sized, made of strips of red and white so that it looked a little like a circus tent with a big *P* on its front. Harold held the brim, and the cap draped down nearly to his knees.

"It's sort of extra extra extra extra large," said Flip, smiling. "Do you like it?"

"It's wonderful," said Harold. He got Conrad to kneel before him and stood on the wooden blocks of the bank to put the cap in place. It was eight times the size of a normal cap, but it seemed clownishly small on the elephant's head. And Conrad, with the strings tied under his chin, looked like a fat and clumsy child, more like Dumbo than a real elephant.

"What does the *P* stand for?" Harold asked.

Flip's head was turned away. "What do you think?"

"Pachyderms?"

"Sure. That's right. The Pachyderms."

She stepped up on the ring bank and started walking around it. "The roses look good in here," she said. "Let's try a game tonight, okay? A whole game, with Conrad pitching."

"He has to work," said Harold.

"Not tonight. We're staying until tomorrow. A two-day show."

Harold scratched his head. "I don't think they're ready for a game."

"But it's their last chance," she said. "Tomorrow night we move to this place that Mr. Hunter knows. It's called Elysium, and it's a big field full of grass and trees. There's a river and lots of space for the horses to run. We spread out the big top and scrub every inch of it. We clean the trucks and everything, 'cause Salem's the next stop. We have to look good in Salem."

"It's too soon," said Harold.

"There's nothing you can do about it." She looked down at him from the ring bank. "The Cannibal King's already gone. It takes him a whole day to mark the trail to Elysium."

Harold sighed. "Then we'd better get to work."

They practiced until the evening show, the wind

blowing warm from the mountains. The elephants were learning, but not very quickly.

And the wind kept rising. At night, with the darkness split only by spotlights, the tent seemed haunted to Harold. The rigging hummed with weird whistles and whispers. The whole tent shook, and the elephants were nervous. They fumbled the ball; they rolled their eyes white when the canvas flogged in ripples, like thunder over their heads. The practice was disastrous.

Flip sat and cried. She sobbed so softly that Harold didn't know at first she was crying. He saw her slumped at the edge of the ring bank, glowing in a spotlight's circle, and thought she was only thinking.

"I wish we had another day," he said.

Then she looked up, and her face was ragged with the tears she had shed. "Well, we *don't!*" she shouted. "And I was *crazy* to think this would ever work. Just crazy." She banged her hands on the wooden blocks. "You don't know how to teach elephants. You didn't know what an elephant *was* just a little while ago."

Harold blinked at her.

"I shoulda listened to Roman," she said. "He told me you couldn't do it."

Harold sagged on his feet.

She was nearly snarling at him. " 'I'm pretty good with animals,' " she said, shooting his own words back at him like arrows. " 'Maybe I could be a lion tamer.' " Then she laughed. It was an awful laugh. "How could I be so *stupid*?"

Harold sniffed. He pushed at his glasses with his fingertip. But he didn't say a word. He didn't say a single word as she got up and ran from the tent.

Conrad came over and nuzzled against him. The trunk breathed and sniffed across his chest, and he held on to it as tightly as he could.

"Can't you learn?" He tipped back his head to look at Conrad's eye. "Can't you try a little harder?"

He went back to work, just him and the elephants and the whispers of the wind. It was midnight when he took the roses to their tent, and the circus lot looked dead and empty. The wind swept dust along and rattled the tent poles. The spotlights in the big top seemed to swing across the canvas, and there was one other glow in all the dark world that Harold could see. A campfire burned at the edge of the field where Thunder Wakes Him must have bedded down. But Harold stayed with the elephants and settled among them in the straw. He slept cuddled up to Conrad, like a tiny white doll held in the elephant's trunk.

And that night the roses disappeared.

It wasn't yet dawn when Harold woke to find an empty tent. In the darkness he groped stupidly through the straw, as though he might somehow have merely overlooked seventeen tons of elephant. Then he stumbled out in his pants, pulling on a shirt, not bothering with his glasses. He shot from the tent into a pale gray glow of fading stars. The mountains were a jagged line of black.

It was easy to follow the trail of the elephants. They had smashed their way into the cook tent and emptied a sack of potatoes. They had trampled through a concession stand and drained the huge pot of water that had boiled cobs of yellow corn. From another stand they'd carried away a lemonade cooler; the whole thing had been torn from its spigot. And then they had wandered off to a corner of the field, where Harold found them as the sun came up—playing baseball by themselves.

Against the craggy, stony shadows, the elephants were big, black shapes standing in the field. They played slowly at first, almost lazily. Conrad dipped his trunk in the lemonade cooler, took the ball and pitched it out. Max Graf swung the bat and hit the ball, and Canary Bird went lumbering off to get it.

Harold watched and felt the sunlight on his back; he saw the mountains turn to red. With each pitch, Conrad shook his head and sneezed. Harold smiled to think the lemonade was tickling him. Then the pace increased, and the ball was pitched faster and batted harder, and the elephants, excited, began to trumpet.

Mr. Hunter came to watch. So did Wicks and Flip and Mr. Happy. So did the Frizzles, with their gray hair woolly from sleeping. They all stood in a row with the sun behind them, watching the enormous elephants playing a game for boys.

More people came, clowns and acrobats. The whole circus came to watch the roses, everyone but the freaks. Even the old Indian came, and he said—with tears in his eyes—that the elephants had looked like buffalo from a distance.

"Splendid," said Mr. Hunter. "You've done it, boy. Congratulations and felicitations. A hundred—a thousand!—felicitations."

Harold grinned. He felt hands thump him on the back. Wicks thumped him twice, then left to make breakfast, and the crowd slowly dwindled. Soon only Harold was left, but he didn't mind at all. He sat on the grass; he didn't have to practice. He sat watching and laughing as the elephants played baseball.

He didn't get up until the second bell sounded for breakfast. Then he found the tent so full of people, so busy, that he stood at the door looking in.

For some reason, no one was sitting. They stood in a huge bunch, like Canada geese on an autumn field, all talking at once. Harold squinted, letting his eyes adjust to the shadows. A face turned toward him, then another, and the tent that had shook with voices fell silent almost instantly. There was a peal of laughter, then nothing. Everyone was staring at him.

"Come in," shouted Mr. Hunter. "Harold, don't be shy!"

Then arms lifted, holding glasses. A cheer started and rang to the top of the tent. Wicks shouted, "Harold, you're first in the line."

And Harold felt as though cold water was pouring on his head. He was living his dream, exactly as the Gypsy Magda had said he would.

Chapter

45

All that morning, clouds rolled in from the west. They crept across the mountains and blotted them out. They covered the sky, and the rain started halfway through the matinee. It fell with an incredible roar on the big top. It flooded the field and streamed underneath the tent flaps, turning the sawdust ring to a brown sludge.

The old Indian splashed through his slow routine, then rode his chestnut horse out from the ring. He took off his headdress and put on a slicker. "I'll see you in Elysium," he told Harold.

"What about the evening show?" asked Harold.

"I don't have time." He was already moving off, into the rain. "I have a long ride to the valley of the Snake."

It was just as well that he missed it. The evening show was a disaster, the sort of night that Mr. Hunter called a lash-up.

A clown's firecracker exploded too soon, blowing the fake nose right from his face. He writhed on the ground as the people laughed and cheered, thinking it all a part of the act. Mr. Frizzle, at the performers' entrance, sent two other clowns into the ring to bring him off on a stretcher.

Then Mr. Frizzle himself tumbled from his trapeze.

He missed a handhold and hurtled down, bouncing from the rigging to land in the sawdust of the ring. His wife, her face stark white, swung above him, back and forth, like a tolling human bell. He was lucky and only twisted an ankle, but he wouldn't be back in the air in time for Salem.

And everyone waited for the third thing to happen.

"They go in threes," said Mr. Hunter. "It's always the same: a terrible trio of tragedy."

The tiny audience went out to a deluge that soaked them in an instant. No one stopped at the sideshow. No one could; the tents were like islands in a sea of mud. And the rain never stopped as the calliope played the breaking-down song.

On Conrad's back, Harold skidded poles and canvas through mud as thick as chocolate pudding. The trucks, when they left in a convoy, were like clods of dirt crawling through the rain.

Harold sprawled exhausted in his seat as the Diamond T growled through the darkness. The wipers swept back and forth, but the water from his clothes made the glass just as wet on the inside. Beside him, Wicks shifted gears.

"So you did it," said the cook. "You got those big, dumb things playing baseball. And just in time, I guess."

"I hope so," said Harold. "I won't know for sure until Salem."

"Well, Flip thinks you did it. She's pretty happy, isn't she?"

Harold shrugged. He had hardly seen her since the night before, when she'd fled crying from the tent.

"I see," said Wicks. "She's a nice kid, but she doesn't think about other people."

"Oh, she's good to *me,*" said Harold.

"'Cause it suits her. You can make Flip famous with those elephants. You can make her rich. She's *got* to be good to you."

"What do you mean?" asked Harold.

"Those elephants belonged to her daddy. When he died, Mr. Hunter took them, sort of. Said he'd buy them over time, a little bit every week. It was kind of nice of him then; they weren't worth much, a bunch of crummy dancing elephants. But now he owes her a bundle, 'cause of course he never paid for them."

The truck jolted, then swayed around a corner. "Now he's got no choice. He has to pay her, see?"

"But that's good," said Harold.

"Good for Flip. Not so good for Mr. Green."

Harold lifted his head at the sound of that name. He had wondered for a long time about the mysterious Mr. Green. "Where is he?" he asked.

"*What* is he, you mean," said Wicks.

"Huh?"

"*Lincoln* Green?" Wicks raised an eyebrow. "*Jackson* Lincoln Green?"

Harold shook his head.

"Money, kid." Wicks laughed. "Mr. Hunter thought his circus sounded better if he tacked on another name: Hunter and Green's. But there's too much Hunter and not enough green."

Harold sat glumly in his seat. He couldn't believe all Flip wanted was to make the elephants more valuable.

"Hey, don't be a sad sack," said Wicks. "It's not just Flip who's counting on those elephants. It's me and you and everyone. If they play ball in Salem, we'll all be in clover."

Chapter
46

The convoy left the rain behind and carried on in silvery moonlight. It wove through forests and foothills, bending north and south again. Then it crossed the mountains and started down toward the great, flat plain of the Snake River. It crossed the mountains as Harold slept.

He was disappointed when he woke and saw them behind him, black against the morning sun, awesome in their size. As the trucks threaded down toward the river, he looked back at every turn. "Did we really go over those?" he asked.

"Over them?" Wicks laughed his mean laugh. "Are you out of your mind? You go *through* them, kid. You go around them."

"Oh," said Harold. He'd thought the road would climb to their very summits, jagging up and down across the backbone of America. "But we're almost there now, aren't we? We're almost in Oregon now."

"Getting close," said Wicks.

"How close?"

"Tomorrow night. We'll leave Elysium in the evening, and the next thing you know, we'll be over the line."

Harold stared ahead. He saw one of the Cannibal

King's arrows fixed to a tree. The road twisted up a hill, down toward a bridge where a burst of arrows appeared along the railing. Then Wicks shifted down through his gears, and the Diamond T swung to the left, following the convoy down a steep grade.

A dark pine forest closed around them. The road narrowed until branches scraped with a screech down the side of the truck. Other roads crossed theirs in all directions, and the red arrows were everywhere. Then the trees fell away on his right, and Harold looked down a hundred feet to a vast green field below him.

"Elysium," said the cook.

A river twisted through it. A steam train, puffing smoke, crawled across a trestle. Then the trees closed in again, and the Diamond T, its motor growling, went down the hill, around a bend and out to the field of grass. It was so green and thick that Harold wanted only to lie in it, to stretch out on his back and do nothing at all.

He watched through the windshield as the convoy stopped in a ragged line. Doors flew open, and a swarm of people flung themselves into the grass. But Mr. Hunter came striding down, shouting orders and waving his hands.

"Pitch the cook tent," he said. "Let's go, everyone. Get the canvas out, the elephants ready."

He was met with a chorus of groans from the roustabouts and riggers. Little clumps of dirt sailed toward him from every direction. But the people got up and started to work.

Harold stepped down from the cab and met Wicks behind the truck. They opened the doors, and the smell of elephants came out. A fat bee buzzed around

Harold's head, flying spirals past his hair when he tried to chase it off.

Wicks laughed. "This place is full of bees."

Max Graf and Canary Bird were set free to root through the field. Harold felt sorry for Conrad, who turned his eyes balefully toward the grass as he knelt to get his harness on. "Don't worry. You'll have lots of time to play," said Harold.

All along the line of trucks, doors were creaking, panels thudding open. Flip turned the horses loose; she sent them away with a shout, and they galloped off with the mountains behind them, their white manes flying.

The tents were pitched slowly, cautiously, with a great deal of shouting and anger. Roustabouts who sang at their work every day now went at it like sulking mules. There were a tension and an awful feeling of dread; everyone, from Mr. Hunter down to the boy who inflated balloons, knew that another accident would happen soon to complete the string of three.

Harold was especially careful. He had lived his dream; he had seen the beast that feeds with its tail. He was sure a death would follow, as certainly as the man in trouble had come from the storm. And somehow, he thought, it would have to involve Roman, the angry boy in the Gypsy Magda's crystal ball. He rode Conrad with an unusual caution, plodding through his labors.

Worried riggers fumbled at their work. A guy rope on the cook tent snapped loose from its stake, and the heavy center pole swung wildly side to side. Workers scrambled from the canvas at its base like fleas from a wet dog as it tilted, swayed and toppled over, nearly crushing Wicks. A job that usually took an hour stretched to three on this day, and by noon the heat was staggering.

When at last the tents were up, people talked in only grunts and shouts. The roustabouts did their laundry in the little stream, and an argument over a pair of socks ended in a fistfight.

Harold led the elephants to a willow grove beside the river. They tore the branches off and gorged themselves; they lashed at their backs with the fronds.

It was too hot to play baseball. Harold lay in the grass, his back against a tree. The sun made mirages out of the trees and the mountains around them. The air shimmered in the heat so that Flip, when she came, looked as shiny as an angel.

"You're not practicing," she said.

"The heat," said Harold. He waited for her to snap at him, to tell him to get up anyway.

But she laughed. "It is kinda hot," she said, and wiped her forehead with her sleeve. "I guess we can wait until evening."

"Aren't you angry?" asked Harold.

"No. Of course not," she said.

Harold frowned; he would never understand her. Then she sat beside him and twirled her finger in the grass.

"Harold," she said. "There's something I haven't told you." Her hair fell over her eyes. "When my father died—"

"Mr. Hunter took the elephants. I know," said Harold.

Her head snapped up. She looked at him, then went back to twirling grass. "Yeah. But that's not all. You see, I got pretty close to Roman then. Pretty close, and . . ."

Harold felt his heart sink. He could actually feel it falling, just snapping away from whatever held it and plopping into his stomach like a big pudding.

"Well, we're sorta going to get married," said Flip.

Harold wondered if his would be the death that followed, if he would just drop dead with a broken heart. He said, "How do you 'sorta' get married?"

For a moment she blushed. "We're waiting for a bit. We decided that we'd better wait until—"

She stopped.

But Harold knew the rest. "Until you get some money."

"Yeah." She sighed. But then she faced him squarely and took his hands. "But listen, Harold. You can't think I was just trying to use you, 'cause I wasn't. You're a nice guy, just the sweetest guy, and I really do like you lots."

He tried to turn his head away so that she wouldn't see him crying. But she leaned across him.

"I *do*," she said. "Why do you think I'm telling you now? Why don't I wait until Salem?"

"Because I've taught the elephants everything," said Harold. "I've got them all ready, and anyone can do the rest. Anyone!"

"No," she said. "Oh, no. It's because you *are* such a nice guy. I thought how happy you'd be in Salem, and then how sad you'd get when you learned about Roman. That's why I'm doing it: so you won't be sad."

"Gosh, thanks," said Harold. "Gee, it's great not being sad."

She almost laughed. She *did* smile. Then she took

288

his glasses off and folded them. She wiped his tears away with her fingers. "You have the most incredible eyes," she said, very gently.

Harold shivered. No one had ever looked right in his eyes without the glasses there in front.

"You won't believe me now," said Flip. "But it's true; I wish I'd met you sooner. I wish I'd met you a year ago."

The Ghost sighed. "You wouldn't have liked me then," he said. "No one liked me then."

They sat together for a little while. Her tanned fingers rested on his white ones. A bee came buzzing between them and darted off across the grass. The elephants covered themselves with willow branches. Then Flip got up. She said, "I better go."

Harold stayed where he was. Hours passed, and he didn't move. He didn't even look up until he heard a splashing in the water.

Through a tunnel the willows made, their branches overhanging, rode Thunder Wakes Him in his feathered bonnet, his lance held at a slant. The big chestnut horse plodded wearily along, stumbling on stones that clinked and rumbled underneath the surface.

The old Indian urged the horse up to the grass, stepped down, and took his medicine bundle from its back. He put it on the ground, and the horse sagged, exhausted, its head and tail drooping down, its knees half bent.

"I had to run him hard," the old Indian said. "We came a ways—a long ways—and this is the first time that we have stopped."

"Since I saw you last?"

"Yes."

Harold leaned his head against the willow trunk. "Gosh," he said.

The old Indian sat beside him, just where Flip had sat. "You look sad," he said.

"No wonder," said Harold. His girlfriend was going to get married.

"I just passed the camp of the Cannibal King. He asked if I had seen you."

"Where is he?" asked Harold.

"Downriver. His trailer is pushed among the trees."

Harold shifted sideways as the old Indian leaned against the tree. Their shoulders touched.

"Are you frightened to meet him?" asked Thunder Wakes Him. "It is all right to be frightened about something that is hard to do."

"I don't think I'm frightened," said Harold. "I'm sort of . . . I don't know. Sort of worried, I guess."

The old Indian nodded. He faced east and Harold faced north. "I was like that with General Custer when the warriors came and said he was riding toward us. 'The Son of the Morning Star!' they shouted; he was just beyond the hills. Oh, I had a terrible fear that day. I put on my war paint, and my hands were shaking so that I drew my straight lines like lightning bolts. I gave away everything that I owned—my horses, my wives, my lodge, a pretty rawhide doll I was given as a child. I said, 'Here, take it all; I won't be back for this.' I thought the Son of the Morning Star would kill me just by looking at me, he was that big and that powerful. Fire and bullets would come from his eyes, that was what I thought."

Harold turned his head. He saw the old Indian in profile, his hooked nose and his braids hanging down.

"And then I saw him dead by the Little Bighorn, I saw him dead on the prairie grass, and I thought that the sun must have shrunk him like a raisin; he was a little man, that was all. He was just a little man with a big mustache, a funny man to look at."

The old Indian rubbed his shoulders against the poplar bark. "So you see, there is nothing to be frightened of. A man is only a man, no matter what you call him."

Harold swallowed. "Will you watch the elephants?" he asked.

"Yes," said Thunder Wakes Him.

Chapter 47

Harold walked down the stream. He hoped to follow it straight to Oola Boola Mambo but had to
veer away when he saw a group of people in the river
and thought Flip might be among them. Suddenly
there seemed a lot of people he didn't want to see,
including Flip and Roman and the Gypsy Magda. He
crossed the grass on a route that circled wide around
the cook tent. He was the Ghost again, stumbling over
the field, tiny and white in the vastness of it. He
skulked from tree to tree and hurried, when he had to,
across the open spaces, with the toes of his boots stub-
bing on the ground, his hands reaching out for the
next bit of shelter.

His eyes twitched. The grass was a blur at his feet.

He wished he had ridden the elephant. On Conrad
he could have gone straight to the painted trailer, right
to its door like a rajah to meet a sultan. On Conrad he
would be grand and important, not the shy, frightened
boy he was on the ground.

But it was too late to go back. Already he stood at
the Diamond T, resting by the rear wheels. There was
only a gap of twenty yards he had to cross, an open
space of grass and trees, and he'd reach the cottonwoods that grew along the river. He could see the

Airstream trailer at the edge of those trees, the Gypsy Magda's truck beside it, and a gleaming black shape that had to be the Cannibal King's enormous car.

Harold launched himself across the gap. He stumbled around a tree and around another, clutching their trunks. He held on to them as a climber would, finding handholds on a treacherous slope. He reached a third tree, a fourth, and peered around it at the cottonwoods, then down at Princess Minikin.

She sat in the shade below the branches, holding a comic book that looked as big as poster boards in her doll-like hands. "Well, look who's here," she said. "Hi, kiddo. I haven't seen you in the longest time."

"I've been really busy," Harold said.

"Oh, I know you have. Everyone's talking about it." She rolled the comic into a tube. "The greatest thing they've ever seen. And poor Flip; she's just beside herself. She can hardly wait to get to Salem and show it to the scouts."

"The scouts?" said Harold.

"Why, sure. Barnum and Bailey always sends a pair of scouts to Salem."

Harold felt a twinge inside. Flip still hadn't told him everything.

"It's big of you to do that," said Tina. "I always knew you were a swell guy, but to set her up like this so she can get away from here? Gosh, a lot of people just wouldn't do that."

"No, I guess they wouldn't," said Harold.

"Everyone here likes her so much; I guess Mr. Hunter will miss her like nuts, the poor dumb lug."

Harold nodded. He sat on the grass beside the little princess.

"It's swell of you, it really is." She tapped her toes with the comic book. "Say, she'll be famous now, and wouldn't her parents be so proud? The Pharaohs! And those elephants with their cute hats, that great big *P* in front."

Ghosts never cry. He told himself that as the trees and the trucks and the tents grew fuzzy around him. So she had fooled him; all along she'd fooled him with promises and lies, brushing away his fears with her charming little smile and her charming little touches. Her unnatural charm, he realized. *Beware the ones with unnatural charm.* And all along he'd thought the Gypsy Magda had meant the freaks.

"Say, what's the matter?" Tina asked. "Gosh, you look awful. You look so sad."

She stood up. Her strange face was wrinkled with worry. "Didn't you know?" she said. "Oh, Harold, didn't you know all this?"

He shook his head. He didn't know anything.

"Gee, I'm sorry," she said.

"It doesn't matter." He tried to laugh, but only snorted dribbles through his nose.

She took his hand and pulled against it, such a little tug that she made him smile. "Never you mind, Harold," she said. "She's not so great anyway. Just a snippet, that's what she is. Say, you come and sit with us, and maybe Samuel will give you a squeeze."

"I was going to meet the Cannibal King," he said.

"You were? Oh, gee, I'm glad to hear that. You go and see him and then come by. All right?"

He let her pull him up, then stood beside her in a slouch, so as not to seem too tall. "What should I say?" he asked. "What should I do?"

"Just go up and say hi."

"To a king?"

"It's what *I* do," she said.

"But you're a real princess," said Harold.

She looked up at him, smiling at first and then serious. "Say," she said, "you don't believe that, do you?"

"You're not?" he asked.

She put both her hands on his. "You poor guy," she said. "That's just a gimmick, just a hook. They call me Princess Minikin to get the people in, because it's not enough to say, 'Come and see the little midget lady.' Gosh, Harold, I didn't think you believed it."

"And Samuel?" he asked. "Isn't he a fossil?"

"No," she said, her little head shaking sadly.

Harold sighed. He slouched down even more. "I'm stupid," he said. "I'm dumb as a post."

"You're not!" said Tina. "You're a real sweet guy who believes what people tell you. You see the good part of everything, and maybe sometimes you get a little mixed up, but gee, I think you're swell."

Chapter

48

Harold walked toward the cottonwoods, toward the black car that caught the sun on its fenders. Somewhere behind it was the trailer, its painted sides blurred too closely with the forest. And then he heard the banging.

It was loud and steady. Not the boom of a drum, but a thudding like the roustabouts' sledges. It stopped, and door hinges creaked.

Harold stood by the car. On the front of its hood was a chrome bird so beautifully made that it might have been real. But it had snapped from its little silver stand, lying now with one wing touching the metal, dangling by a wire. And the rest of the car was just as shiny and just as battered as the bird. The fenders that swooped down into wide running boards were dented and torn. The sparkling grille was shattered in the middle, and one of the lights that stuck out from the car like bug's eyes was missing altogether. A bit of fur was stuck to the wheel well; a cluster of feathers was wedged in the bumper.

He walked right around the car. There were dents everywhere, but they'd been polished and waxed as though they didn't exist. Then he bent down to peer into the driver's window. And just as his hands touched the glass, he heard a shout from the forest.

Branches crackled and broke. Harold spun around. And out from the cottonwoods came the Cannibal King, slashing a long machete over his head. Under his arm he carried a skull that was stained an awful bloodred at the back. He was naked to the waist.

Harold fell against the car. He gasped huge breaths.

But the Cannibal King ran right past him, then back in a circle, thrashing at the air with his glistening machete. "Get away!" he shouted. "Go on, get out of here!"

Then suddenly he stopped, his head tilted slightly to the left. His eyes were the same watery blue as Harold's. And the Ghost and the Cannibal King both seemed to gaze off toward the trees, but studied each other with the same curious look. It was almost as though only one of them was real and the other a reflection in a funhouse mirror.

Harold gazed at the man he had come so far to see, at the wild and unruly hair, at the bulging arms, at the rolls of fat that reminded him of an overfilled cone of ice cream scoops. They were white—all white—even whiter, he thought, than him.

The Cannibal King twitched. He tossed his head, then sliced his machete through the air above it, and up again, beside his ear. "Bees," he said. "Geez, I hate bees."

Harold smiled. He heard the bee whining around the Cannibal King. He saw that the skull under his arm wasn't really a skull, but half a watermelon so pale that it was almost white.

The Cannibal King smiled back. "Hello," he said. "I'm the Cannibal King."

"I'm Harold," said Harold. "I came from Liberty. I came all this way to find you."

"You didn't look too hard, eh?"

"I tried," said Harold. "I—"

"It's okay. I understand."

The bee came to Harold. It circled his head, and he swatted it away. The bee dropped low to the ground, zigzagging from the forest to the sunshine.

"Would you like to come to Oola Boola Mambo?"

Harold grinned. He nodded and followed the Cannibal King between the cottonwoods, toward the little trailer that he now sensed was all there'd ever been of Oola Boola Mambo. "You're not really a cannibal," he said to the broad white back in front of him. "Are you?"

The white hair shook. "But I wish I was. Sometimes, eh? There's a lot of people I wouldn't mind stewing in a pot."

"That language you speak," said Harold. "What is that?"

"Rand McNally," said the King. "I rattle off the names of islands, eh? I made up some words myself."

"The box of bones?"

"Fake," he said. "Everything's fake. It's all a part of the show."

In less than a minute they came to the trailer. The door was open, the grass below it strewn with arcs of watermelon rinds, their inside curves worried down to lime-green linings.

"You want some?" asked the Cannibal King. He

held out the huge half that Harold had thought was a skull.

"Sure."

The machete glinted. The blade rushed up and, swooping down, sliced a wedge away. The point squished in through the red pulp, and the Cannibal King lifted it and held it out.

"Thanks," said Harold.

Another wedge flew off, and Harold sat with the Cannibal King on the steps of Oola Boola Mambo. They leaned forward to let the juice dribble on the ground.

"Do your eyes hurt?" asked the Cannibal King. "In the sun, I mean, eh? Do they hurt?"

"Yes," said Harold.

"Do things look funny to you? Sort of blurred, and you see them best sideways?"

"Yes." Harold nodded with the watermelon.

"And the other kids. Do they tease you? They call you names, eh?"

"You bet," said Harold.

"Buggers, eh?" The Cannibal King ate his watermelon in only three bites, then tossed away the rind. "Well, you know something? It gets easier, Harold. A little bit, anyway. Those kids grow up and they start seeing that they've got all sorts of things wrong with them, too. Then they stop calling you Snowman and Frosty, because they're afraid you'll turn on them—eh?—and call them Big Ears or something. You see how it works?"

"Yes, sir," said Harold. No one had ever called him Frosty or Snowman, and he found himself smiling at the picture it gave him: the Cannibal King bulging and white like a snowman.

"And you know something else?" The Cannibal King wiped his mouth with the back of his hand. "Sometimes I'm glad I'm on the inside of that tent instead of outside gawking in. It's hard to explain. But me and Samuel and Tina and so on, at least we're fake on the *out*side. Those other people, they're fake on the *in*side. You see what I'm saying?"

"I think so," said Harold. He remembered looking at Samuel by the swollen river, looking at those dark eyes and seeing a different person behind the hair and ugliness.

"Those other people," said the Cannibal King, "they're normal to look at, but inside they're *really* freaks. All twisted up, ugly, mean little freaks."

"I know," said Harold.

The Cannibal King smiled. "I know you know." He stood up, and the trailer bounced flat on its springs. "So, you want to come inside?"

"Sure," said Harold. "For a minute."

The Cannibal King went first. He squeezed himself into a corner to let Harold fit through the door. "Welcome to Oola Boola Mambo," he said.

Harold didn't admit that he'd already seen inside it. He let the Cannibal King go proudly from one belonging to another. But all the time, he stared at the table. There was a jigsaw puzzle there, half finished, a big, heavy mallet resting on top of the pieces. It was a picture of boys playing hockey on a winter field.

"I do jigsaws," said the Cannibal King.

"How do you see them?" asked Harold.

"Wow!" The Cannibal King slapped his forehead.

"No one's ever asked me that before. No one, Harold. They think it's a dumb thing for a grown man to do, but they don't know how hard it is when you can't see the little pieces. It's a brainteaser, eh? Well, you know something? I do it by feel, Harold. I do some of it with my eyes closed."

Harold squinted at the picture. He leaned over it, touching it, and saw that some of the pieces were jammed into place—into the wrong places—hammered down with their little cardboard tabs all bent and broken.

"I've done others," said the Cannibal King.

Harold looked again at the pictures on the wall. Every one was fuzzy, because the pieces didn't line up.

"They remind me of my home," said the Cannibal King. "I come from Canada. From a little town in Canada."

Harold moved from picture to picture. He passed *voyageurs* in a bark canoe and stopped in front of the red-coated man that he saw now as a Mountie on a fine black horse. They were pictures of Canada, all shaky and blurred. They were exactly as the Cannibal King would have seen them in life. The older man's eyes, Harold thought sadly, were even worse than his own.

"How do you drive?" he asked.

"Slowly," said the Cannibal King. "Like this." He looked at Harold with his eyes squinted, his cheeks almost touching his eyebrows. "I get terrible headaches, but I like driving, eh? I like the freedom of that."

"Me too," said Harold.

"Well, that's about it." The Cannibal King seemed

embarrassed now. "That's all there is to Oola Boola Mambo." He got a T-shirt and tugged it over his head. "Now let's go see your friends."

They walked together through the trees, two cream-colored people with hair like sunlight, one small and frail, one huge and fat. They both ate pieces of watermelon and dropped the rinds behind them.

"Holy smokes!" said Samuel, rising from a chair. "It's the Stone People of Oola Boola Mango."

The Cannibal King laughed. "Mambo," he said.

"Mumbo jumbo, you mean," said Samuel.

The Cannibal King cuffed Samuel on the arm, and Samuel cuffed him back, and the two of them wrestled like bear cubs. Then Samuel pulled away and smiled at Harold. "Welcome back," he said.

It was almost evening. The waves of heat were gone, and Harold saw that his arms had goose bumps in the coolness from the mountains. Tina was there, and the Gypsy Magda, and they came toward him.

"Jolly jam!" shouted Samuel. "Come on!" He waved them in. "Let's squeeze this little geezer."

They crowded around him, and Harold cried as they rocked and hugged him. And then they all turned away for a moment, to let him wipe his eyes, and they sat together in the grove of trees. He felt a part of the group, shoved into it like one of the Cannibal King's jigsaw pieces.

"So, Harold," said the Cannibal King. "How did you come to be here, eh?" And Harold started to tell him. But Tina interrupted, and then Samuel, and they talked about the trip he'd made, every mile of every day.

"Remember the filling station?" Samuel asked, and talked about that.

"And remember the farmer?" said Tina, and talked about *that*.

"And remember," said Samuel, "when we stopped by that schoolyard? The one with the swings and the roundabout?"

"Oh, I loved that roundabout," said Tina.

"And then we played baseball," said Samuel. "Didn't we, Harold?"

"Yes." He nodded. "We played Five Hundred."

"And the Gypsy Magda got lost in the grass."

Bells and bracelets jangled. "Ach, I did not," said the Gypsy Magda. "I only played at getting lost."

Samuel laughed. He sighed, and it seemed to take the breath from everyone. They all sat there, smiling at their shoes.

Harold rubbed his arms. He stood up and stretched. "I have to get back," he said. "The elephants are loose."

"The elephants are loose!" cried the Cannibal King, in a laughing way. "You even talk like one of the Stone People."

Harold smiled. He felt shy, standing with everyone sitting. "I'm not supposed to leave them," he said.

"We understand," said Tina.

The Cannibal King too stood up. "Is it true?" he asked. "Do they play baseball?"

"Yes," said Harold. "They're pretty good."

"And they're going to play in Salem?"

"I don't know." He kicked the grass with his boot. "I don't know what to do about that."

"Let it happen," said the Gypsy Magda. "The future is like the grass you stand on; if you try to cut it down, it only grows again. But faster."

"Do you really know the future?" Harold asked.

She nodded. "Yes, I do."

"How old are you?" he asked. She seemed, to him, as old as Earth. But she smiled now, and in her withered and toothless face he saw that she was too shy to tell him, and that she was far, far younger than he had ever thought.

"Twice your age," she said. "A little less, maybe. A little less than twice your age. But now you had better go."

Harold started off across the field. He heard Samuel say, "Wait a minute. You know what I'd really like to do? I'd like to play baseball with an elephant."

"Yeah, so would I," said Tina. "Can we do it, Harold? Can we all go?"

Harold turned back. "Sure," he said.

"Let's take my car," said the Cannibal King.

They piled into it, all in the front, and drove across the field in that big, bashed-up boat of a car. Jostled by the ruts and holes, laughing like children, they passed the cook tent and headed for the willows.

They plowed through grass as high as the fenders. The six horses galloped across their path from left to right, and the elephants appeared ahead, reaching with their trunks for the highest branches.

"It's like Africa here," said Samuel.

"Oh, you lug." Tina laughed. "You've never been to Africa."

The old Indian came out to meet them from the little grove of trees. He held up a hand, his fingers spread apart, as the Cannibal King stopped the car.

"Hi, Bob!" shouted Samuel, tumbling from a door. "Hey, Bob!" said the Cannibal King, coming out another.

The old Indian nodded. "What are you doing?" he asked.

"We're going to play baseball," said Tina. "Say, you want to play?"

"Sure," he said. "How do you play baseball?"

Harold got the bat and ball, and the elephants came on the run, trumpeting eagerly. He drew out a diamond with the end of the bat, and for bases they put down their shoes. Samuel's, being the biggest, made the pitcher's mound. He set them carefully in place. "What are the teams?" he asked.

"I don't know," said Harold.

"How about the freaks against the elephants?"

Harold frowned. "Which team am I on?"

"What do you think?" said Samuel. "The elephants, of course."

The Cannibal King was the pitcher, and the elephants batted. They hit long, looping drives and went trundling around the bases. They bugled past first, then bugled past second, squashing the shoes as they ran in a great jiggle of hide.

Like the old Indian, the Gypsy Magda had never played baseball. She stood in deep right field, and every time the ball was hit she ran toward it with her scarves flowing back, her bracelets and bells all a-tinkle. The freaks shouted and laughed; they tagged the elephants out by their knees and their tails. Even Tina tagged out Conrad, running behind him from second to third, flinging herself forward to touch his massive heel.

The laughter and the trumpeting brought other people to the corner of the field. Wicks came and played second base; Mr. Hunter came, as thin as the bat itself, and knocked the ball right across the river. The roustabouts joined in; Mr. Frizzle came on his crutches, swatting at the ball like a golfer. People who hadn't done more than grumble at each other for almost a day now played side by side, the best of friends again. They switched teams, and switched again, as the score went up and up.

And the elephants fielded and batted. The elephants stampeded around the bases.

Then Flip came, and Roman was with her, and they stood at the edge of the trees, only watching the game.

Harold was waiting to bat. He saw Samuel crouched at third, swaying on his shoeless, hair-covered feet. Wicks was running for the elephants, and he waited on third for Conrad to bat. Never before had the two of them said so much as a word outside of the cook tent, but now they joked together, and Samuel's crooked teeth flashed in a grin.

Mr. Hunter pitched. His thin arm whipped the ball across the plate. Conrad swung at it; he swung harder than the Sultan of Swat. He swung so hard that he reeled around in a half circle as the ball went whistling past. A jeer, a laugh, a cheer and a trumpet: They rose together from the field, one tremendous sound that filled the valley of the Snake and echoed from the mountains.

"It's something to see," said Thunder Wakes Him, next in line past Harold. "I saw a million buffalo pass here once; they took six days going by. Once I saw the valley—every blade of grass—burning in a fire. Once I saw a wagon train draw up in a circle here, and a man played a real piano as the others danced a ballroom dance. But I never thought I would see anything like this."

"It's wonderful," said Harold.

Conrad thumped the bat on the ground. Mr. Hunter pitched again. The elephant swung. And with a sound like cannons the ball went soaring far across the field. Conrad headed off for first.

"Drop the bat!" shouted twenty voices.

The old Indian sighed. "Do you know what you have done?" he asked.

"It's not me, really," said Harold. "It's the elephants."

"No, my friend." The old Indian put his hand on Harold's shoulder. "It's you. You have brought the people together. You are just like White Buffalo Woman. You have made all the people one."

"Not everyone," said Harold. "Not quite."

He stepped out of the batters' line and shambled across the field. It was getting dark and the shadows fooled him. He tripped and caught himself and carried on. He crossed to the trees, to Flip and Roman.

They were standing close together, but Flip moved half a step away.

"Hi, Harold," she said.

"Hi," he told her.

Roman only glowered at him.

"You did it, huh?" Flip grinned with unnatural charm. "You got them ready, and a day early."

"Think the scouts will like it?" Harold asked.

Her eyes went wide, her eyebrows up. "You know all that?" she asked.

"Most, I think."

"The Gypsy Magda, right? I knew she'd tell you."

"Tell me what?"

"That she made me go and talk to you."

Harold smiled to think the Gypsy Magda had tried to help him. "No, she didn't tell me that," he said. Then he squinted sideways at Flip. "You should come and play."

"You want me to?"

"I guess. You were pretty nice to me, and . . ." He shrugged. "A lot of people weren't. Not right then."

"You're sweet, you know that?" She leaned forward as though she meant to kiss him, but Harold pulled away.

"Roman can play too. I don't care."

"No way," said Roman. "I'm not going near those elephants. Not now and not never."

"Oh?" said Harold. "I thought you'd have to look after them from now on. I thought you'd have to wash them and dress them and clean up their stables and everything. I thought you'd be the elephant boy for Flip and the Pharaohs."

"In a pig's eye," said Roman. He backed away. "Screw you, Whitey."

"Wait!" cried Flip.

"And you, too," shouted Roman. He kept on going. "I'm not going to be anybody's stable boy."

In a moment he was gone. Then Flip pouted and stamped her foot on the grass. "Well, thanks a lot," she said. "Who told you he'd be the stable boy?"

"No one," said Harold. "I was just making trouble, I think."

Chapter
49

The sun was nearly down; the shadows of the players stretched in purple bands along the grass. The game might have ended then if someone had kept track of the score. But nobody had, and so an extra inning was played in a clear and starry twilight.

With one out, Harold batted. He closed his eyes and batted, and Harold never missed.

The ball bounced off Samuel's shoes. It shot between Wicks' legs and caromed off Mr. Frizzle's crutch. Harold headed for first.

The Cannibal King chased down the ball in center field. He threw it to the Gypsy Magda, who was jingling in from the right. She fumbled it, and Harold headed for second amid such a shouting and a cheering that he imagined himself running for the Dodgers.

A roustabout snatched the ball and threw it underhand to second, where Tina waited with her hands held out. Harold raced the ball. He couldn't hope to see it in the fading light, against a sprinkle of stars that seemed to him to whirl across the sky. But he *felt* it there, and he hurried, and he and the ball arrived pretty much together.

"You're out!" shouted Tina. She capered around the shoes. "You're out, kiddo! You're out like a light!"

"Safe!" shouted the old Indian.

It started quite a ruckus. Everyone but the Gypsy Magda argued that he was safe or out, all at the same time, all at the tops of their voices. Conrad, who was waiting with the bat, thumped the plate and whistled like a steam train.

Mr. Hunter made the ruling; he made all the rulings that seemed too close to call. "The boy was clearly at the shoes," he said. "I saw him hasten there, and I say the boy is safe."

The freaks groaned. The elephants trumpeted—all the players on that side trumpeted like elephants.

The ball made its way from hand to hand, back toward the pitcher. Tina was grinning up at Harold. "Gee, I'm proud of you, kiddo," she said. "I've never been so happy in all my life."

Then Conrad hit a pop fly. The red-and-yellow ball went up like a rocket, straight from the plate, and the freaks closed in on Samuel's giant shoes. Side by side on second base, Harold and Tina watched with amazement as the players tumbled into the infield. The Gypsy Magda went by with her bracelets jangling. The Cannibal King slid past like a great white bar of soap. And the ball disappeared against the stars.

Conrad dropped the bat. It was the first time that he had ever done it. He dropped the bat and lumbered off to first.

"Stop!" shouted Harold. He'd never thought of teaching rules to roses. "Go back. Go back."

But Conrad was only gaining speed. His ears flapping, his head shaking, he trundled on.

And the ball fell out of the stars.

"Catch the elephant out!" shouted Wicks. An

immense shout swelled through the freaks. "Catch the elephant out!"

Conrad rounded first. Tilted over, his feet hammering, he swept around the corner with his trunk scraping on the ground.

"Stop!" shouted Harold.

Tina doubled up with laughter. "You'd better run," she said. "He's going to overtake you."

Harold thrust his hands out. "Go back!" he shouted, laughing himself.

"Run, kiddo!" Tina pushed him. Hunched down, she shoved him with her shoulder and caught him on the knees.

The Gypsy Magda spun around, her scarves in a dark swirl. "No!" she screamed.

Harold stumbled. He sprawled across the ground.

Tina laughed. "Hey, kiddo!" she shouted, and pummeled at his shoulder.

Conrad veered slightly from his path. He skidded to a stop, rearing until his head was impossibly high and his trunk even higher, curled back to his forehead. He trumpeted once, with the most furious, frightening sound that anyone there had ever heard. And then he came battering down.

He came down like an avalanche on top of the little woman who seemed to be hitting Harold.

There was a scream: a short, awful scream. The elephant trampled over the shoes, over the base, over Tina. His gigantic gray feet rose and fell, bashing at the ground. The bottoms of them sagged as they lifted, tightened as they fell, turning slowly red with blood.

And the ball plopped onto the field and trickled back toward the plate.

Chapter

50

Samuel held the tiny princess. He raised her little shoulders from the grass and let her head fall across his lap. From the waist down, it was as though she wasn't there. Her little black dress was flat as paper on the ground.

"Hey, Samuel," she said. Her arms reached up; her hands took hold of Samuel's fur. Her face was white and taut with pain. She tried to smile but only winced.

"You'll have to do it yourself," she said. "You'll have to get the house and put the curtains up." She squeezed her fingers in his fur. "And don't forget your cuckoo clock."

"Oh, Tina," said Samuel. Tears ran down his horrid jowls, down his thickly matted beard. "You're going to be okay," he said. "Just hang on. You're going to be okay."

"Squeeze me," she said. "Give me a good old geezer-squeezer, Samuel."

He wrapped himself around her. He swayed and crooned, and all the time he shook with sobs.

"That's good," she said. "That's nice." Her voice was fading.

Harold stared right into her eyes, into her face, which was turned toward him.

"Say," she said. "Is Harold here?"

"Yes," said Harold. He dropped beside her on his knees. People pressed around him, silent as the stars.

"Where are you, kiddo?"

"Here," he said.

She took a hand from Samuel's fur, and Harold grasped it tightly. "I'm sorry," he said. "Oh, geez, I'm sorry."

"Don't feel bad." She twitched and groaned. A spot of blood bubbled on her lip. "It's okay, Harold. I'm okay. Sort of tired anyway. I was sort of tired."

Her hand tightened in Harold's fist. "Go see your mama," she said. "Okay? She'll miss you, kiddo." Then her eyes closed, and she slumped back in Samuel's arms.

"Tina," said Harold. "Oh, Tina, please."

"Shhh." Samuel brought her higher in his lap. His claws nearly covered her chest. "She's gone now," he said.

Harold sat back. He couldn't believe she was dead, not so quickly as that, not in the time it took a baseball to rise and fall again.

"Yes, she's gone." Samuel looked up at all the faces, his claws kneading and pressing at Tina. "Could you go away now?" he asked. "Everybody? She didn't like to be looked at. She didn't like people staring."

They wandered away in quiet groups. They muttered apologies and touched Samuel's shoulder as they passed. Then only Harold was left. He stood up and saw the Gypsy Magda watching him. "Bring her back!" he shouted.

The Gypsy Magda didn't move. Harold ran to her—he ran *at* her—and clutched her scarves in his fists. "Bring her *back*," he said again, and pushed with his arms. The bracelets jangled.

"Do it!" he cried. "You did it for the farmer's girl, now do it for her."

The Gypsy Magda held him. She hugged him as he fell against her, sobbing in her scarves.

"Can't you bring her back?" he asked.

"To what?" she said. "Look at her and tell me: Do you think she would want to live like that?"

Harold shuddered. He didn't look at Tina.

"She could never run again. She could never walk," said the Gypsy Magda. "She could never sit on her apple box or rock in a rocking chair. No, it is not what she would want."

Harold groaned, but he didn't argue. And he let the Gypsy Magda lead him away.

Her hand on his shoulder, she took him to the grove of willows. They stopped there, and Harold looked back.

Samuel was a little black dot in the empty field. With the stars above him, the grass and the mountains around him, he looked like a part of the land, like a hunched stone that had been there forever.

"I wish I could help him," said Harold.

"There is nothing you can do," said the Gypsy Magda. "He must sit and remember things. He must work the sadness from himself."

Far across the field, an orange light flashed in the darkness. Then Harold heard a gunshot, and the sound made him wince. It was followed by a thud, a hopeless-sounding thump of something toppling to the grass.

Tears filled Harold's eyes. He thought of Conrad

hitting the ball for the first time, of Conrad trumpeting to his rescue by the river. He remembered the touch of the elephant's trunk and the deep, caring look in his eyes. He wondered if Conrad had danced again as the gun pointed at him. Then he thought of Conrad falling, crumpling to his knees, folding to the ground with a shudder and a sigh.

Suddenly it was too much for him, his hopes in ruins. He buried his face in the Gypsy Magda's scarves. "I don't understand," he said. "You saw the angry boy in your crystal ball. You saw Roman there."

"No," she said. "I saw you."

"Me?"

"You were seething with anger."

"Oh, gosh. Then it's my fault," said Harold. "Everything that's happened. It's all my fault."

"No," said the Gypsy Magda. "You taught the elephants what no one else could teach them. And Tina, you gave her happiness. A great happiness. And—you must believe me—happiness is worth many times more than years."

"But you saw it coming," said Harold. "You tried to warn me."

"I saw only a bit of it." Her bracelets rubbed on Harold's arm. "It is all I ever see. There was nothing you could do to change it."

They stayed together until the moon rose. Then she guided Harold to the cottonwoods, to the big Airstream, where she left him. Harold lay on the sofa, but he couldn't sleep. He was too aware of the empty room at the back, of Samuel tossing endlessly, and sometimes sobbing.

315

Chapter
51

In the morning he said goodbye. He walked through the field from person to person. He said goodbye to Wicks, to the Frizzles, to Mr. Happy, who hugged him for a moment. He said goodbye to the drummer and the trombone player, to Max Graf and Canary Bird. Then he came to Mr. Hunter and said goodbye to him.

"So you're leaving us," said Mr. Hunter.

"Yes, sir," said Harold.

"I suspect a lot of people will, once we're done in Salem. Or maybe not." He shrugged. "It might be a new beginning, a start of something splendid. Who can see the future?"

Harold looked up. Mr. Hunter bent over him but didn't put his hands in his pockets. And Harold realized that he would never be paid for the work he had done. He would never meet Mr. Lincoln Green.

He started back toward the Airstream. He shook hands with Esther but didn't know what to do with Wallo. "Goodbye," he said. "Good luck."

Wallo grinned. "Same to you."

He said goodbye to the Cannibal King. On the steps of Oola Boola Mambo, they sat one above the other like a strange white totem pole. "You came a long way," said the Cannibal King. "I hope you weren't too disappointed."

"Gosh, no," said Harold.

"You know something?" The Cannibal King, on the upper step, put his hands on Harold's shoulders. "I was a grown man before I could look in a mirror. That's nuts, eh?"

Harold shook his head. "No," he said.

"And I used to dream that I was different. Like I was someone else, eh? I thought it stopped, but last night I dreamed it again."

"I do that all the time," said Harold.

"But you know something?" The Cannibal King leaned forward. "I dreamed that I was you."

Harold smiled. He stood up, and he shook hands with the Cannibal King. Then he walked on, through the cottonwood grove, to say his last goodbye, the hardest of them all.

The Gypsy Magda came to meet him, tinkling with bells. She hugged him, and Samuel hugged them both. They rocked together in a little circle that seemed far too small without Tina.

"Where will you go?" asked Samuel.

"Home, I guess," said Harold.

Samuel squeezed him. "I think that's good."

Fur-covered hands rubbed at Harold's back. He closed his eyes. "What will happen to Flip?" he asked the Gypsy Magda.

"I do not know," she said. "I think maybe she will stay with Mr. Hunter. I think maybe she will find that she still has a family here."

"And me?" he asked.

"Whatever you do, you will do well," she said.

He let himself be rocked and held. Samuel's fur reminded him of Honey's, and he longed to touch it again. "I'd better go," he said, pulling from the circle.

"Take this," said Samuel. His hand was suddenly holding money, the roll of dollar bills that had come from selling postcards.

"I can get home," said Harold.

"You can get home a lot faster with money." He pressed the roll into Harold's palm. "That's what Tina would want."

The circus broke camp soon after that. The trucks pulled out in a convoy, climbing back toward the mountains. They left behind them a big square of turned-over ground and, beside it, a smaller one—a tiny one—marked by a plain white cross. They left behind them the old Indian. And Harold the Ghost.

The boy and the Indian sat by the stream, under a willow. The old Indian had his feet on his medicine bundle.

"Are you going to Salem?" asked Harold.

"No," said Thunder Wakes Him. "I would have liked to, though. I have never been west of the Cascades."

"Then what will you do?"

"Oh, I might ride south. Camp by the Humboldt for a week or two, if I can find a place by myself." Thunder Wakes Him plucked a stem of grass. He split it into four and let the pieces fall from his fingers. "I'll catch the circus coming back."

Harold nodded.

"Can I give you a ride?"

"No, thanks. I want to walk awhile, and then catch a train, I think."

The old Indian whistled for his chestnut horse. He took his feet from the medicine bundle. But when he stood he grunted, and a little look of pain flashed across his face. "It is hard to get old," he said. "No longer can I do the things I did when I was only eighty."

The horse had crossed the river. It came down to the opposite bank and waited there for its rider.

"Well, I'll see you, Harold," said Thunder Wakes Him.

"Yeah. See you," Harold said.

The old Indian stooped to pick up his bundle. Again he winced, and the roll of hide and leather dropped from his hand, unrolling on the slope. Little pots and jars scattered across the grass.

"My medicine!" cried Thunder Wakes Him.

Harold scrambled after them, and the touch of the cold glass jars made him suddenly homesick. His mother kept a row of them in the little cabinet in the bathroom. As a boy, he had built castles of the ones she had emptied. He liked the feel of them again, and only slowly packed them back. But the old Indian threw them on the leather and rolled the bundle around them.

"Now you know," said the old Indian.

"Know what?" asked Harold, though he did.

The old Indian smiled. "You are a good person, my little white friend." He took his bundle and walked down to the river, into the water that rose to his knees. He waded toward the chestnut horse, stepping awkwardly over the stones, and in the middle he slipped. For an instant, he was flat above the surface, for another instant underneath it. And then he stood

319

again, dripping wet, his buckskins blackened by the stream.

The water, where it flowed around him, carried on. It eddied down along the banks, down toward the ocean. It carried a stain of red that dripped from the old Indian's face, from his hands, leaving him white underneath.

The old Indian looked at the back of his hands. His long gray braids hung across his face. "It's a miracle," he said, and laughed. "When you get stuck being something else, it is hard to get unstuck."

Harold nodded. Then he turned his back on old Bob and started his journey home.

Chapter
52

Harold the Ghost came home to Liberty on a steam train. It stopped at the old, dust-covered station, and he walked up through the town to his home.

He carried his bundle on his shoulder, the bat for a handle. He looked like the same boy who had left Liberty weeks before, but he wasn't the same at all. He walked steadily, quickly, his head held high. And when he met the children running down to see why the train had stopped, he neither slowed nor lowered his head. He just kept walking.

"Hey, it's the Ghost!" shouted Dusty Kearns. "It's Harold the Ghost!" The children swept down in a line and swarmed around him. A girl said, "We thought you were dead." And Dusty cried, "He looks like he is!"

They tugged at his clothes and snatched at his bundle. But Harold felt bigger and stronger than he ever had, and he walked along in silence as the children circled him.

"Where have you been?" they asked. "What were you doing?"

Harold kept walking. The bundle hung heavily over his shoulder.

"You been hiding?" asked Dusty. "Looks like you've been hiding under a rock."

Harold smiled. He took off his little round glasses and touched his eyes with the back of his hand, then put them on again. His hair stood up in white tufts.

The circle grew wider around him. It grew wider and silent. A girl fell into step beside him. "Did you go off with the circus, Harold?" she asked. "Is that where you've been?"

Harold shrugged up his bundle and kept on walking. He thought of Princess Minikin, always happy, laughing her way through crowds; of poor Samuel, who hated being thought a freak; of the Cannibal King as a fat little boy crying because he'd been called a snowman. He thought of the old Indian pretending to be something else, and then of Tina again—the best of them all—telling him it was hard to be different.

He stopped in the street, in the circle of children. He looked around the blurs of faces and saw them looking back, wondering where he had been, seeing that somehow he had changed. *You're no better or worse than anyone else,* the Gypsy Magda had told him. But he *was* better now; he was better than he used to be.

Harold the Ghost shifted his bundle to his other shoulder and set off again along the street. The children stood away before him, all but Dusty Kearns. In overalls streaked with grass stains, his scruffy boots laid open down the tongues, Dusty stood and stared. His freckled face was set in a hard, mean look. His hair was like coppery wool.

"Where have you been, Maggot?" he asked.

Harold stopped. He was surprised to see that he was a little bit taller than the rancher's boy, who stood like

322

Roman Pinski, legs apart and shoulders back, puffed like a pigeon to make himself seem bigger than he really was. He had so many freckles that his face looked smeared with brown and pink, and his hair was nearly as red as the juggling clown's.

It seemed to Harold that years had passed since he'd lain on the prairie and wished he looked like that. He'd thought no one would tease him if he looked like Dusty Kearns. Now he imagined that they would, but only in different ways. It was the inside of him they were teasing, not the part they saw.

"Huh?" said Dusty. "Where did you go?"

He had gone to Oregon to meet the Cannibal King. He had gone all the way to the mountains and back. But all he said was, "A long way." He said, "I've gone a long way, and I'm tired now, and I just want to go home."

Dusty Kearns rolled his hands into fists. For a moment it was hard to tell what he meant to do. Then he tucked his thumbs into the straps of his overalls and kicked at the dirt with his boot. He reminded Harold of a barking dog that had been told suddenly to shut up. Through his freckles he blushed a strange red. "Aw, let the baby go home," he mumbled. Then he stood away, and Harold walked past him.

The buildings of Liberty grew large in the Ghost's round glasses. His bundle thumping at his back, he passed the empty door of Kline and Sons and turned toward his house. He walked up the same streets he had gone down in the darkness on the night that the old Indian had taken him off across the prairie. He passed through the gate and started up the path. But the closer he came to the house, the more slowly he walked, until he reached the foot of the steps and stopped altogether.

Staring up at the house, the Ghost felt the same blur of emotions he'd felt on the circus lot when he'd come across the trailer of the Cannibal King for the very first time. He wanted to go in, and he wanted to run away. He wished he could *know* what waited inside.

Harold stood there for a minute or more. Then he trudged up the steps and across the porch. Sunlight gleamed on the doorknob, but in places the brass was worn to brown where hands had grasped it. The Ghost felt sad to think that it remembered, more strongly than he did, the touch of his father and his brother. Then he put his hand where theirs had been, turned the knob and pushed open the door.

"Ma?" he shouted. The house seemed to swallow his voice. "Ma? I'm home."

He let his bundle swing down to the floor. He walked through the hall, staring through doorways, looking for changes, as though he'd been gone for years. He came to the kitchen, calling for Honey, but there was no dog there to greet him. There was only a bare, clean patch of floor beside the stove, where Honey's blanket had always been stretched carefully square. The food dish was gone. The water bowl was empty.

"Ma!" he shouted. "Ma?"

Heavy steps came down the stairs. They came faster and faster, and the door thudded open, and his mother stood there in its frame. She was pasty, and she seemed older, but she didn't come any closer.

"Where have you *been*?" she said. "Where on *earth* have you been?"

"Don't be angry," he said. "Please don't be angry, Ma."

"Angry?" she said. "I should whip the tar from you."

Then her mouth started shaking; her eyes blinked open and shut. And Harold saw, for a moment, the younger, prettier mother he had known years ago, before the war killed his father and took his brother away. He saw her as clearly as he'd seen the sad little man trapped inside Samuel's body.

She was the same person he had always known. And he remembered how she had kissed his father goodbye at the start of the war, how she had wept on the platform as the train started east down the tracks. He remembered the way she had thrashed on the floor with a little piece of blue paper balled in her fist, shrieking like a madwoman at the telegram that said his father had died. Memories poured through his mind in an instant: how she had cried every morning and every night for more than a year, then finally smiled when Walter Beesley came to the door with a huge bunch of bright yellow daisies; how she had danced at her wedding; how she had begged him to be nicer to Walter. He remembered the day she took his father's picture from the mantel, the day he said, "I hate you." He saw her down on her knees, tugging at David's uniform, shouting at him not to go. And he saw her crumple in a faint when the second telegram came; he remembered so much in that instant.

"I'm sorry, Ma," he said. "I'm sorry for everything."

She came across the room, her arms reaching out. She crossed it faster than Harold did, and they met in a hot, sweaty hug. She cried as she rubbed her hands across his back.

"Where were you?" she asked.

"I was playing baseball, Ma," he said. "I was playing baseball with elephants, Ma, with a princess and a man like a fossil. But I'm back now, Ma. I'm home again."

Harold felt a pressure on his legs. He looked down and Honey was there, leaning against him, her head turned up and her tongue hanging out.

"That poor dog," said Mrs. Beesley. She sniffed and laughed. "That poor old flea-bitten dog. She's hardly come out of your room since the day you left. Won't sleep or eat anywhere else but up in your room."

Harold reached down to pet her, but his mother tightened him in another crushing hug. She squeezed him even harder than Samuel had. She pushed him away to see him, then squeezed him again. "We were frightened," she said. "God, we were frightened, your father and me."

"I want to see him," said Harold. "I've got an idea about Kline and Sons. I want to open it again. I want—"

"Tell me later," she said. "Oh, I just want to hold you."

Acknowledgments

Like most stories, *Ghost Boy* doesn't really begin with the first sentence on the first page. It starts instead in another book, with a title I've forgotten, in a paragraph or two about an English circus in which the elephants played cricket. In that very real circus, the elephants enjoyed their little game immensely but pouted when they lost.

I liked that image and mentioned it one day to my father. He surprised me by telling me what the elephants wore, and how they held the cricket bat, and how they lumbered up and down the pitch. He talked very fondly about it, because he remembered seeing it as a boy. The baseball game in this story is based on what he told me, and the story grew from there, through the help of many others.

Details of the circus come from two British-born friends, Barry White and John the Hermit. Barry had captured elephants in Kenya and knew firsthand their favorite ways of trampling people. The Hermit remembered the mud and smells of a circus lot and the mysteries of Gypsies.

The story was transposed to postwar America through the help of librarian Kathleen Larkin of Prince Rupert, British Columbia. She found answers to countless questions, down to such details as whether army trucks had glove boxes. Her husband, J. Kevin

Ash, brought my elephants to life when he introduced me to three of them as they passed through Prince Rupert in a Shriners' circus sponsored by his club.

The writing was helped along by my wife, Kristin Miller, and my very good friend Bruce Wishart. My agent, Jane Jordan Browne, suggested several changes and then found an excellent place for the story with Delacorte Press. There I was lucky to work with two wonderful editors: Lauri Hornik, who guided *Ghost Boy* into a major revision, and Françoise Bui, who saw it through its final changes.

From the first word I wrote, I saw Harold Kline as an albino. But I threw away almost a hundred pages when I realized that there was more to albinism than just a whiteness of skin. For teaching me the realities of the condition—which changed the story completely—I owe many thanks to NOAH, the National Organization of Albinism and Hypopigmentation, and especially to one of its members, an inspiring young man named Eric Downes. Eric told me some very personal things in a very patient way and suggested new directions in which my story could grow. He very kindly read the final manuscript and provided this clarification:

"Although Harold Kline has albinism, he must always be considered an individual. There are over a hundred different DNA mutations which can cause albinism. No two albinos are alike, just as no two people with regular vision and skin pigmentation are alike. Some albinos have a small amount of pigment in their skin, some have none. Some albinos see 20/40 (very close to the 'perfect' 20/20), some see 20/400. Harold is intended to be only a person with albinism, not a representation of every albino."

For more information on albinism, NOAH can be found at www. albinism.org.

About the Author

Iain Lawrence passed a large part of his childhood on the Canadian prairies. Summer vacations spent camping and trailering through western Canada and Montana inspired the setting of *Ghost Boy*. Always a fan of small circuses, Lawrence once had a job tearing down a traveling big top. The job lasted one night and earned him five dollars.

Iain Lawrence is the author of two award-winning books for young readers: *The Wreckers*, an Edgar Allan Poe Award Nominee, and its companion *The Smugglers*, both published by Delacorte Press.